Berkley Prime Crime titles by Jimmie Ruth Evans

FLAMINGO FATALE
MURDER OVER EASY
BEST SERVED COLD

Best Served Cold

Jimmie Ruth Evans

BERKLEY PRIME CRIME, NEW YORK

THE BERKLEY PUBLISHING GROUP
Published by the Penguin Group
Penguin Group (USA) Inc.
375 Hudson Street, New York, New York 10014, USA
Penguin Group (Canada), 90 Eglinton Avenue East, Suite 700, Toronto, Ontario M4P 2Y3, Canada
(a division of Pearson Penguin Canada Inc.)
Penguin Books Ltd., 80 Strand, London WC2R 0RL, England
Penguin Group Ireland, 25 St. Stephen's Green, Dublin 2, Ireland (a division of Penguin Books Ltd.)
Penguin Group (Australia), 250 Camberwell Road, Camberwell, Victoria 3124, Australia
(a division of Pearson Australia Group Pty. Ltd.)
Penguin Books India Pvt. Ltd., 11 Community Centre, Panchsheel Park, New Delhi—110 017, India
Penguin Group (NZ), Cnr. Airborne and Rosedale Roads, Albany, Auckland 1310, New Zealand
(a division of Pearson New Zealand Ltd.)
Penguin Books (South Africa) (Pty.) Ltd., 24 Sturdee Avenue, Rosebank, Johannesburg 2196,
South Africa

Penguin Books Ltd., Registered Offices: 80 Strand, London WC2R 0RL, England

This is a work of fiction. Names, characters, places, and incidents either are the product of the author's imagination or are used fictitiously, and any resemblance to actual persons, living or dead, business establishments, events, or locales is entirely coincidental. The publisher does not have any control over and does not assume any responsibility for author or third-party websites or their content.

PUBLISHER'S NOTE: The recipes contained in this book are to be followed exactly as written. The publisher is not responsible for your specific health or allergy needs that may require medical supervision. The publisher is not responsible for any adverse reactions to the recipes contained in this book.

BEST SERVED COLD

A Berkley Prime Crime Book / published by arrangement with the author

PRINTING HISTORY
Berkley Prime Crime mass-market edition / January 2007

Copyright © 2007 by Dean James.
Cover art by Paul Slater.
Cover design by Judith Lagerman.
Interior text design by Kristin del Rosario.

ISBN: 978-0-425-21349-0

BERKLEY® PRIME CRIME
Berkley Prime Crime Books are published by The Berkley Publishing Group,
a division of Penguin Group (USA) Inc.,
375 Hudson Street, New York, New York 10014.
The name BERKLEY PRIME CRIME and the BERKLEY PRIME CRIME design are trademarks belonging to Penguin Group (USA) Inc.

PRINTED IN THE UNITED STATES OF AMERICA

10 9 8 7 6 5 4 3 2 1

For Natalee Rosenstein,
this book, our ninth together,
with grateful appreciation for many years of patience,
encouragement, opportunities, and support.
Thanks for giving Wanda Nell
and the gang their chance.

Acknowledgments

Thanks, as always, to my agent Nancy Yost; you can find a picture of her in the dictionary under the word *irrepressible*. That's a great quality in an agent, believe me.

Thanks to the team at Berkley, including of course Natalee Rosenstein and her assistant, Michelle Vega, who do their best with each book. I particularly appreciate Michelle's enthusiasm for these books and what she does to help make them the best they can be.

Thanks also to my cheerleaders who never fail to encourage me: Tejas Englesmith, Julie Wray Herman, and Patricia Orr. Knowing you three are always on my side keeps me going when I need it most, which is just about every day.

Thanks to Barbara Douglas for reading the manuscripts and offering suggestions. Your input is valuable, and I hope you realize that!

Finally, a very special thanks to a good friend and terrific writer, Carolyn Haines, who listened to my plot woes and very quickly helped me find a solution. Carolyn's generosity, creative and otherwise, is an unfailing inspiration.

One

Wanda Nell Culpepper forced herself to stay right by the cash register and not intervene. Gladys Gordon was old enough to look after herself.

Maybe if the woman had even the little-bittiest bit of a sense of humor, Wanda Nell reflected, she wouldn't find herself in these situations.

Perry Howell, a tall, handsome man in his early thirties, spoke again. "Now, Miss Gladys, surely you know a fellow just can't help trying to flirt with a fine lady like you." His eyes sparkled with mischief as he stared up into the waitress's face.

After three months on the evening shift at the Kountry Kitchen, Gladys Gordon still hadn't figured out how to handle jokers like Perry Howell. Wanda Nell sighed. Gladys was so danged dead serious about everything. Right now she was staring at Perry Howell in horror.

"You're young enough to be my son," Gladys said, her voice huffy. "You got no business trying to get smart with me." Her face bright red, she turned and stalked off. In amusement mixed with irritation, Wanda Nell watched her go. She picked up the tea pitcher from the counter behind her and walked around to Perry Howell's table.

"You shouldn't pick on her like that, Perry," Wanda Nell told him softly as she filled his glass. "It's like shooting fish in a barrel."

Unrepentant, Howell winked at Wanda Nell. "Now, Miss Wanda Nell, if *you* was to give me the time of day, I wouldn't be so desperate trying to make time with Miss Prissy Britches back there."

"I'm not that desperate either, Perry Howell," Wanda Nell retorted, smiling, "but when you're the last man on Earth, I might give you a chance."

"This joker giving you a hard time?"

Startled, Wanda Nell turned to look up into the glowering face of Melvin Arbuckle, her boss and the owner of the Kountry Kitchen. In the three months since the murder of one of his waitresses, Melvin had been real touchy. He needed to get his own sense of humor back, but Fayetta Sutton's death had hit him harder than Wanda Nell had reckoned it would.

"Everything's fine, Melvin," Wanda Nell said, her voice firm. Perry Howell had bristled slightly at Melvin's tone, and Wanda Nell didn't want this silliness to erupt into something else. "Perry was just about to pay his check and get on home."

She fixed Howell with a stern look, and he wilted, just like one of her children. She was only six or seven years older than he was, but tonight she felt old enough to be his mother.

Howell stood up, pulled a couple of dollars out of his pocket, and dropped them on the table. He followed Wanda Nell to the cash register while Melvin wandered off to chat with another customer.

"Dang, but he's got a bug up his butt," Howell muttered as he handed Wanda Nell his money.

Making change, Wanda Nell just shrugged. "He's been through a lot, Perry. Don't take it personal. He'll be okay, just needs a little more time."

"I guess," Perry said sourly. "But maybe I'll start eating out at the Holiday Inn for awhile. I hear they got a real sexy waitress out there."

"You do that," Wanda Nell said as he walked away. "Jerk," she muttered under her breath. She glanced at her watch as the door shut behind Howell. Only eight-thirty. Would this night ever end?

She was feeling dead on her feet. It had been a long, hard week, and she was plumb worn out. Her youngest, Juliet, was back in school, and Miranda, her middle child, had gotten fired two days ago from her job at Budget Mart. Wanda Nell was about ready to wring Miranda's neck, but she didn't want her grandson, Lavon, to be an orphan.

Coming out of her reverie for a moment, Wanda Nell noticed one of her customers waving at her. Picking up the tea pitcher again, she went to fill his glass and shoot the breeze a little.

While Wanda Nell was chatting with Junior Farley and his new lady friend, she saw Gladys Gordon clump by on the way to greet a man who had just walked in the front door.

Turning away from the table, Wanda Nell got a good look at the man. Surprised, she almost dropped the tea pitcher on the floor. She stared for a moment, then took a step forward. She couldn't believe her eyes.

"Rusty," she finally said. "What are you doing back in Tullahoma? Why didn't you call?"

"I wasn't sure I was gonna see you, Wanda Nell," her brother answered. He looked away from her. "Last time I was here, you didn't have much good to say to me."

Wanda Nell's temper flared just thinking about it. She had last seen her younger brother six years ago when their mother died after a long battle with breast cancer. Furious that her brother had ignored all their mother's appeals to come home one last time before she died, Wanda Nell lit into him the minute he set foot in the funeral home. She told him at length what she thought about his callous behavior, all her grief and anger at their mother's death washing over her like a tidal wave.

Immediately after the funeral, Rusty headed back to Nashville, where he had been living for several years, and Wanda Nell hadn't heard from him since. She tried calling him a few times, to make peace with him, but he rebuffed every effort she made.

Now she was getting angry all over again, just thinking about his neglect of their mother. She forced herself to calm down, though. She didn't want to make an ugly scene right here in front of everybody.

"You were right, Wanda Nell," Rusty said softly. "I should've come back to see Mama. I didn't treat her right, and I'll go to my grave with that." Finally he looked back into his sister's face.

The sharp words Wanda Nell wanted to say died in her throat. The pain and misery she could see in her brother's face cut right through her. With surprise, she noted how tired and worn he looked. He was a little over two years younger than she was, but right now he could pass for fifty-eight instead of thirty-eight.

"How'd you know where to find me?" She reached over and set the tea pitcher on the counter near the cash register.

"Miranda," Rusty said. "I went to your trailer first, and she told me where you was working."

"Have you had anything to eat?"

Rusty shook his head. "I'm about to starve. I ain't had much since I left Nashville."

"Then come on back here and sit down," Wanda Nell said, turning to lead the way into the rear dining room.

She pointed to a table, and Rusty pulled out a chair and sat down. "What would you like to drink? Tea, or maybe some coffee?"

"What I really want is a shot of bourbon," Rusty said, almost smiling, "but I reckon I'll settle for a glass of milk."

"Okay," Wanda Nell said. "Anything special you'd like to eat?"

Rusty shrugged. "Whatever you got, it don't matter much."

"You just sit there and relax, and I'll get you fixed up," Wanda Nell said. "I'll be right back with you some milk."

Rusty rubbed his face tiredly. "Where's the restroom?"

Wanda Nell pointed. "To the left there, just around that wall."

In the kitchen, she ordered a chicken-fried steak dinner with mashed potatoes and green beans. As a kid, Rusty had always been partial to country-fried steak, and Wanda Nell hoped he still was. She poured a large glass of milk and took it back to his table. She waited for him a moment, but he was still in the restroom.

Wanda Nell walked back to the front dining room to check on her remaining two tables there. Business was fairly slow tonight, and it didn't look like they'd get many more people in before closing time at ten.

Just as well, she thought. Maybe Melvin would let her off early, so she and Rusty could talk a little before she headed to Budget Mart for her overnight shift.

Rusty was sitting in his chair, sipping at his milk, when she walked into the back dining room again. "Food'll be out in a few minutes," she told him. "Chicken-fried steak, mashed potatoes, and green beans. Sound okay?"

He smiled. "Thanks. That sounds real good right about now."

Wanda Nell took a moment to examine him more closely. His reddish-blond hair had faded almost to white except for a few spots, and his dusting of freckles stood out against the paleness of his thin face. For a moment, he was someone she didn't know, a complete stranger. Where was her brother? This man just didn't look like the brother she remembered.

She didn't know what to say to him, feeling suddenly awkward. He didn't say anything either, and the silence between them grew longer and more strained.

"Ain't you gonna introduce me?"

Melvin Arbuckle's voice was a welcome intrusion. Wanda Nell turned to him in relief.

"Melvin, this is my brother Rusty. Rusty Rosamond. He's really Raymond, but we always called him Rusty. And this here's my boss, Melvin Arbuckle, Rusty. He owns the Kountry Kitchen."

Standing, Rusty offered his hand, and Melvin shook it. "Pleased to meet you, Rusty," Melvin said. He motioned for Rusty to take his seat.

"Likewise," Rusty answered, sitting down.

"I didn't realize Wanda Nell had a brother," Melvin said, cutting his eyes sideways at Wanda Nell. "I don't think I ever heard tell of you."

Rusty shrugged. "I been living in Nashville for about ten years now, and I don't make it back to Tullahoma much."

"Nashville," Melvin said. "That's a real nice town. I been up there a couple of times. What do you do up there?"

"I write songs," Rusty said. "I write 'em, but I don't sell too many of 'em." He laughed bitterly. "Mostly I work whatever job I can get."

Wanda Nell stared at her brother in surprise. "I didn't know you wanted to be a songwriter."

Rusty shrugged again. "I guess there's a lot we don't know about each other, Wanda Nell." He had an odd glint in his eyes. "Like you being a grandma, and Miranda having a baby. That sure was a surprise."

"You mean because his daddy's black," Wanda Nell said evenly. "Well, it don't matter who his daddy is, Lavon is my grandson, and I love him. I don't want to hear anything from you about it. You got that?"

Rusty's mouth had set in a firm line while Wanda Nell was speaking. "Whatever you say, Wanda Nell." He looked to Melvin. "That's my big sister for you, always telling me what to do and how to think, without even asking me what I really think."

"*Big* sister?" Melvin asked in surprise.

"Rusty's two years younger than me," Wanda Nell said.

"Yeah, I just got more miles on me than she does," Rusty said. "Big Sis was always the lucky one in the family, not me."

Turning away, Wanda Nell just rolled her eyes. It wouldn't do a bit of good to say anything. Rusty was always feeling sorry for himself. Didn't matter what happened to anybody else, something worse was always happening to Rusty. She headed to the kitchen to get his food.

Why had he suddenly turned up in Tullahoma? Wanda Nell wondered about that as she picked up his steaming plate. Was he in some kind of trouble? He didn't look too good. Maybe he was ill. She sure didn't think he'd come home just because he'd been missing her.

Back at the table, she set the plate down in front of Rusty. "Dig in," she said. "And it's on me, so if you want anything else, order it." He didn't look any too prosperous, either, and maybe he could use a free meal or two. It was the least she could do.

"Thanks," Rusty said, his voice husky. His eyes avoiding hers, he picked up his knife and fork and started cutting into the chicken-fried steak.

"I'll be back in a minute," Wanda Nell said. "I'm just going to check on my tables, and then maybe we can talk a little while you eat."

Not waiting for a response, she walked into the front dining room. Junior Farley and his girlfriend had left and Wanda Nell started clearing the table, pocketing the generous tip. The two men at her other table left, and by the time she finished clearing that table and got back to Rusty, he had wolfed down almost the entire plateful of food.

"You were hungry," Wanda Nell commented. "How about seconds? Or maybe some dessert? I think we still got some apple pie left."

"Apple pie sounds good," Rusty answered, "and some more milk."

Wanda Nell nodded, picking up his glass.

A couple minutes later she was back with a piece of apple pie, a scoop of vanilla ice cream on the top, and a full glass of milk. She set them in front of her brother, then sat down across from him at the table.

Rusty stuck a forkful of the pie into his mouth and smiled around it. "Delicious," he said as he chewed.

Wanda Nell waited a moment while he had several more bites of pie and ice cream. "I'm glad to see you, Rusty. And you know you're welcome to stay with me and the girls. Juliet can move in with me, and you can have her room."

Rusty shook his head. "Thanks, Wanda Nell, I appreciate that. But I don't want to put y'all out none. Besides, I already got me a place to stay."

"Where?" Wanda Nell asked in surprise.

"Right next door." He grinned. "That neighbor lady of yours is something else."

Wanda Nell relaxed. Her best friend and next-door neighbor at the trailer park, Mayrene Lancaster, *was* something else. Generous to a fault, for one thing, especially if she'd offered Rusty the use of her guest room.

"Mayrene's a good friend," Wanda Nell said. "I guess she must have been there when you stopped by my trailer."

Rusty nodded. "She came over right after I got there. Guess she was checking up on the girls." He had another bite of pie. "When she found out who I was and that I was aiming to visit for a few days, she said I should stay with her. Even gave me a key to her trailer." He stuck the last bit of pie and ice cream into his mouth, then washed it down with milk.

"That's real sweet of her," Wanda Nell said. "Mayrene's real generous, so you be nice to her, you hear?"

Rusty rolled his eyes at her. "I ain't five years old no more, Wanda Nell. I know how to behave nice for somebody like your friend. I ain't gonna embarrass you."

"I know," Wanda Nell said, feeling guilty. "Sorry." It sure was easy, dropping back into old habits. She'd always been bossy with Rusty.

Rusty fiddled with his fork, tracing patterns in the melted ice cream on his plate. Wanda Nell watched him for a moment, then drew a deep breath. Might as well get on with it, she thought.

"So what brings you back to Tullahoma?"

Rusty didn't say anything.

"I'm glad to see you, Rusty, I really am," Wanda Nell said softly. "With Mama and Daddy gone, there's just you and me and my kids, after all." She paused, struck by a sudden thought. "You got anybody up there in Nashville?

A wife, or kids, or somebody else?" She was appalled to realize that she had no idea how he'd answer.

"Yeah, there's someone," Rusty said. "We been together for a few years now." A shadow crossed his face.

"Why didn't you bring her with you?" *If it is a her*, Wanda Nell added silently. Maybe it wasn't a her, but a him, and Rusty was afraid Wanda Nell would react badly to the news. She had to stifle a laugh at that thought. Wait till Rusty found out about his nephew, her son T.J.

"She wasn't able to come," Rusty said.

"That's too bad," Wanda Nell said. "I'd sure like to meet her."

Rusty nodded. "Maybe some other time." He shifted restlessly in his chair. "Look, Wanda Nell, I'm only gonna be here a few days, probably. I don't want to argue with you no more, okay?"

"I don't want to argue with you either, Rusty," Wanda Nell said.

"I just need to take care of some things here, some old business," Rusty said, not meeting her eyes. "Nothing you need to worry about, okay?"

"Is it something I can help you with?" Wanda Nell asked cautiously. Rusty was in a strange mood, and she didn't know how he'd react.

Rusty stood up. "No, it's nothing you can help me with, so don't be worrying about it. Thanks for the meal, Wanda Nell, I appreciate it. But I'm real tired, and I guess I'll head on back to the trailer park and get to bed."

"All right." Wanda Nell stood also, and she stepped closer to her brother, aiming to give him a hug. But he shied away from her, and she stopped, feeling awkward and stupid.

"I'll see you tomorrow sometime," Rusty said. Without a backward glance, he walked away.

Troubled, Wanda Nell watched him go.

Two

Wanda Nell leaned tiredly against her locker for a moment, feeling the welcome cool of the metal on her forehead. She had put in her eight hours at Budget Mart, and she was ready to go home and climb into bed. Thank the Lord, after her shift at the Kountry Kitchen tonight, she had Sunday off. She needed it.

She opened the locker and extracted her purse. Muttering good-bye to her coworkers, she left the locker room and made her way out of the store.

The September morning was warm but cloudy. They could use a little rain after two weeks of sun and heat, and Wanda Nell didn't want to have to get out in the yard again and water her flowerbeds. She could always make Miranda do it, but sometimes it just didn't seem worth the battle.

Thoughts of Miranda made her head hurt as she turned the key in the ignition of her red Cavalier. She still couldn't believe the girl had been such a fool as to think her mother wouldn't find out she was skipping work. Really, sometimes she was afraid her middle child was about as smart as a clod of dirt. Miranda never thought about the consequences of anything.

She could hear Miranda's voice even now, whining. "I wasn't meaning to miss so much work, Mama, I really wasn't, but I just couldn't help it. I just been feeling tired and bad all the time, and when I tried to tell you, you wouldn't listen. And then that old Miz Putman, well, she's had it in for me right from the first day. She shouldn't've fired me like that."

"Honey, you missed six of the last nine days you were supposed to work, and Miz Putman had every right to fire you, you acting like that," Wanda Nell said, trying hard to hold on to her temper. "And if you felt that bad, you should have gone to see the doctor, instead of hiding out with that girlfriend of yours."

"I didn't wanna go to the doctor," Miranda said, her mouth set in mulish lines.

Wanda Nell had a sudden, terrible thought. "Miranda, you're not pregnant, are you?" *Please, Lord,* she begged, *don't let her be pregnant again.*

Miranda had sworn up and down she wasn't pregnant, and anyway, how could she be, she never went anywhere to meet any boys, and on and on until she was crying from feeling so sorry for herself.

Wanda Nell had had to walk away from her, for fear of either slapping her or saying something she'd have cause to regret. She had thought Miranda was finally beginning to shape up the last few months, and then Miranda went and pulled a fool stunt like this. What was she going to do with that girl?

Wanda Nell pulled out onto the highway toward home, the Kozy Kove Trailer Park out by the lake. There was very little traffic out on this early Saturday morning. She had made this drive so many times in recent years, she could probably do it with her eyes closed. She was tempted to close them now, but she forced herself to focus on driving. She didn't need to be running off the road into a ditch.

Try as she might, though, she couldn't turn her mind away from thoughts of her family. If Miranda wasn't headache enough, now Rusty had turned up, acting strange. She considered that a moment. It had been so long since she'd spent any time with her brother, she wasn't sure what was strange for him anymore.

Even so, there was something sly about him, something that made her uneasy. What kind of business could he have here in Tullahoma when he hadn't lived here in over ten years? Who did he even know anymore? Had he been keeping in touch with somebody all these years? She didn't like the sound of it.

Unless he decided to confide in her, she didn't see much way of finding out what he was up to. They had been close when they were kids, but about the time their daddy died, when Wanda Nell was almost seventeen and Rusty was fifteen, they had both changed. Their daddy's death had hit them hard, and they had each ended up doing foolish things.

Wanda Nell sighed, pushing away the thoughts of those long-ago mistakes. Even after twenty-three years, she still missed her daddy. If he hadn't died so young, from a heart attack at forty-two, things might have been so different.

But there wasn't much use in looking back and crying over spilt milk, her mama would have said. *Wipe up the milk, and get on with it.* Wanda Nell smiled for a moment. She could almost hear her mama's voice in the car with her.

As she turned off the highway onto the lake road, Wanda Nell laughed. Trouble was, on a good day she had more than enough milk to wipe up. She didn't need any more just now.

A few minutes later, she was home, parking her car beside her double-wide trailer. A battered Toyota pickup with Tennessee plates was parked at the end of Mayrene Lancaster's trailer.

As Wanda Nell climbed wearily out of the car, Mayrene poked her head out of the door of her trailer. "Hey there, girl, how are you?"

"Morning, Mayrene," Wanda Nell said, suppressing a yawn. "Pretty dang worn out. How about you?"

"I'm okay," Mayrene said, stepping out of the trailer onto the little porch and pulling the door shut behind her. "Your brother's still asleep."

"I appreciate you putting him up like this," Wanda Nell said. "I hope he's not gonna be any trouble."

Mayrene flapped her hand in a dismissive gesture. "He ain't no trouble. And you're crowded enough already, you don't need nobody else over there. I'm glad to do it."

Wanda Nell leaned against her car for a moment. "Tell Rusty for me, if you don't mind, I'm gonna sleep for a while, but he's welcome to come over whenever he wants. I'll talk to the girls about him, and he can help himself to whatever's in the fridge."

"I don't think you need to worry about looking after him," Mayrene said. "I heard him talking on his cell phone last night, and it sounded to me like he was planning to be pretty busy today."

"Oh, really," Wanda Nell said, her curiosity piqued. "Did you hear him say just what it was he's gonna be doing?"

Mayrene shook her head. "Not really. I wasn't intending to be getting into his business, but I was coming down the hall to check on him, make sure he had everything, and that's when I heard him talking." She paused. "He didn't have the door closed, and I couldn't help it."

Wanda Nell suppressed a grin. Mayrene wouldn't admit she'd probably been listening in on purpose, but Wanda Nell didn't care. She wanted to know what Rusty was up to herself, and if this was the only way she could find out, so be it.

"Could you tell who he was talking to?"

Again Mayrene shook her head. "He mentioned the name Tony, but I don't think that's who he was talking to. Whoever this Tony is, Rusty sure don't like him much."

Wanda Nell thought it over a minute. She couldn't remember anybody right off the bat named Tony that her brother might have known. Maybe she'd look through her high school yearbooks later on, if she could find them. Right now she was too tired.

"Anything else?" Wanda Nell asked after a big yawn.

Mayrene hesitated. "I'm not sure, but I think he said something like, 'You better believe I'm gonna use it, and I don't give a rat's ass what you want.' And that was it."

Wanda Nell had no idea what it meant, but it didn't sound too good. It sounded like Rusty was threatening someone. But why?

She pushed herself away from the car. She had to get some sleep, and when she was rested, she would feel more like tackling her brother.

"Keep your ears open for me, Mayrene," she said. "Something strange is going on with Rusty, and I don't know what it is."

"Sure thing, honey," Mayrene said. "I don't know him at all, but he does seem to be acting a little weird." She made a shooing gesture with her hands. "Now you get on in there and get some rest. Don't worry about none of this right now."

Wanda Nell waved her thanks as she turned and mounted the steps to the front door of her trailer.

She unlocked the door, pushed it open, and stepped inside. Easing the door shut behind her, she stood still for a moment and listened. Everything was quiet.

Resisting the impulse to check on Miranda and her

grandson, she instead turned down the hall where her bedroom and Juliet's room lay. She did poke her head in Juliet's room for a moment, and Juliet was sound asleep, her long, fair hair almost covering the teddy bear, Alexander, clutched in her right arm.

Wanda Nell smiled and blew a kiss toward her sleeping daughter. Thank the Lord, Juliet never gave her any trouble.

In her own room she pulled off her clothes and dropped them in the laundry hamper. After slipping into her nightgown, she crawled into bed and was asleep in less than five minutes.

Sometime later she surfaced to hear the steady beat of rain against the windows. She glanced at the clock on her nightstand, surprised to note that it was nearly two-thirty. She'd been so tired she'd slept soundly for over seven hours.

Sitting up in the bed, she yawned and stretched. She actually felt rested for once. Climbing out of bed, she slipped on her housecoat and padded out into the hall. She peered into Juliet's room, but it was empty.

After a stop in the bathroom she shared with Juliet, she continued into the living room. The trailer was quiet, except for the drumming of the rain.

Wanda Nell frowned for a moment, until she remembered that Juliet was supposed to be at the library, working on a project for school. Miranda had probably taken Lavon and gone off to visit one of her friends. *She better be back with the car in time for me to go to work*, Wanda Nell thought sourly.

In the kitchen she poured herself a large glass of Diet Coke and sat at the table drinking until she felt more awake. Her stomach was starting to growl a bit, and she got up and rummaged in the fridge for something to eat.

There was some leftover ham and potato salad, and she decided that would do just fine.

She was eating and considering what to do about finding Miranda another job when she became aware of loud voices outside. The rain had slacked off, and she could hear the angry tones of two men arguing.

Alarmed, she got up from her chair and peered out her kitchen window. Rusty was standing in the doorway of Mayrene's trailer, his face reddened and twisted into a scowl. He was listening, arms crossed over his chest, to a man who stood at the foot of Mayrene's steps.

Wanda Nell recognized him with a start. She knew that bald head and tubby body. They belonged to Bert Vines, her insurance agent. What the heck was he doing here, and why was he hollering at her brother like that?

She couldn't make out what they were saying, so she raised the kitchen window quietly.

"I done told you what I want," Rusty said, his voice harsh and clear in the spattering rain. "And you better do what I say. There ain't no room for negotiation."

Bert Vines uttered several choice obscenities, and Wanda Nell flinched. Then he shouted, "I'll see you in hell first, you bastard!"

Turning quickly, he almost slipped on the slick concrete, but he righted himself. Moments later, Wanda Nell heard a car door slam. Then the car roared off.

She stared out the kitchen window at her brother. He stood there for a moment, completely still, then he turned and went back inside the trailer.

Wanda Nell's stomach began to ache. What was Rusty up to? And what was she going to do about it?

Three

Wanda Nell stared through the kitchen window at Mayrene's trailer trying to decide what to do. Should she confront Rusty right now about what she had overheard? Would he even talk to her about it?

Turning away from the window, she picked up the phone and punched in Mayrene's number. She heard several rings before Rusty picked up.

"Rusty, it's me, Wanda Nell."

"Where are you?" Rusty's voice was gruff.

"I'm at home," Wanda Nell said, surprised. "Where'd you think I'd be?"

He breathed hard into the phone. "I reckon I thought you'd gone to work. Your car's not out there."

"I been sleeping after my shift at Budget Mart," Wanda Nell said. "Miranda's gone off in my car somewhere."

He grunted. Then after a pause, he said, "Well, what do you want?"

To slap you upside the head, Wanda Nell thought irritably, but she didn't say it to him. Instead, she said, "I thought maybe you could come over here for awhile, and we could talk. It's been a long time, Rusty, and I think there's some things we should talk about."

"I got things I got to do."

"Well, can't they wait just a little while?" Wanda Nell didn't want to sound like she was pleading with him, but he was being so danged obstinate.

His tone was grudging when he finally replied. "I guess so. I'll come over for a few minutes."

"Good," Wanda Nell said. "Give me about five minutes while I throw on some clothes."

"Whatever." The phone clicked in her ear.

Sighing, she put the phone down. Talking to him was going to be like pulling teeth, but she had to do it.

She hurried down the hall to her bedroom to slip on some jeans and an old shirt. She had about an hour before she'd have to start getting ready for her shift at the Kountry Kitchen. And Miranda had better get herself back here by then.

Wanda Nell was back in the kitchen when she heard a knock at the door. She went to answer it.

Rusty was scowling at her before she even said a word to him. She stepped back and motioned him in. He stomped past her like a little boy being called in from recess. Rolling her eyes at his back, Wanda Nell shut the door.

"Have a seat," she said, pointing him toward the couch.

He plopped down on it and stared at his feet.

"Can I get you something to drink? Or maybe something to eat? Have you had lunch yet?"

"Got any beer?"

"I think so," Wanda Nell said, heading for the kitchen. She tried to keep some on hand for her friend, Jack Pemberton, and for T.J. They both liked Heineken, and she hoped Rusty did, too. Maybe a beer would mellow him out a little.

She returned to the living room with a cold beer for him and more Diet Coke for herself.

"Thanks," Rusty muttered, accepting the bottle. "Good beer." He tilted it up to his lips and drank about half of it.

Wanda Nell sat down in a chair near the couch. After a sip of her drink, she said, "Did you sleep okay? I hope you got some rest, because you sure looked tired last night."

"I slept fine," Rusty said shortly.

"Good," Wanda Nell said, determined to be patient with him, even though he was irritating the hell out of her. "I sure appreciate Mayrene putting you up like that, though you know you're perfectly welcome to stay here with us."

"Yeah," Rusty said, staring at his beer. "I know."

He wasn't going to make it easy for her, Wanda Nell could see. Suppressing a sigh, she said, "I'm sorry, Rusty."

Finally he looked up at her. "Sorry? For what?"

"For being so rough on you when Mama died," Wanda Nell replied. She had been so angry with him at the time she hadn't really thought much about what she was saying to him. She'd been pretty vicious when she'd told him what she thought about his neglect of his mother. "I was so upset about losing her and her dying the way she did, I didn't think about what I was saying to you."

Rusty rolled the beer bottle back and forth between his hands. When he spoke, his voice was rough. "I'm sorry, too, Wanda Nell. I let Mama down, and I'm ashamed of the way I treated her. I don't really blame you for what you said. I been saying worse to myself ever since Mama died."

Wanda Nell wanted to reach out to him, but something about the way he was holding himself warned her that her touch wouldn't be welcome. She stared at him for a moment. How had her little brother turned into this bitter stranger?

"It's time to let go of that," Wanda Nell said gently.

"We both need to move on. We can't undo what's been done, but maybe we can do better from now on."

Rusty drained the rest of his beer. He stuck the empty bottle in her direction. "Got another one?"

"Yeah," Wanda Nell said. She took the bottle into the kitchen and retrieved another one from the fridge. There were two left, and she hoped Rusty wasn't going to want them, too. He got mean when he was drunk. She remembered that all too clearly from some of his escapades when he was a teenager after their daddy died.

She handed him the beer and returned to her seat. Rusty muttered his thanks, then sipped at the beer.

"Are you willing to do that?"

"Do what?" Rusty moved restlessly on the couch.

"Forget the past and try to move on," Wanda Nell said.

"What's the point?" He was avoiding looking at her.

"The point is, we're family," Wanda Nell said, her voice a bit tart. "That should mean something. It did, once upon a time, when Mama and Daddy were alive. I don't think they'd be happy with us not even talking to each other, not even knowing what the other one is doing."

"Yeah, well," Rusty said, shrugging. He drank some more beer.

Wanda Nell hated the bleak look on his face. How was she going to get through to him?

"Family ought to count for something."

"What is you want me to say, Wanda Nell?" Rusty plunked the beer bottle down on her coffee table so hard she was afraid the bottle would shatter. He finally looked right at her. "You want me to say how thrilled I am to be back in the bosom of my family? You want me to say how much I've missed being around you and your kids all these years? That I'm just beside myself with joy to see y'all again? Is that what you want?"

"What I want," Wanda Nell said, holding on to her

temper by the merest thread, "is to figure out what the hell has made you so bitter. What has any of us done to make you hate us so much?"

"I ain't got that much time," Rusty said. He stood up. "I don't think there's anything else to say." He started moving toward the door.

"Now you just hold on a dang minute," Wanda Nell said, standing up. She'd had enough. "I reckon you want me to feel sorry for you, but you seem to be doing a pretty good job of that yourself. *Poor little Rusty.*"

He flinched at the tone of those last three words. Anger blazed in his eyes as he faced her. "That's about what I'd expect from you, Wanda Nell. You never cared about anything but yourself. If I really sat down and told you, I don't think it would matter one little bit to you."

"Is that what you really think of me?" Wanda Nell was so stunned she took a step backward.

For a moment, Rusty looked almost contrite at the effect of his words. Then his face hardened. "Why do you even care? You've got your family. What else do you need? It's too late for you and me to be a loving family, Wanda Nell." He moved toward the door again.

"What were you and Bert Vines arguing about?" Wanda Nell thought maybe she could surprise an answer out of him, because surely that was the last thing he'd expect her to say.

He halted, his hand on the doorknob. He looked back at her, his face grim. "That ain't none of your damn business. It wasn't before, and it sure ain't now. I'll probably be gone in a day or two, so just forget about it. It ain't got nothing to do with you." He opened the door and walked out. The door slammed behind him.

Wanda Nell felt like throwing something at the door, but that wouldn't accomplish anything. Even though they hadn't seen each other in a long time, Rusty still knew how to get her riled up.

She wanted to grab hold of him and shake some sense into him. She just couldn't figure out what the heck had made him so bitter toward her. They both had a rough time after their daddy died and Rusty ran a bit wild. She'd had her own wild moments. She blushed to think about some of them now.

Deep in thought, she wandered back into the kitchen to refill her drink. It was only a few months after her daddy died that she found out she was pregnant. For a while she'd been afraid to tell her mama, worried about laying another burden on Mrs. Rosamond. Things were tight financially, and she should have been thinking about work rather than having a baby and getting married.

Maybe that was part of it, Wanda Nell reckoned. When Wanda Nell finally confessed her pregnancy, Mrs. Rosamond had directed most of her attention to her daughter and dealing with the Culpepper family. Wanda Nell shuddered every time she remembered the night she and Bobby Ray had gone to talk to the elder Culpeppers to tell them they were getting married, and why. If Lucretia Culpepper could have struck her dead right then and there, she surely would have. Wanda Nell had never faced such hate in her life as she did that night.

She had been too caught up in her own problems to give much thought to Rusty, and now she could see how he might still be hurt by that long-ago neglect.

But was that all it was?

She didn't know the answer to that, after thinking about it for a few minutes and trying to dredge her memory. She'd just have to work on Rusty and keep trying to talk to him.

The sound of a car pulling into the carport beside the

trailer brought her firmly back to the present. She glanced at the clock. Miranda was cutting it a bit fine, but Wanda Nell could make it to work on time. She headed for the shower.

Fifteen minutes later, refreshed and dressed for work, she found Miranda and her grandson Lavon in the kitchen. Lavon was crying, his face red and tear-stained. Miranda was doing her best to ignore him while she talked on the phone.

On seeing his grandmother, Lavon stopped crying and began hiccuping instead. Wanda Nell picked him up from the floor and kissed his cheeks, tasting the tears. She spoke soothingly to him, and soon his hiccups ceased. He hugged her neck and laid his head on her shoulder.

Wanda Nell glared at her daughter. Miranda kept her back to them, speaking in a low voice.

"Miranda!"

Miranda's back hunched up. She muttered something into the phone, hung it up, then turned to face her mother.

Wanda Nell paid no attention to the defiant look on Miranda's face. "What do you mean, letting this baby cry and carry on like that while you're on the phone? Can't you see he's tired and needs to be put down for a nap?"

"I had to talk to somebody," Miranda said, her face set in sullen lines.

"And that was more important than seeing to your baby?"

Miranda flinched at the tone in her mother's voice.

Upset by the arguing, Lavon began whimpering. Annoyed with herself, Wanda Nell consoled him. "Come on, sweetie pie, I'm gonna put you down for a nap." She kept talking to him as she took him down the hall to the bedroom he shared with his mother.

Wanda Nell had to bite back more harsh words when she discovered that his diaper was filthy and soaking wet.

"No wonder you're crying," she said under her breath. Quickly she dropped the diaper into the pail beside his crib, then commenced cleaning him and putting him into a fresh diaper.

Soothed by his grandmother's loving care, Lavon calmed and soon curled up with his stuffed bunny. Wanda Nell pulled a blanket over them and watched her grandson for a moment. His eyes closed, and he dropped right off to sleep.

She tiptoed out of the room and closed the door softly behind her. Her face set in stern lines, she went back to the kitchen.

Miranda was on the phone again, but the minute she heard her mother behind her, she put the receiver back on the hook. Slowly she turned to face her mother.

"That baby's diaper was filthy," Wanda Nell said, holding on hard to her temper, "and it looked like he'd been that way for longer than he should've been. How would you like it if you had to go around like that?"

Miranda flushed. "I'm sorry, Mama."

"You dang well oughta be, Miranda. You've got to take care of him. I can't be here every minute watching over the two of you, and you can't make Juliet do it for you. You hear me?"

"Yes, Mama." Miranda's head had dropped, and her voice was so low Wanda Nell could barely hear her.

Wanda Nell took a deep breath. Then she stepped forward and wrapped her arms around her daughter. Miranda stood stiffly for a moment, then she settled into her mother's embrace.

"I know it's hard, sweetie," Wanda Nell said softly. "You wanna be out having fun with your friends, and instead, you've got a baby to look after." She stroked Miranda's bowed head. "I know what it's like, because I wasn't much older than you are now when T.J. was born.

But Lavon is a baby, honey, and he needs you to look after him. You're his mama, and you've got to be somebody he can count on."

"I know, Mama," Miranda said, her voice muffled. She pulled away and looked into her mother's face. "I'll try harder, I promise."

"Good," Wanda Nell said. "Now, go wash your face. I've got to get to work. If you need me, call me, okay?"

Miranda nodded. She walked past her mother and headed for the bathroom.

Wanda Nell stared blankly at the kitchen cabinets. What was she going to do with that girl? How many times was she going to have to give her the same lecture? She kept thinking maybe Miranda was becoming more responsible, and then she'd do something like this.

Her head beginning to ache, Wanda Nell grabbed her purse and car keys. Time to get to work.

Four

Things were really hopping at the Kountry Kitchen that evening. Saturday nights were usually the busiest, and Wanda Nell didn't have much time to worry about Miranda or Rusty. The steady flow of customers kept her, Gladys Gordon, and Ruby Garner, the other night-shift waitresses, constantly on the move. Melvin was going back and forth, running the cash register and busing tables.

Around nine the crowd started to thin out, and Wanda Nell took a quick bathroom break. When she came back, Ruby Garner said, "Some guy back there's asking for you, Wanda Nell. The table in the back left corner."

"Thanks," Wanda Nell said. She cast a quick glance over her tables in the front dining room before heading to the rear of the restaurant. She glanced toward the corner Ruby had indicated, and she almost stopped dead in her tracks from surprise. She got a sick feeling in her stomach.

Bert Vines looked up as she approached. His face was set in grim lines.

"Evening, Bert," Wanda Nell said. "What can I get for you?"

Vines jerked his head toward the empty chair beside him. "Why don't you set yourself down here for a minute, Wanda Nell. You and me's got some talking to do."

The feeling in her stomach got worse as Wanda Nell did what Bert asked. This had to have something to do with Rusty. What the hell was going on?

"What about?" Wanda Nell was surprised to hear her voice come out steady.

"That sonofabitchin' brother of yours," Bert said hotly. His face flushed a deep red. "You need to tell him to get the hell back to Nashville and stay there. He's got no business in Tullahoma."

"Just what is going on here, Bert?" Wanda Nell didn't like Bert's tone one little bit, and her temper was on the rise. She made an effort to hang on to it. "Why are you so interested in what Rusty's doing here? What business is it of yours?"

"He's making it my business," Bert replied shortly. "And he's gonna find himself in deep shit if he keeps on. He's messing with the wrong people."

"And who would they be?"

Bert dropped his gaze. "That ain't your business either, Wanda Nell. I got a lot of respect for you, and I remember what a fine man your daddy was. That's the reason I'm coming to you."

"I guess I appreciate that, Bert," Wanda Nell said, "but I'm having a hard time figuring out what kind of business Rusty has with you. He's been in Nashville a long time."

"He's coming back here and stirring up things he oughta leave alone," Bert said, still not looking at her. "That's all I can tell you. You take it from me, you'll all be better off if he hightails it back to Nashville first thing tomorrow."

"This don't make much sense," Wanda Nell said. Her

mind was racing. What kind of connection did Rusty
have with Bert Vines? They had known each other in
school, of course, although Bert had been a year behind
her and a year ahead of Rusty. To her knowledge, Rusty
and Bert had never been close friends.

"It don't have to make sense to you," Bert said. "Just
trust me. It'll be better for everybody if Rusty goes back
to Nashville and leaves well enough alone."

"I don't know what I can do about it. Rusty won't listen to anything I have to say," Wanda Nell told him after
a moment. She felt like banging his head on the table until he told her what was going on, but that wouldn't do
any good. "Maybe if you tell me what it is he's trying to
do, I can figure out how to talk to him."

"You don't want to know," Bert said. "And you better do something about it, or you ain't gonna like the
consequences."

"Don't you threaten me, Bert Vines," Wanda Nell said.
She started to say something else, but she felt a hand on
her shoulder. Surprised, she turned her head to see her
son, T.J., standing there, and beside him, Hamilton "Tuck"
Tucker.

"What's going on here, Mama?" T.J. asked. "Evening,
Mr. Vines. Everything okay?"

Bert Vines stood up. "Just giving your mama a little
friendly advice, T.J. You might tell her to listen to what I
said."

"I'd be a little more careful about how I gave *advice*,
Bert," Tuck said, his tone icy. "It didn't sound too friendly
to me."

Bert's lip curled as he regarded Tuck. "I sure don't
need advice from the likes of you two." He pushed past
Tuck and stalked away.

"What a jackass," Tuck said mildly. "I guess word's

been getting around town about you and me, judging from that little remark." He winked at T.J., and T.J. smiled and shook his head.

T.J. squeezed his mother's shoulder lightly. "What's going on here, Mama?" He moved to the chair vacated by Bert Vines and sat down. Tuck took the chair across the table from Wanda Nell.

"We came by for a late dinner," Tuck explained, "and Ruby sent us back here. We heard what sounded like Bert threatening you over something."

Wanda Nell took a deep breath and tried to calm down. She didn't want to get any more of her family involved in whatever mess Rusty was stirring up, but she couldn't evade their questions. She also didn't like the way Bert Vines had reacted toward T.J. and Tuck, but she was just going to have to get used to that, if she ever could.

"My brother Rusty is back in town," Wanda Nell said, "and evidently he's been stirring some people up, including Bert. I don't know what the heck's going on, but it doesn't sound good, whatever it is."

"Uncle Rusty?" T.J. was astonished. "It's been years since he came back. Wasn't the last time when Grandmama Rosamond died?"

Wanda Nell nodded. "That's about the only time Rusty's been back since he left town over ten years ago, and I don't know what brought him back now." She turned to Tuck. "My brother and I don't get along too well."

"Sorry to hear that," Tuck said. "It sure sounds like he's causing some trouble."

"Yeah, he is," Wanda Nell said, leaning tiredly back in her chair. "And I don't know what to do about it. Heck, I don't even know what it is he's doing. I tried to talk to him about it, and I tried getting something out of Bert. But neither one of 'em will tell me anything."

"You want me to try talking to Uncle Rusty, Mama?"

"Thank you, honey," she said. "If I thought it would do any good, I'd ask you to do that. But I don't think anybody can get through to Rusty. He's so bitter towards me, I don't think he'd pay any attention to you."

"What if a lawyer talked to him?" Tuck asked. "Think that would do any good?"

"It might," Wanda Nell said, "but I hate to get you involved in this mess."

Tuck grinned. "If I'm part of the family, Wanda Nell, it's my mess too, I reckon."

Wanda Nell smiled back at him. He truly was part of the family. He adored T.J., and as far as Wanda Nell could tell, T.J. adored him. She still couldn't quite believe it, but when she saw the two of them together, she tried not to think about it. They seemed so happy together, and that was all that really mattered to her.

"You are part of the family," Wanda Nell said softly, "and we're proud to have you."

Tuck winked at her. "I'm the lucky one."

T.J. groaned. "I think I'm going into sugar shock right here."

Making a face at her son, Wanda Nell stood up. "Y'all said you came to eat, so let's get you something before we start closing up. What'll you have?"

Wanda Nell took their orders to the kitchen, then brought them tea and water. Apparently sensing that Wanda Nell didn't want to talk any more about her brother, neither T.J. nor Tuck brought up the subject again. Wanda Nell was relieved not to have to talk about it.

Around ten, when they were ready to leave, they each gave her a quick kiss on the cheek before heading up front to pay Melvin at the cash register.

"Y'all be careful," Wanda Nell said softly. She couldn't

help herself. They were both well able to take care of themselves, but it didn't stop her worrying.

T.J. turned back to grin at her, and for a moment she saw, not her son, but her dead ex-husband. T.J. was the spitting image of his daddy at that age, and Wanda Nell felt a fleeting pang of grief for Bobby Ray.

Shaking off her morbid thoughts, she concentrated on cleaning up the table. She pocketed the generous tip with a sigh and a shake of the head. No matter how many times she fussed at them about it, they always left her way too much. She took half of it and surreptitiously stuck it on one of Ruby's tables. Ruby could always use the extra money for her classes.

By the time she got in her car to drive home, it was nearly ten-thirty. She rolled her shoulders for a moment before she cranked the car. Maybe she'd take a hot shower when she got home. That would help ease the tension a bit and let her sleep.

She had turned off the highway onto the lake road when her cell phone rang in her purse, startling her. One hand on the wheel, she stuck the other hand into her purse, probing for the phone.

She wasn't fast enough. The phone had stopped ringing by the time she had it in hand. Fumbling with the phone, she punched buttons until she could see who the missed call was from, and her heart skipped a beat. It was her home phone number. Trembling, she hit speed dial.

All she got was a busy signal. She dropped the phone back into her purse and concentrated on driving the last couple of miles to the trailer park. She was driving too fast, but she knew the road well, and there was no other traffic.

About three minutes later she pulled into the driveway of the trailer park. Her trailer was the first one to the right after the park entrance. Her headlights hit the side of a car parked in front of her trailer, and she slammed on her brakes in shock.

Wanda Nell jumped out of her car, her heart in her mouth. What was a sheriff's department car doing in front of her trailer?

Five

Wanda Nell thrust open the door of her trailer and stepped inside. Her racing pulse began to slow. Juliet, Miranda, and Lavon were sitting on the couch, apparently unharmed. Sitting across from them, however, was one of Wanda Nell's least favorite people.

"Elmer Lee, what the heck are you doing here?"

Sheriff's Deputy Elmer Lee Johnson stood up and scowled at Wanda Nell. "And good evening to you, Wanda Nell. I'm fine, how've you been?"

"Stop trying to be cute, Elmer Lee," Wanda Nell said. "Girls, are you okay? What's happened?"

"They're fine," Elmer Lee said before either Miranda or Juliet could respond. Lavon was chattering and holding out his arms, and Wanda Nell walked over to scoop him up into her arms. She kissed his cheeks and nodded her head at his babbling. Maybe soon they'd be able to understood what he was talking about.

"So is this some kind of social call?" Wanda Nell kept her voice cool, though just the sight of Elmer Lee standing so casually in her living room made her head ache. In her experience, Elmer Lee's presence usually meant trouble of some sort.

"No, it's business, Wanda Nell," Elmer Lee said. "Why don't you sit down for a minute, and let me talk to you."

More uneasy than ever, Wanda Nell complied with his request. What if something had happened to T.J. or Tuck? The awful thought struck her, and her mouth went dry.

"I'm just looking for some information," Elmer Lee said. "I hear your brother Rusty's back in town."

Wanda Nell took a deep breath and relaxed slightly in her chair. She might have known it had something to do with Rusty. "Yeah, he's back for a visit."

"You know where I might find him?"

Wanda Nell shrugged. "He's staying with Mayrene next door, and if he's not there, well, I don't know where he is. Out gallivanting around somewhere, probably getting drunk."

"Mighty high opinion you have of your brother," Elmer Lee said. "Gallivanting around and getting drunk. But now I think about it, I reckon you're right. I remember some of the hijinks he got up to before he left town, what, ten years ago?"

Wanda Nell nodded. "Yeah, about ten years ago. He's been living in Nashville recently." She rocked Lavon gently in her lap. "How come you want to talk to him? He was never a buddy of yours."

"He's been running around town stirring people up. Some people it don't do to stir up, if you get my drift. I think I ought to have a little talk with him before things get ugly."

"What do you mean, get ugly?" Lavon reacted to the note of alarm in his grandmother's voice and started to whimper. Wanda Nell did her best to soothe him while she waited for an answer.

"Sounds like he's been threatening some people," Elmer Lee said. "And I aim to stop him before something happens."

"What people? Has Bert Vines been talking to you?"

Elmer Lee scowled. That answered the question for her, despite what he said next. "I can't say who, but that don't matter. Rusty just can't go around bothering people."

Wanda Nell wanted to throw something at his head, preferably something hard and pointed. "I don't know what to tell you," she finally said. "Rusty's got something on his mind, I know that, but he's not talking to me about it. I just know I don't want to see anybody get hurt."

"Neither do I," Elmer Lee said, standing up. "Then I guess you've told me about all you know, or else all you're gonna tell me."

"I'm not lying to you, Elmer Lee," Wanda Nell retorted. "I know it's hard for you to believe that, but I don't have a clue what's going on." She stood up and handed Lavon to his mother. The girls had been sitting wide-eyed and, in Miranda's case, open-mouthed during her exchange with Elmer Lee.

Elmer Lee strode to the door. Wanda Nell followed him. As he opened the door, the deputy regarded her for a moment. The stern look on his face softened slightly. "I know you may not believe me, Wanda Nell, but I'm just trying to help. I don't want to see you or your family in any kind of trouble."

"Thank you," she said. "I appreciate that." She wasn't quite sure what to make of Elmer Lee trying to be friendly. Was he sincere? Or was he just trying to lull her into relaxing her guard around him?

"When you see Rusty, you tell him I want to talk to him," Elmer Lee said.

"Okay," Wanda Nell replied. She shut the door after him and stood there a moment, lost in thought.

"Mama, what's Uncle Rusty doing?"

Miranda's voice brought Wanda Nell out of her reverie. She turned to look at her daughters. "I'm not sure, honey. I don't know if it's anything we need to worry about, but if your uncle comes around here when I'm not home, y'all be careful. I don't think he'd ever harm you, but it don't hurt to be careful."

"He was real nice to me when I talked to him this morning," Juliet said. "He even gave me a ride to the library so Miranda didn't have to." She frowned. "I'm sorry, Mama, but I thought it was okay, him being my uncle."

"It was okay, honey," Wanda Nell said, "but from now on, I think you'd better not accept any rides from him." Her heart ached at having to warn her daughters about her own brother, but the safety of her children and grandson had to come first. "Everything's gonna get straightened out, and we won't have to worry about any of it. Y'all just get ready for bed, okay?"

Juliet gave her a hug and a kiss before heading to her bedroom. Miranda stood, Lavon on her hip, watching her mother uncertainly.

"What is it, honey?" Wanda Nell could tell Miranda wanted to talk about something.

"I didn't wanna say nothing in front of Juliet," Miranda said, "because I don't think she noticed it, Mama. But I thought I oughta tell you."

"Tell me what?" Wanda Nell's voice came out sharper than she intended, and Miranda scowled. "Sorry, honey, I'm just tired and worried. What do want to tell me?"

"It's about Uncle Rusty," Miranda said, frowning. "Maybe it don't mean a thing, but I just thought it was strange."

"What?" Wanda Nell forced herself to be patient. Miranda was a slow thinker, and a slow talker, and it didn't do any good to try to hurry her along.

"It was the way he looked at Lavon," Miranda said. She paused, obviously struggling for the words she wanted. "You know how most people around here look at me and Lavon, like we was something the cat threw up." Her brow furrowed in anger. "Like it was any of their business who Lavon's daddy is."

"I know, honey," Wanda Nell said gently. They had faced a lot of uncomfortable moments because of the color of Lavon's skin. "Did Rusty do or say something nasty to you and Lavon?"

Miranda shook her head. "No, he didn't. He just had this funny look on his face. Then he reached out like he wanted to hold Lavon, but Lavon was shy with him and wouldn't let him."

Wanda Nell frowned. It did sound a bit odd, not like what she imagined Rusty's reaction would be.

"He just looked real sad for a minute," Miranda said. "Then he said something really strange."

"What did he say?" Wanda Nell prompted her after Miranda trailed off.

Frowning, Miranda thought. "Well, it was something like, 'I hope you have a better time of it, little man.' What did he mean by that, Mama?"

"I have no idea," Wanda Nell said, totally puzzled. Maybe Rusty had something wrong with his head. She had read about cases where people with brain tumors did and said strange things. Could that be what was wrong with her brother?

"Anyway," Miranda continued, "I just thought I should tell you. Come on, baby, let's go get ready for bed." She kissed Lavon on the forehead. "Goodnight, Mama."

"Good night, honey," Wanda Nell said. "Good night, Lavon."

"Night," said Lavon clearly, startling both his mother and his grandmother. They grinned and said good night again to the baby, and he started chanting the word *night* over and over. Laughing, Miranda took him off to bed.

Still smiling over the baby's accomplishment, Wanda Nell walked into the kitchen and picked up the phone. She punched in a number and waited for a response.

"You weren't in bed yet, were you?" she asked when Mayrene answered.

"Naw, I'm still up puttering around," Mayrene said. "What's going on with you?"

Quickly Wanda Nell filled her in on Elmer Lee's visit. Mayrene whistled when she had finished. "I was back in my room with the TV on and I didn't hear a thing. What do you reckon your brother's up to?"

"I sure wish I knew," Wanda Nell said. "I don't like the sound of this. If somebody's complaining about him to the sheriff's department, then he's really getting somebody riled up. And that can't be good."

"No," Mayrene agreed. "I ain't seen him since this morning, so I don't know what he's been up to. And he ain't showed up yet."

"I figure Elmer Lee's probably sitting out there on the road somewhere, waiting for him to come home," Wanda Nell said.

"Maybe it'll be a good thing if Elmer Lee gets hold of him before something happens," Mayrene said.

"I guess so," Wanda Nell said. "But if you do hear him come in sometime tonight, will you call me? I want to talk to him, and if I have to slap him upside the head five hundred times, I'm going to find out what he thinks he's doing."

Mayrene laughed. "Well, either I'll hold him down while you slap him, or I'll just let Old Reliable do the talking for you."

Wanda Nell snorted. *Mayrene and her shotgun.* Mayrene thought she could do anything and get anything she wanted as long as she had that danged gun in her hands. So far she pretty much did. Wanda Nell wasn't too worried about her.

"If it comes to that," Wanda Nell said, "we'll really be in trouble."

After telling her not to worry too much, Mayrene said good night and hung up the phone.

Wanda Nell wandered back to her bedroom. She thought about taking a hot shower, but she was now so tired she didn't feel like making the effort. Instead she took off her clothes, got into her nightgown, and crawled into bed.

She fell asleep almost as soon as her head hit the pillow and slept soundly until she was awakened sometime later by a pounding at the door.

Bleary-eyed, she glanced at the bedside clock. It was just barely seven o'clock.

Climbing out of bed, she threw on a robe and padded to the front door.

The minute she opened it, she knew she was in for bad news.

Elmer Lee stood there, a grim scowl on his face.

Six

"I need to talk to Rusty," Elmer Lee said, pushing his way inside the trailer. "Where is he?"

Annoyed by Elmer Lee's rudeness, Wanda Nell slammed the door before she thought about it. She winced at the sound, hoping it wouldn't wake up the girls and Lavon.

"How in the Sam Hill should I know?" Wanda Nell said, folding her arms across her chest. She didn't feel comfortable standing there in her robe and nightgown with Elmer Lee. "We went through all this last night, Elmer Lee. Did you check next door with Mayrene?"

"I did," Elmer Lee said, "and he ain't been there all night. Have you heard from him?"

"No," Wanda Nell said. "What's so urgent now? You weren't behaving like this last night."

"Last night I wasn't investigating a murder," Elmer Lee said baldly.

"A murder?" Wanda Nell could barely whisper the words. She stumbled over to a chair and plopped down on it. She pulled her robe tightly across her and stuck her hands under her arms to warm them. Her body suddenly went ice cold. Surely this couldn't be happening again.

"Yeah," Elmer Lee said, "and Rusty may have something to do with it. I need to talk to him."

"Who was murdered?" Wanda Nell tried hard to keep her voice steady.

Elmer Lee regarded her silently for a moment. "Reggie Campbell. You know him?"

Wanda Nell thought about it. She tilted her head, looking up at Elmer Lee. Then it hit her. "He was in Rusty's class in high school, I think. And his brother is a veterinarian."

"Yeah. Dr. Tony Campbell. Reggie ran a gas station out on the highway that his mama owns."

"Tony Campbell," Wanda Nell said. "He divorced his wife and then married that niece of Bert Vines, didn't he? She's about the same age as his daughter." She couldn't keep the disgust out of her voice.

"I ain't here to discuss who Dr. Campbell is married to," Elmer Lee said, his impatience barely under control. "I need to find Rusty and talk to him. You sure you ain't seen him or heard from him since last night?"

"No," Wanda Nell said. "Why are you so set on finding Rusty? Why do you think he knows anything about a murder?"

Elmer Lee hesitated briefly before he spoke. "Because witnesses saw Rusty and Reggie having a knock-down drag-out about midnight. This morning somebody found Reggie's body with the back of his head caved in and called the sheriff's department."

Wanda Nell stared mutely up at him.

"I shouldn't even be telling you any of this, Wanda Nell," Elmer Lee said.

Wanda Nell resisted the urge to ask him why the heck he was doing it then.

"Things are looking pretty bad for Rusty," Elmer Lee continued. "I need to find him and find him fast. Campbell's brother's already raising hell over it."

"And you want me just to turn my brother in, is that it?" Wanda Nell got up from her chair. Warmed by fear and anger, she stuck her face in Elmer Lee's. "If my brother killed a man, then he has to face up to it and take what's coming to him. But I'm not gonna sit by and watch somebody railroad him just because it's convenient."

"What the hell do you mean by that?" Elmer Lee's face reddened.

"I been sitting here remembering a few things about Reggie Campbell," Wanda Nell said. "Seems to me there ought to be a pretty damn long line of suspects for killing him. It ain't been that long since that girl living with him ended up in the hospital. Mayrene told me all about it, because the girl's mama gets her hair done at the beauty shop where Mayrene works. And from what I hear, she's just the latest one he's beat up on."

The skin tightened on Elmer Lee's face. He took a step back from Wanda Nell.

"Seems to me you ought to be looking at a lot of other people besides my brother," Wanda Nell went on. "Reggie Campbell was a nasty, worthless excuse for a man, and there was probably plenty of people in Tullahoma wanted him dead." She paused to draw a breath. "I know his mama owns just about half this town, but I don't care how much money she's got. Nobody's gonna railroad my brother, you got that?" She sat down in her chair, trying to get her temper under control.

"I ain't looking to railroad nobody," Elmer Lee said. "I didn't say Rusty was the only suspect, but I ain't gonna comment any further'n that. One way or another, I'm gonna find him, and he's gonna talk. If he's guilty, he's gonna have to pay for it. But if he ain't guilty, then we're gonna find out who is."

"Damn right we are," Wanda Nell said.

"Now hold on there a minute, Wanda Nell," Elmer Lee said, his face flushing red with annoyance. "Just 'cause I said 'we' just now don't mean I want you poking your nose into this like you did before."

Wanda Nell smiled sweetly up at him, ignoring the finger he was shaking in her face. "That's your tale, Elmer Lee. I'm sitting on mine."

"You just better hope you don't end up in jail for interfering in this investigation," Elmer Lee said. "But I know talking to you don't do one blame bit of good. You're as stubborn as any hundred mules I know."

"Why, Elmer Lee, you do say the sweetest things." She grinned at him, determined to goad him.

To her surprise, he threw back his head and laughed, a deep, rolling sound. "Yeah, and one of these days, you maybe'll be lucky enough to hear some more."

Leaving Wanda Nell speechless for once, he turned and marched out of the trailer, closing the door with quiet firmness after him. She heard his boots clomping down the steps, then the opening of the car door and, moments later, the engine roaring to life.

As the sounds of the car faded in the distance, Wanda Nell sat in her chair, deep in thought. She didn't want to delve too deeply into what Elmer Lee had meant by that last remark. She didn't have any time in her life to deal with something that complicated. Besides, she could never think of Elmer Lee that way, not in a million years.

Firmly she forced her thoughts away from Elmer Lee and onto the subject of her brother. Where the heck could Rusty be? And had he killed Reggie Campbell?

Wanda Nell didn't want to think of her brother as a murderer, although she knew he was capable of violent outbursts. Back in high school, after their daddy died, he'd gotten into trouble for fighting several times. He had the same hair-trigger temper she'd been cursed with, and now she worried he had finally gone too far.

The phone rang, but for a moment she ignored it. Her head ached from tiredness and stress, and all she wanted to do was climb back into bed and forget everything and everybody. The phone continued to ring insistently, and she dragged herself into the kitchen to answer it.

"Hello."

"Hey, Wanda Nell, it's Rusty."

Wanda Nell almost dropped the phone.

"Where are you?" she asked.

"I been taking care of some things," Rusty said, actually sounding cheerful and almost friendly. "I'll probably be back sometime tonight. You think maybe . . ."

The rest of what he said was lost in a burst of static.

"What'd you say?" Wanda Nell asked.

There was no response.

"Can you hear me, Rusty?"

Still no response.

"Call me back right away, if you can hear me. I really need to talk to you."

She paused a moment, but the line was dead. She hung up the phone.

Leaning against the kitchen counter, she waited with her hand on the phone. A minute, two minutes, passed, and Rusty didn't call back.

He had been on his cell phone, and he was probably in some area where reception wasn't so good. Cell phones worked pretty well in Tullahoma, but once you got out into parts of the county, especially if there were any hills, sometimes service was real spotty.

Wanda Nell considered the little Rusty had said. From the tone of his voice, he had sounded more upbeat than he had been since he came back. He sure didn't sound like he'd murdered somebody in cold blood, or that he thought the cops were after him.

She took heart at that. Her brother had never been much good at hiding his feelings, and she didn't think he'd learned how to do it that well in the years since she'd seen him.

For once Wanda Nell wished she'd splurged a little and paid for extras like caller ID, but between the regular phone bill and her cell phone, she was paying more than she liked already. She didn't have Rusty's cell number, and unless he called her back sometime today, she had no way of talking to him until he returned that evening.

Sighing, Wanda Nell walked away from the phone and considered what to do next. Should she call Elmer Lee and let him know she'd heard from her brother? And that he didn't sound like he'd killed anybody?

No, she decided, she wasn't going to call Elmer Lee. At least not yet. She wanted a chance to talk to Rusty first. She yawned.

Right now she was going back to bed to get some sleep. Stopping only to down a couple aspirin for her headache, Wanda Nell climbed into bed. Sleep didn't come easily. Deep down, she was still worried about Rusty and what she should do about the trouble he was apparently stirring up.

Finally she dropped off to sleep, and when she woke up again, groggy and still tired, it was nearly two o'clock. She could hear faint sounds emanating from other parts of the trailer. Her worries about her brother returned, now that she was awake again. She tried to push her concerns to the back of her mind, at least for a while.

Twenty minutes later, refreshed by a shower and dressed in a comfortable pair of jeans and a T-shirt adorned by a faded picture of Reba McEntire, Wanda Nell wandered into the kitchen. Juliet, her blonde hair pulled back into a ponytail, was munching on a sandwich while Lavon stuffed his face with macaroni and cheese. His small brown face was smeared with cheese, and he smiled happily at his grandmother.

Wanda Nell greeted her daughter and grandson, kissing the boy on the forehead and doing her best to avoid his sticky fingers. Lavon chattered away at her, and Wanda Nell listened intently. Much of what he said now was clear, and he was acquiring new words pretty quickly. Miranda had been very slow to talk, and for a while, Wanda Nell had worried that Lavon might be like his mother.

"He's been talking a mile a minute," Juliet said laughingly. "Now that he's got started talking, it's hard to get him to be quiet."

"Oolie," Lavon said, commanding his aunt's attention. That was the closest he could come at the moment to Juliet's name.

"Yes, sweetie pie?" Juliet said, and Lavon needed little more encouragement to gabble away at her, something to do with his bunny sitting in the high chair beside him.

"I think that bunny better have a bath real soon," Wanda Nell said, eyeing the cheese-smeared rabbit with disfavor. "In fact, I think they both need a good bath." She pulled a can of Diet Coke out of the refrigerator, opened it, and sipped from it.

Juliet laughed. "Well, I'll give Lavon a bath after we're finished with lunch, and I'll do my best with the bunny."

"Where's Miranda?" Wanda Nell asked. "I thought she was going to be here this afternoon. She should be giving Lavon his bath, not you."

Juliet shrugged. "It's okay, Mama. I don't mind a bit."

"You didn't answer my question," Wanda Nell said in a mild tone.

Juliet flushed slightly. "Miranda went out with some

friends. Somebody's having a picnic out by the lake, and she asked if I'd look after Lavon so she could go. I truly don't mind, Mama."

Wanda Nell shook her head. "That's not the point, honey. I know you don't mind. But Miranda's taking advantage of you, because she knows you'll look after Lavon for her. This is the third Sunday in a row she's done this, and I'd be willing to bet she did the same thing yesterday."

Juliet didn't say anything and avoided looking at her mother.

"I guess I'll have to talk to her again," Wanda Nell said.

"It doesn't really matter that much, Mama," Juliet said. "I'm at home most of the time on the weekends anyway, and I don't mind staying home with Lavon. I don't really have anything else to do."

Juliet didn't sound sorry for herself, Wanda Nell was relieved to hear. Her youngest child was pretty but shy. So far she didn't seem to be that interested in boys, unlike her sister. Miranda had been boy-crazy from the time she was twelve. Wanda Nell figured maybe she ought to be counting her blessings and not fussing too much about Juliet staying home. At least that way she wouldn't end up like her sister, unmarried, with a baby, and expecting everyone else to take care of her.

"Isn't Mr. Pemberton coming over sometime this afternoon?" Juliet smiled innocently at her mother.

"Oh Lord," Wanda Nell said. "He sure is, and I'd forgotten about it, so much has been going on."

"Like what?"

Wanda Nell regarded her daughter. She'd just as soon keep all this mess away from her children, but she realized there was not much point in trying. Briefly, she explained the situation to Juliet.

"Oh Mama, that's awful," Juliet said. She got up and put her plate in the sink, then pulled Lavon and his bunny out of the high chair. "Do you think Uncle Rusty really did it?"

"No, I don't," Wanda Nell said. "But we're all gonna need to be careful until all this is sorted out."

"Yes'm," Juliet said. She twisted her head to keep Lavon's cheesy hands away from her ponytail. "Come on, sweetie, let's go have a bath."

"Holler if you need me," Wanda Nell called after them. She made herself a sandwich and sat at the table eating it while she thought about her date with Jack Pemberton.

They were supposed to drive over to Greenwood for a movie and dinner afterward, but after that call from Rusty, she wasn't sure she wanted to be away from home this afternoon and evening. She really ought to be here when and if Rusty actually showed up.

Jack would be awfully disappointed. They didn't get many chances to be together because of her work schedule, so the times they did have were special to both of them. Wanda Nell was disappointed herself. She would have enjoyed a few hours away from her responsibilities to spend with an attractive and attentive man.

Maybe Jack wouldn't mind coming over for dinner and watching a movie here while she waited for her brother to appear. If she explained the situation to him, she was sure he'd understand. That was one of the things she liked best about Jack. He was a caring and understanding man. Still, it was irritating to have to rearrange her plans.

Sighing, Wanda Nell got up from the table and went to the phone. Better break the news now.

Seven

Wanda Nell handed Jack Pemberton the beer she had brought him and sat down on the sofa with him. Holding the beer in his right hand, he slipped his left arm around Wanda Nell's shoulders and pulled her closer to him. Sighing, Wanda Nell laid her head against his shoulder. "Feels nice," she murmured.

"Sure does," Jack whispered as his lips brushed the top of her head.

"I'm sorry we couldn't go to Greenwood like we planned," Wanda Nell said, her head still nestled against him. "You're gonna get mighty sick and tired of my family if this keeps up."

Jack laughed, a low, pleasant sound. "One thing about you, honey; it's never dull." He sipped from his beer.

"Dull sounds kinda nice now and then," Wanda Nell said, her tone wry.

Jack set his beer down on the table beside the sofa. Capturing Wanda Nell's right hand in his, he brought it to his lips and kissed it softly. Then he shifted a bit on the couch so that he could turn his face to hers. She smiled as he pulled off his glasses. He always did that before he kissed her.

After a few very satisfying minutes, Wanda Nell reluctantly pulled away, and Jack put his glasses back on. He started to speak, but Wanda Nell, knowing what he was going to say, touched his lips lightly with her forefinger. She was pretty sure she loved him too, but she wasn't anywhere near ready for that kind of complication in her life. So far, Jack had been very willing to take things easy, and she hoped he could bear with her a while longer.

"I'd better get in the kitchen and check on dinner," Wanda Nell said, her voice husky.

"I'll come with you," Jack said, shifting his tall, lean frame off the couch.

Wanda Nell, not used to having a man offering to help her with dinner, sat on the couch a moment and watched Jack as he walked toward the kitchen. He looked mighty good in those tight jeans and cowboy boots, she had to admit.

She sighed as she got off the couch. *Better keep your mind on something else, girl*, she told herself. *No use getting all heated up over something you aren't ready for yet, no matter how much you think you might want it.* Then she laughed softly to herself as she followed Jack into the kitchen.

"How many are you expecting for dinner?" Jack asked.

Wanda Nell checked the roast she had cooking in the oven. It would be done pretty soon.

"Well, you and me and Juliet and Lavon, for sure. T.J. and Tuck might drop by later." Would Rusty turn up? She started worrying again about where he was and what he could be up to.

"They seem to be doing pretty well," Jack said. "Are you getting more used to them being a couple?"

Wanda Nell shrugged, trying to keep thoughts of Rusty from intruding so much. "I guess. It's so obvious when they're around me—how much they care about each other, I mean. And if T.J.'s happy and settled down, then that makes me happy." She frowned. "But you know how people can be around this town."

"Yeah," Jack said. "But neither one of them is going out of his way to stir up trouble. They're both pretty sensible."

Wanda Nell shrugged again. "I just keep praying nothing bad happens, but I know there's not much I can do about it." She pointed toward the sink full of potatoes she had washed earlier. "If you really want to help, you can start by peeling those. That is, if you want any mashed potatoes for dinner."

"Yes, ma'am," Jack said, saluting smartly. He picked up the knife lying by the sink and set to work. "Do you think Miranda will be back for dinner?"

"I never know with that girl," Wanda Nell said, lifting the lid on the pot of green beans she had cooking on the stove. She added a little water before replacing the lid. "She may show up or she may not. When she's out having a good time, she sure don't think much about anybody else." She opened a package of rolls and started arranging them on a cookie sheet. Which one should she be more concerned about, Rusty or Miranda? She'd like to give both of them a good talking-to.

"Have you thought about trying to get her back to school so she can get her diploma?" Jack was peeling the potatoes expertly, Wanda Nell noted with appreciation. She had been pleased to discover he was quite handy in the kitchen.

Brushing the rolls with some soft butter, Wanda Nell laughed a little bitterly. "I'd like her to, but she was always a pretty poor student. She never liked school, and most of the time she just barely passed."

"Did you ever have her tested to see if maybe she's dyslexic, or has some other kind of learning disability?"

"Yeah," Wanda Nell said, "but they didn't find anything wrong with her." She shook her head. "It's a sad thing to have say about your own child, but I can't help it: Miranda's just not that smart. I don't know what happened with her, because Juliet's real smart, and so is T.J. when he gets motivated."

"That makes it tougher on you," Jack said. He had finished peeling the potatoes, and now he dropped them into a pan of water and set them on the stove. He punched the burner on and turned to watch Wanda Nell as she put the rolls into the oven.

"It's just the way it is," Wanda Nell said. "I keep hoping Miranda will grow up a little, and maybe she will at some point." She shut the door of the oven. "But enough of that. I appreciate the fact that you're concerned about all of us, but I don't want you feeling like you have to take all that on."

"I know, honey," Jack said. He placed a hand on each of her shoulders and looked down into her face. "But you're part of a package deal, and it's no use telling me otherwise." He grinned. "At least your part of the package is pretty damn sexy."

Wanda Nell grinned back at him. "And so is yours, mister, but don't you be letting that go to your head."

Jack drew her into his arms for a kiss, and for a few moments Wanda Nell lost track of everything other than herself and Jack.

"Well, well," a voice drawled, "looks like you found yourself a feller, Wanda Nell. You gonna introduce me, or are you just gonna stand there all day with his tongue down your throat?"

Surprised, Wanda Nell jerked away from Jack's arms and regarded her brother with a rapidly deepening blush.

"Don't be a jackass, Rusty," she snapped. "I don't appreciate you being vulgar and trying to embarrass me in front of a friend."

"Sor-*ree*," Rusty said, throwing his hands up in mock apology. "Didn't know I was going to set all that off. Cool down, sis, I don't mean nothing by it."

Wanda Nell glowered at him for a moment, but she knew arguing any further wouldn't accomplish a danged thing. Taking a deep breath, she said, "Rusty, this is my friend Jack Pemberton. Jack, this is my little brother, Rusty Rosamond." She put some emphasis on the word *little* and had the satisfaction of seeing Rusty scowl.

"How do you do?" Jack stuck out his hand, and Rusty took it. "It's good to meet you."

"Glad to meet you," Rusty said. He stuck his hand in his pocket and regarded his sister and Jack blandly.

"You made it back in time for dinner," Wanda Nell said, determined to be polite.

"Good," Rusty said. "I ain't had much to eat today, and I sure could use a good meal. I reckon you must've learned to cook pretty good by now."

"Wanda Nell's a fine cook," Jack said, with a quiet edge to his voice.

Wanda Nell shot him a quick look. She could see he wasn't too impressed with Rusty, not that she could blame him. Rusty was acting like a jerk, and he knew it. He just didn't care. Wanda Nell wasn't sure why she should either. She was tired of Rusty's attitude.

"Where've you been, Rusty?" Wanda Nell said. "Did you know the sheriff's department is looking for you?"

"What the hell for?" Rusty demanded, obviously surprised.

"Somebody got murdered," Wanda Nell said, watching him closely. Was he really surprised by what she was telling him, or was he putting on an act?

"Murdered?" Rusty stared at her. "What the hell kind of joke is this, Wanda Nell? Who got murdered?"

Beside her, Wanda Nell could feel Jack tense up. He was about to say something. She put a warning hand on his arm. She had told him all about this earlier, so it wasn't a surprise to him. He relaxed.

"Somebody you had an argument with," Wanda Nell said. "There was a witness to it."

"I'll be damned," Rusty said, his face going blank. He fumbled for a chair and pulled it back from the table. Dropping down into it, he just stared at his sister.

Wanda Nell didn't say anything.

After a moment, Rusty spoke. "Who got killed?"

"You mean you had an argument with more than one person yesterday?"

"Don't try to be cute," Rusty snapped. "Who the hell got killed?"

"Reggie Campbell," Wanda Nell said, continuing to watch him closely.

"I'll be damned," Rusty said again, his voice soft and strained.

"What do you know about it?" Wanda Nell stepped closer to the table, her arms folded across her chest.

"*I* didn't do it," Rusty said, "but . . ."

"But *what*? You know who did?" Wanda Nell put her hands palms down on the table and leaned toward her brother. "If you know who did it, Rusty, you better get over to the sheriff's department right now and tell them. Otherwise you're gonna find yourself in jail."

"But I didn't do it," Rusty said, his face suffusing with blood. "I tell you, it wasn't me. You gotta believe me, Wanda Nell." He shook his head. "But I doubt you will, knowing the high opinion you have of me."

"Don't start feeling sorry for yourself," Wanda Nell snapped. "That ain't gonna help nobody."

Suddenly they all became aware of loud knocking on the door.

"I'll go see who it is," Jack offered, and Wanda Nell nodded.

"I swear I didn't do it, Wanda Nell," Rusty said. For once, he sounded like the little brother she had always loved, the one who trusted his big sister to help him out of trouble. "You gotta believe me," he repeated.

"I do," Wanda Nell said simply, and then she wanted to cry at the look on Rusty's face.

"Glad to see you, Rusty."

Rusty turned in his chair.

Elmer Lee Johnson stood there, one hand on the gun at his side.

Eight

"It's been a long time, Rusty," Elmer Lee said.

Rusty stared at him, not saying a word.

"Were you hiding out in the woods behind the trailer, Elmer Lee?" Wanda Nell tried to keep her voice cool.

Jack walked by Elmer Lee and came to stand by Wanda Nell. This time it was he who put a warning hand on her arm. She noticed it but didn't let it stop her.

"Well, here he is. What are you waiting for?"

"Calm down, Wanda Nell," Elmer Lee said. "I just want to talk to Rusty." He might have been talking about watching a football game with a buddy, he was so relaxed.

"What you want to talk about?" When Rusty finally spoke, his voice came out hoarse.

"I reckon your sister's done told you why I want to talk to you," Elmer Lee replied. "But I think maybe you ought to come with me down to the sheriff's department. We can have us a nice long talk there with nobody butting in." He looked pointedly at Wanda Nell. "Y'all can just go on with what you're doing and not worry about ol' Rusty here."

Wanda Nell ignored that last little sally. "I know a real

good lawyer, Rusty. You want me to call him and have him meet you down there?"

"I ain't got money for a lawyer," Rusty said bleakly.

"Don't worry about that," Wanda Nell said. "This lawyer's a member of the family, practically, and I know he'd be willing to help you out."

Rusty frowned at that, obviously wondering what she meant. He glanced curiously at Jack, who shook his head. "Not me," he said.

"No need to be getting a lawyer involved in all of this," Elmer Lee said. "Leastways, not just yet. Come on now, Rusty. Let's get going. I'll ride with you, okay? And we can have us a nice little chat on the way."

Rusty got up from the table. Wanda Nell walked around to where he stood and wrapped her arms around him. For a moment he was stiff in her arms, then he put his arms awkwardly around his sister and returned her hug. Releasing him, Wanda Nell whispered in his ear. "I'm gonna call the lawyer. Don't worry."

Rusty nodded to show that he had heard. Elmer Lee, waiting less patiently now, reached out and tapped Rusty on the shoulder.

"I'm coming," Rusty said. He turned and followed Elmer Lee to the door. Jack went with them to see them out.

Wanda Nell immediately grabbed the phone and punched in Tuck Tucker's cell phone number. "Come on, answer," she grumbled into the receiver after three rings.

Tuck answered on the next ring. "Hello, Hamilton Tucker speaking."

"Hey, Tuck, it's Wanda Nell."

"Hey, Wanda Nell. We're gonna be on our way over there in about ten minutes. That okay?"

Wanda Nell hated to spoil Tuck's Sunday evening, but Rusty needed his help. She didn't trust Elmer Lee and his little *let's be pals* act. The sooner Tuck got down to the sheriff's department, the better. Quickly she filled Tuck in on what had happened.

"I'm on the way right now," Tuck promised. "Don't worry about your brother. It's a good sign that Elmer Lee let him bring his truck. That means they probably aren't planning to hold him."

"Thanks, Tuck. I'm gonna owe you big time for this."

"We'll work it out in Sunday evening dinners," Tuck said, and Wanda Nell had to smile as she said good-bye.

"Thank the Lord for Tuck," Wanda Nell said.

Jack smiled. "Kinda nice having him to call on, isn't it? He's a great guy, but then so is T.J."

Wanda Nell smiled her thanks at him. Her eye fell on the oven. "Oh my Lord, the roast!"

Fearing the roast had burned to a crisp, she hurried over to check on it. Opening the oven door, she peered in. "Whew. It's okay. I was afraid I'd let it burn up with all this going on." She reached for her oven mitts and took the roast out and set it on the trivet on the counter.

"Smells great," Jack said. "I like it well done anyway."

Wanda Nell drew off the oven mitts and dropped them on the counter beside the roast. Jack came to her and folded her into his arms. "Are you okay?" he asked.

"Yeah," she replied. "I'm okay." She enjoyed the warmth of his arms around her. He felt strong and safe.

"What about your brother?" Jack said. He pulled back enough to peer into her face. "Do you believe him?"

Wanda Nell nodded. "I don't know why I do, or even why I should, but I do. I don't think he killed that man."

"But?" Jack asked.

He was getting to know her pretty well, Wanda Nell realized. He had caught the hint of uncertainty in her voice.

"But," Wanda Nell said, drawing away from him, "I do think he knows something about it. He may even know who did it. I'm not sure."

"He never answered your question when you asked him that," Jack said. He went to the stove and checked on the potatoes. He picked up a fork and stuck it in one of them. "I think these are done." He turned the burner off.

"Let them sit for a few minutes," Wanda Nell said. "I don't feel like finishing them right this minute." She sat down at the table.

"You sit there and try to relax a few minutes," Jack said. "I'm perfectly capable of making mashed potatoes." He grinned. "It's actually one of my specialties."

"Have at it," Wanda Nell said, smiling faintly.

She watched as he drained the water from the pot, then retrieved milk, sour cream, and butter from the refrigerator. While he worked, she enjoyed the sight of him perfectly at home in her kitchen, boyishly handsome and intent on his task.

"I saw him yesterday," Jack said as he searched in a drawer for her mashing tool.

"Who?" Wanda Nell asked, startled. "Rusty?"

"Yeah," Jack said. He had found the masher and set to work on the potatoes.

"Where?"

"At the high school," Jack said. "I was there part of the afternoon, working on cleaning out one of the cupboards in my room. Something I should have done before school started. When I was leaving, I guess it was about four o'clock, I decided I'd take a walk around the football field. You know, clear my head a little and get some exercise."

He picked up the sour cream and spooned a large dollop into the potatoes, then added some butter. He continued mashing. "You have to go by the fieldhouse to get to the field, at least coming from the building where I was," Jack explained. "I was about fifty feet or so from the fieldhouse when the door opened and this guy came out.

He stopped in the doorway for a moment, spoke to someone, then stalked off. From what I could see, he looked pretty angry."

"And that was Rusty?"

Jack nodded.

"Did he see you?"

"No, I don't think so," Jack answered. "The afternoon sun would have been in his face, and I doubt he noticed me."

"Did you see who he was talking to?"

"Yeah, it was Scott Simpson," Jack said. "The football coach. He was standing in the doorway when I walked by. He had a nasty look on his face, and he wasn't too happy to see me walking by just then."

"What did he do?"

"Nothing except slam the door shut," Jack said, shrugging. "Does your brother know Simpson?"

Wanda Nell nodded. "Yeah, they were in high school together. I think Scott was a year ahead of Rusty, but they certainly knew each other."

"Good friends?" Jack took the masher to the sink and rinsed it.

"No, I don't think so," Wanda Nell said, raising her voice to be heard over the running water. "Scott hung out with a different crowd, I think."

"Then I wonder why your brother went to see him," Jack said as he dried his hands on a towel.

Wanda Nell shook her head. Then a thought struck her. "Tony Campbell," she said slowly.

"The veterinarian?"

"Yeah. He and Scott were both on the football team in high school," Wanda Nell said, remembering. "I think they were good friends."

"And it was Tony Campbell's brother who was murdered."

"That means there's a link somewhere among all of them," Wanda Nell said.

"Sounds reasonable to me," Jack replied. He sat down at the table with her. "But what kind of link?"

Wanda Nell shook her head. "That I don't know."

"Are you going to try to find out?"

Wanda Nell regarded him squarely. She had heard the note of concern in his voice. "Yeah, I'm going to have to. Unless Rusty tells me what this is all about, and I don't think he's going to, then I'll have to try to find out for myself." She frowned. "I could try talking to Tony Campbell or Bert Vines, but I don't think they'd tell me anything. I haven't seen Tony in a long time, not since our old dog had to be put to sleep."

"No, they probably wouldn't talk to you," Jack said. He too frowned. "And I don't think it's such a good idea to antagonize them, at least not until we have a better idea what's going on here." He regarded her sternly. "And when I say 'we,' I mean 'we.' I think you should be careful about running around by yourself."

Wanda Nell smiled at him. "I appreciate your concern, Jack, and I can promise you I'm not going to do anything foolish. If I need backup, I'll make sure you're with me. Or else Mayrene and her shotgun."

They both grinned at that. Mayrene and her shotgun had been very helpful to Wanda Nell a few times when she'd found herself in tight spots. There wasn't much that scared Mayrene, at least that Wanda Nell had ever seen. Especially when Mayrene had her hands on Old Faithful.

"How are you going to find out what you need to know, then?"

Wanda Nell had been thinking about that. "I know someone who might know, someone who can maybe tell me how all these people are connected."

"Who?"

"Was Miss Ernestine Carpenter still teaching at the high school when you started?"

Jack shook his head. "No, I think she retired a year or two before I was hired." He grinned broadly. "But I've heard about her. She's a legend."

Wanda Nell laughed. "She probably is. She taught me when I was in school, and she was pretty tough. She always knew what was going on and who was in trouble or even who might be about to get into trouble." She looked down at her hands. "She was a good friend to me when I needed someone to talk to, someone outside my own family."

"She sounds like a good person."

"She is. She was always one of those teachers you had to respect, because she expected things of you. She was tough on us, and she expected us to do our best. But if we had problems, we could talk to her. She wasn't self-righteous, like some of the teachers were." Wanda Nell had bitter experience with the self-righteous ones, because when she turned up pregnant in her senior year, she quickly found out who they were.

"Then I guess you'll try to go see her," Jack said. "Want me to come with you?"

"No, I think I'd better talk to her on my own," Wanda Nell said after a moment's thought. "I'd like for you to meet her sometime, though. You'd like her, and I think she'd like you, too."

"Well, anything I can do to help, you just let me know." Jack stood up. "Guess we'd better finish getting dinner ready. The troops are arriving." He nodded at someone standing behind Wanda Nell.

Juliet, with Lavon holding her hand and walking beside her, came into the kitchen. Lavon started telling his grandmother all about his bunny, and Juliet turned him over to Wanda Nell. While Wanda Nell kept the baby occupied,

Juliet and Jack set the table, and before long they were enjoying a hearty dinner.

All through dinner and the movie they watched afterward on TV, Wanda Nell fretted alternately over her brother and Miranda. She wondered what was going on at the sheriff's department and whether Rusty would end up arrested. T.J. had turned up for dinner about half an hour after they had sat down at the table, and all he was able to tell her was that Tuck was at the sheriff's department. Then she worried about Miranda. Where was she, and what was she up to?

Miranda came in at nine, and Wanda Nell could tell right away she had been drinking. Deciding she wouldn't make an issue of it tonight, Wanda Nell just told her to go to bed and they'd talk in the morning. Miranda acted like she wanted to argue with her mother, but one look at Wanda Nell's face and she meekly ambled off to her bedroom.

Trying to concentrate on Jack and the movie they were watching, Wanda Nell did her best to relax and forget about family problems for a while, but she was only partially successful. At about nine-thirty, Tuck called, to Wanda Nell's relief.

"Did they keep Rusty in jail?"

"No," Tuck said, "they really didn't have enough evidence to arrest him. Plus they turned up someone who saw Campbell alive after your brother left him."

"Does that mean he's in the clear?"

"No. He's still a person of interest to the investigation, and it was clear to me, and to the sheriff's department, that your brother's not telling all he knows. He's hiding something, but none of us could get it out of him."

"Where is he now?"

"He ought to be there in a few minutes," Tuck said. "He told me he was going back to Mayrene's to go to bed."

"I'll talk to him and see if I can get him to tell me anything," Wanda Nell said.

"I hope you can," Tuck said, "because he could be in a lot of trouble if he's keeping something back. They may yet arrest him."

Wanda Nell thanked him for his help, and he brushed that aside. He asked to speak to T.J., and Wanda Nell called her son from the living room.

T.J. left a few minutes later, and Jack went right after that. Wanda Nell waited anxiously for the sound of Rusty's truck, but by ten-thirty, he still hadn't turned up. She debated calling Tuck or even the sheriff's department, but finally, with a heavy heart, she went to bed and had a restless night.

Nine

Wanda Nell grimaced when she examined herself in the mirror the next morning around six-thirty. After the night she'd had, she wasn't surprised she looked like death warmed over. She splashed her face with some cold water, then dried herself.

Slipping on her robe, she stepped into the hall and checked to see that Juliet was awake. "Are you doing homework, honey?"

Juliet turned away from the computer screen and smiled. "No, Mama, I was just checking my e-mail before school. Marijane Marter wants me to help her with her English project in study hall today, and I was just e-mailing her back."

"Okay," Wanda Nell said, "but don't be too long. You've still got to get dressed and have your breakfast before the school bus gets here in about an hour."

"I'll be done in a minute," Juliet promised her.

Wanda Nell watched her daughter for a moment, blonde head bent toward the computer screen. She felt completely out of date because she had no idea how to use the computer, and she was still trying to figure out exactly what e-mail was and how it all worked. She kept meaning to sit down and have Juliet teach her about the computer, but there never seemed to be enough time.

Sighing, she headed down the hall toward the kitchen. She peered out the window to see if Rusty's truck was anywhere around. She didn't see it. Sighing again, she picked up the phone and punched in Mayrene's number. All her worries about her brother were coming back with a vengeance.

"Morning," Mayrene said in response to Wanda Nell's greeting. "Where's that brother of yours done got to, Wanda Nell? He never did show up last night."

"I don't have the foggiest notion," Wanda Nell said. "Elmer Lee Johnson showed up and took him down to the sheriff's department last night." She explained why and listened to Mayrene's shocked response. "I called Tuck to go look after him, and the last I heard from Tuck was that he was sending Rusty home. He never made it back here as far as I know. I don't know what's happened or where he could be."

"Are you worried something bad happened to him?"

Wanda Nell hesitated. "I just don't know. Seeing as it's Rusty we're talking about, I wouldn't be surprised if he's already back in Nashville by now. It would be like him to run away from trouble. He's done it before."

"Maybe," Mayrene said. "But what if he didn't? Where could he be?"

"That's what's got me worrying," Wanda Nell said, her head aching slightly. "What if he's had some kind of accident? He could be lying in a ditch somewhere needing help. I've been trying to decide whether to call Elmer Lee, but if Rusty's just run off to Nashville, I don't want to get him into trouble." That was the guilt talking, she knew. She had let Rusty down in the past, and she didn't want to cause more bad feelings between them.

Mayrene snorted into the phone. "If he's done run off to Nashville, then he's going to be in trouble anyway. I don't think Elmer Lee wants him gallivanting out of the state, for Pete's sake. You'd better go ahead and call Elmer Lee, just in case something else has done happened."

"You're right," Wanda Nell said, strengthened in her resolve by her friend's firm tone.

"Call me the minute you hear something. I'll be leaving about eight-thirty to get to work, so you can reach me after that at the beauty shop," Mayrene said, and Wanda Nell said she would.

Moments later she was connected with the sheriff's department, and she gave her name and asked for Elmer Lee. The dispatcher put her on hold while he determined whether Deputy Johnson was available.

After nearly three minutes, Elmer Lee came on the line. "What is it, Wanda Nell? Something wrong?"

Wanda Nell took a deep breath. "Rusty never made it back here last night, and I'm worried something might have happened. Do you know where he is?"

Elmer Lee swore into the phone, and Wanda Nell held the receiver away from her ear for a moment.

"I guess you don't know where he is, either," she said. The pain in her head intensified.

"No, I sure as hell don't," Elmer Lee said, his tone grim, "but I'm damn sure going to."

"Maybe he went back to Nashville," Wanda Nell said, rubbing a hand across her eyes.

"I don't think so," Elmer Lee said slowly. "When I told him he had to stay in Tullahoma for a while, he said he didn't plan on going anywhere."

Wanda Nell's heart sank. "Then something's happened to him."

"Now, don't go borrowing trouble, Wanda Nell,"

Elmer Lee said, his tone softening. "I bet ol' Rusty's safe and sound somewhere with an old friend. He'll turn up before long."

"I hope you're right," Wanda Nell said. But what if whoever killed Reggie Campbell had killed Rusty? She pushed that thought away quickly. It didn't bear thinking about. "Call me the minute you find him."

"I will," Elmer Lee promised. "And you call me right away, too, if he turns up there. Okay?"

"Okay," Wanda Nell said, then placed the receiver on the hook. Rubbing her temples with her fingertips, her eyes closed, she stood there for a couple of minutes trying to ease her headache.

It didn't work. Wanda Nell found a bottle of aspirin in the cabinet over the sink, opened it, and rolled a couple of pills into her palm. Next she got a glass and filled it with Diet Coke. Maybe the combination of caffeine and aspirin would knock the headache out. Something had to, or she was going to have to go back to bed.

Fifteen minutes later when Juliet came into the kitchen for breakfast, Wanda Nell was feeling better. She had already set cereal and a bowl and spoon on the table for Juliet, and as her daughter sat down at the table, she retrieved the milk from the fridge.

"Are you okay, Mama?" Juliet asked as she poured milk over her Honey Nut Cheerios. "You look real tired."

"I'm okay, honey," Wanda Nell said. She filled her glass with Diet Coke again and sat down across from Juliet. "I didn't sleep real well last night, but I'll be okay."

"What's wrong? Is it Miranda?" Juliet asked between mouthfuls of cereal.

"Your uncle Rusty never came back last night."

Juliet's eyes widened in surprise. "Do you think something's happened to him?" She dropped her spoon in the bowl, and a tiny drop of milk splashed onto the table. Barely taking her eyes off her mother, she rubbed at the milk with a finger, then stuck the finger in her mouth.

"I hope not, honey," Wanda Nell said. "But I just don't know. I don't want to think the worst, so I'm just going to hope and pray he turns up soon, and that he's not hurt or anything."

"Me too, Mama," Juliet said. She resumed eating.

"You try not to worry about it and concentrate on school," Wanda Nell said.

Juliet nodded.

Miranda had still not put in an appearance by the time Juliet went outside to wait for the bus, so Wanda Nell tiptoed down the hall to check on Lavon. He was playing quietly in his crib, but he started chattering happily when he saw his grandmother in the doorway. He held out his arms for her.

Miranda was sound asleep and snoring, lying on her back in a tangle of sheets. Wanda Nell left her alone while she tended to the baby. As she suspected, his diaper was soaking wet. She changed him, not caring how much noise either she or Lavon was making.

Wanda Nell set Lavon on his feet on the floor and watched him toddle off toward the kitchen. He knew it was time for breakfast, and he was hungry. Smiling, she followed him.

Wanda Nell had finished feeding Lavon his cereal when Miranda wandered into the kitchen, rubbing her temples the way Wanda Nell had done earlier. "There's some aspirin in the cabinet over the sink," Wanda Nell said.

Miranda mumbled something as she walked over to help herself to the pain relievers. Once she had taken the aspirin, washed down with a glass of water from the tap, she turned around to face her mother.

"Well?" Miranda demanded, frowning. "Ain't you gonna say something?"

"About what?" Wanda Nell asked, her tone deceptively mild.

Miranda's eyes narrowed in suspicion. "About me coming in late last night."

"And being drunk?"

Miranda shrugged. "I had a few beers, maybe. That was all."

"Who were you with?" Wanda Nell didn't look at her daughter. She focused on wiping Lavon's mouth. The baby blinked his big brown eyes at her.

"Just some friends," Miranda said. "Jeez, it's like living with the damn FBI around here sometimes. All these damn questions."

Wanda Nell slowly got up from her chair and stood in front of Miranda. "As long as you're living under my roof and living off me, Miranda, you're gonna answer any question I feel like asking you. Especially when you go off and leave your baby and nobody knows where you are."

Miranda wouldn't meet her eyes. She kept her head turned away. "Maybe I'll move out then. I could find me a place to live."

"You probably could," Wanda Nell said, holding on to her temper by a hair. "But how would you pay for it? And for food and clothes and everything for you and Lavon? Last I heard, you don't have a job."

"I don't," Miranda said, "but I could go and live with . . . with somebody, and Lavon could stay here with you and Juliet."

Wanda Nell clasped her hands together to keep from either slapping Miranda silly or jerking clumps of her hair out by the roots. "And just who do you think you would go and live with? Have you got a new boyfriend?"

"Yeah, I do." Now Miranda gazed defiantly into her

mother's face. "He wants me to come and stay with him, and I told him I'd think about it."

"And I guess he doesn't want Lavon to come with you?"

Miranda's eyes shifted sideways. She mumbled something.

"What was that?" Wanda Nell said, her voice sharp. "I didn't hear you."

"No, he don't," Miranda said more clearly. She licked her lips while she waited for her mother's response.

Wanda Nell stepped back a couple of paces. "Then I'll give you something to think about, Miranda. You can go and live with this guy, whoever he is. But if you do, I'll go to court and get custody of Lavon, and you won't get him back. In fact, you won't even be able to see him. I'll make sure of that. You'll be on your own, and you'll be stuck with this guy, whoever he is. You can't come back here the first time you have a fight."

Miranda's eyes widened in alarm. "You . . . you wouldn't really do that, would you, Mama?"

Wanda Nell took a deep breath. As usual, it was obvious that Miranda hadn't thought her little plan through.

"Yes, I would, Miranda," Wanda Nell said, though in her heart she wasn't sure if she could really go through with the threat. "You can't walk out on your family and your responsibilities and not expect some kind of consequences." She bit back the words she wanted to add: *You're just like your daddy.*

"Then maybe I'll just go and take Lavon with me," Miranda said, "and you won't ever see either one of us again." Tears welled in her eyes.

"You could do that," Wanda Nell said, fighting hard to keep her voice even. "But I don't think that's what either one of us really wants, is it, honey?"

Miranda began sobbing loudly. "I can't ever do anything right with you, Mama. I'm always wrong. Juliet's your favorite, anyway. You don't even really want me here. All you do is fuss at me all the time." The words came out in short bursts between sobs.

Wanda Nell stood and watched her for a moment. She was tempted to walk away and leave Miranda there. On top of everything else, this was too much. She was so tired of dealing with Miranda and her problems. Plus she felt guiltily aware that Juliet truly was her favorite, though she loved all three of her children fiercely. She simply didn't *like* Miranda most of the time.

Wanda Nell reached out and drew Miranda into her arms. Miranda stood stiff and resistant, but Wanda Nell wouldn't let go. "I do love you, Miranda, and I always will. You're my daughter, and I want what's best for you. Always. But I can't do everything for you. You're almost eighteen now, and you've got to grow up and start acting like an adult."

She released Miranda and took her daughter's chin in her right hand, forcing the girl to look at her.

"The world doesn't owe you a living," she continued. "Nobody's going to take care of you for the rest of your life. What would you do if something happened to me? You've got to start learning how to take care of yourself. And your baby."

Miranda threw her arms around her mother and hugged her tightly. "I'm sorry, Mama. I didn't mean it, what I said about taking Lavon and running off. I wouldn't do that. And you won't kick me out, will you? Please say you won't." She started crying again.

"I won't, honey," Wanda Nell said, stroking her daughter's head. "But you've got to straighten up. You need to get a job."

"I will," Miranda said. "I'll start looking today."

"That's good," Wanda Nell said, praying that Miranda would follow through with her promise. Most of the time she didn't. "Now, you go and wash your face, okay? And come back and have some breakfast. You'll feel better."

"Okay," Miranda said, rubbing her nose. She pulled away from her mother and walked over to Lavon's high chair. She patted his head, then bent to kiss his cheek. "Mama'll be back in a minute, sweetie."

Her headache once again pounding, Wanda Nell watched Miranda go with troubled eyes. Had she finally gotten through to the girl? All she could do was hope.

The phone rang, startling her. Hand trembling, she reached for the receiver.

"Hello."

"Wanda Nell," Elmer Lee said. "That you?"

"Yes," she answered. She could tell by the tone of his voice that something had happened. "What is it?"

Elmer Lee expelled a deep breath into the phone. "We found Rusty's truck."

Ten

For a long moment Wanda Nell couldn't breathe. "And Rusty?" She had to force the words out.

"No sign of him so far." Elmer Lee's words were curt. "One of my deputies found his truck about six miles out of town, on the highway going towards Calhoun City. It was down in a ditch. I've got some men heading out there right now to start looking in the area, and I'll be on my way there in a few minutes myself."

"What do you think happened?" Wanda Nell did her best to keep calm, but it was hard work.

"According to the deputy who found the truck, it don't look like it was in an accident. He said it looked like somebody just let it roll into the ditch." He hesitated a moment. "No sign of blood or anything like that."

"Then maybe that means Rusty's alive."

"Your guess is as good as mine," Elmer Lee said.

"You think maybe he's been kidnapped?"

"Either that, or he's done staged some kind of accident for some reason. You think he'd do that?"

"I don't know," Wanda Nell said. "I just don't know. But

who do you think would want to kidnap him? And why? Surely they ought to know he don't have any money."

"There ain't much use in all this speculating, Wanda Nell," Elmer Lee said. "There's just too much we don't know. Look, I got to head out now. I'll let you know if we turn up anything important. In the meantime, you call me if you hear anything from Rusty yourself."

"I told you I would," Wanda Nell said. "I'm just praying I do, and that Rusty's okay."

"Keep on praying," Elmer Lee said. The phone clicked off.

Wanda Nell hung up her receiver for a moment, then took it off again and punched in Mayrene's number. The phone rang seven or eight times, and finally it dawned on Wanda Nell that Mayrene had left for work.

She glanced at the clock. It was just past eight-thirty, so Mayrene was probably still on the road. She'd call her friend later.

She punched in another number, and after a couple of rings, Tuck Tucker answered his cell phone.

Without preamble, Wanda Nell launched into an account of what had been going on.

"Pretty strange" was Tuck's first comment. "I've got no idea what's going on here, Wanda Nell. I know you're worried about your brother, but for the moment, I don't think there's anything we can do except wait. Hopefully Elmer Lee and his men will turn up something soon, and then we can act on that."

"I guess," Wanda Nell conceded, "but I sure hate sitting here twiddling my thumbs. I feel like there ought to be something I can do."

"Do you have any idea what this strange business is your brother is here about?"

"No," Wanda Nell said. "All I can figure is that it has something to do with the past. Something that must've happened years ago, and now Rusty's back in town to do something about it."

"If we knew more about his reasons for coming back to Tullahoma, we'd have something to work with."

"Bert Vines must know something about it," Wanda Nell said slowly, remembering the scene she had witnessed between Rusty and Bert, plus the strange conversation she'd had with Bert at the Kountry Kitchen.

"I don't know him that well," Tuck said thoughtfully. "Do you think he'll talk to you after that little scene at the restaurant?"

"I don't know. Maybe." Wanda Nell sighed. "I may not have much choice."

"If we decide it's necessary, we can go talk to him," Tuck said. "I've got to get ready for court in a few minutes. In the meantime, let's wait till we hear something more from Deputy Johnson. Call me as soon as you do."

"I will," Wanda Nell said. She hung up the phone, then stood staring at it for a moment, trying to make up her mind.

Miranda spoke from behind her, startling her.

"What's going on, Mama? Who were you talking to?"

Wanda Nell turned around. "Your uncle Rusty's disappeared. They found his truck out on the highway going toward Calhoun City. The sheriff's department is out looking for him now."

"Oh my Lord, Mama," Miranda said, her face registering her shock. "I had no idea."

"Well, don't you worry about it," Wanda Nell said. "Just say your prayers that Rusty turns up safe and sound."

"I will," Miranda promised.

"Look," Wanda Nell said abruptly, "I've got some errands I need to do this morning. You think you and Lavon'll be okay while I'm gone?"

Miranda nodded. "I guess so, Mama. I'm gonna call around and see about a job."

"Good," Wanda Nell said. "Why don't you call out at Budget Mart first and see if they'll take you back?"

"You think they would?" Miranda sounded doubtful.

"They might," Wanda Nell said. "Can't hurt to ask. All they can do is say no. And if they do, then you can try someplace else."

"Okay," Miranda said. "I'll try."

Wanda Nell gave her a quick kiss on the cheek, then headed to her room to get ready. She had a quick shower, taking care not to let her hair get too damp. After applying a bit of makeup, she dressed in a pair of jeans and a nice blouse. She might not have time to come home and change for her shift at the Kountry Kitchen, so she might as well be prepared.

There was no sign of Miranda or Lavon when she went back into the kitchen. She collected her purse and her car keys, made sure her cell phone was on and charged, then went out to her car, carefully locking the trailer's front door behind her.

Tuck might think they should just sit around and wait for the sheriff's department to find out something, but Wanda Nell had no intention of sitting still. She knew Elmer Lee would be aggravated with her when he found out what she was doing, but she didn't really care all that much if Elmer Lee got mad at her. He'd been mad at her before, and he'd get over it.

Her first stop was Bert Vines's insurance office, a few blocks down the highway from the Kountry Kitchen. She pulled her Cavalier into an empty space right in front of the door a few minutes after nine. The facade of the small building was mostly glass, and Wanda Nell could see Bert's secretary, Karen Marter, at her desk. Wanda Nell got out of her car and walked into the office.

"Morning, Karen, how are you?"

The secretary looked up from her computer and smiled. "Well, hey there, Wanda Nell, how are you? Marijane was just telling me this morning that Juliet is going to help her with her English assignment." She pulled a wry face. "Marijane's a good girl, but she has a hard time focusing on her schoolwork."

"I know," Wanda Nell said sympathetically. "When they're that age, you never know just what it is they're thinking about. I'm thanking my lucky stars Juliet's not boy-crazy yet."

Karen laughed. "You are lucky. All Marijane can think about is some skinny boy who's crazy about basketball. Of course, next week it's probably going to be some other boy." She shook her head. "I'll be glad when she's not a teenager no more."

Thinking of her own problem teenager, Wanda Nell sighed inwardly.

"Well, I'm sure you didn't come in to talk about teenagers," Karen said. "Can I help you with something, or do you need to see Bert?"

"I need to talk to Bert, if he's available," Wanda Nell said.

Karen glanced down at her phone console. "He's on the phone, but soon as he's off, you can go on in. Oh, the light just went off." She jerked her head. "Go on in."

"Thanks," Wanda Nell said. She stepped past Karen's desk and knocked on the slightly ajar door to Bert's office.

Bert Vines glanced up at the sound of the knock. His slick salesman's smile faded the minute he recognized Wanda Nell. "Morning, Wanda Nell. Something I can do for you?"

"I sure hope so, Bert," Wanda Nell said. She closed the door carefully behind her, then advanced into the room. From what she could see in the office, Bert was doing really well for himself. The desk and all the furnishings looked expensive, and Bert appeared to be spending plenty of money on himself. Wanda Nell noted the watch he was wearing, as well as the heavy gold-link bracelet he sported on the other wrist. A wave of cologne hit her as she moved closer to the chair in front of the desk.

Bert eyed her warily. "So what can I do for you?"

Wanda Nell didn't answer immediately. She had been thinking about how she should approach Bert, and she had finally decided that making up some story wouldn't work. She might as well tell him the truth and see what that got her.

"I'm here about my brother," Wanda Nell said. "Rusty. You were just talking about him to me the other day."

"What about him?" Bert said. "I think I said all I needed to say then." He opened a box on his desk and extracted a large, dark cigar. He snipped off the end, stuck the cigar in his mouth, then lit it with a gold lighter. Expelling a cloud of fragrant smoke, he said, "I hope you don't mind me smoking."

"No," Wanda Nell said. "Smoke doesn't bother me. And it's your office."

Bert regarded her through the haze he was creating. "So what about your brother?"

"He's disappeared, so things are a little different now," Wanda Nell said. She watched Bert carefully for his reaction. His eyes tightened briefly, but he gave no other sign that the news affected him.

Bert exhaled more smoke. "What do you mean, disappeared? You mean he went back to Nashville or wherever it was?"

"No, I don't think he went back to Nashville," Wanda Nell said. "He was on his way back from the sheriff's department last night, and he just disappeared. They found his truck on the side of the road and no sign of him."

"And why do you think this has anything to do with me?"

"Oh, come on, Bert," Wanda Nell said. "You were talking to him just the other day. I saw you leaving the trailer park."

Bert took the cigar out of his mouth and regarded the ash on the tip. He continued to study the cigar as he spoke. "Now that you mention it, I do recall talking to Rusty. What about it?"

"Y'all were arguing about something, not just *talking*," Wanda Nell said, "and I can't help but wonder if what y'all were arguing about has something to do with him disappearing."

Bert sat and puffed on the cigar for at least a minute before he answered. "Rusty and me were just talking over old times, Wanda Nell. Nothing special about that. We disagreed on something, that's all. Nothing important." He shifted in his chair. "Now, if you don't mind, I have some work to do."

"I do mind, Bert," Wanda Nell said, her voice taking on an edge. "I don't know whether you know it, but somebody murdered Reggie Campbell." She could see that he already knew. "And now with Rusty disappearing, I think something strange is going on."

"Maybe Rusty did it, and he's run off," Bert said. "Did you ever think about that?" He tapped the ash from his cigar into an ornate crystal ashtray on the corner of his desk.

"He could've," Wanda Nell said. "But I don't think my brother's a killer. I think maybe somebody kidnapped my brother, but I don't know why. I want to know what you know about it."

"Why should I know anything?"

"If you don't, why were you hollering at Rusty?" Wanda Nell said. "Near as I can recall, you said something like, 'I'll see you in hell first, you bastard.'" She paused. "What was it Rusty wanted from you?"

Bert's face paled, but he remained impassive, exhaling smoke. "I don't really have anything to say to you, Wanda Nell. I think you'd better get on and let me get to work."

"Well, Bert, you can either talk to me, or you can talk to the sheriff's department," Wanda Nell said. "What's it going to be?"

Bert stared hard at her for a moment, his eyes glittering with hatred. He put his cigar in the ashtray and leaned back in his chair. "I've been thinking about that policy you're carrying on your trailer, Wanda Nell. I'm not sure it's really enough, you know? I mean, if something was to happen to it, I don't think your insurance would be near enough. Maybe we should be thinking about more insurance."

Wanda Nell didn't back down from the thinly veiled threat. "I don't think anything's going to be happening to my trailer anytime soon, Bert. But if it does, insurance is going to be the least of my worries, and yours. You understand me?"

Sticking the cigar back in his mouth, Bert remained silent.

"Have it your way," Wanda Nell said, standing up. "You know something, and sooner or later it's going to come out. You'd better think about that, and what's going to happen to you when it does."

She left the office, resisting the temptation to slam the door behind her. She couldn't believe the bastard was threatening her.

"Everything okay?" Karen Marter asked.

Wanda Nell hadn't been paying any attention to the secretary, she was so intent on just getting out of Bert Vines's office. She paused for a moment and took a deep breath. "I'm okay," she said. "I'll be seeing you. I've got a lot to do today."

She waved good-bye to Karen and didn't wait for a response.

Climbing into her car, she sat in it for a moment, staring blankly into space. "Guess I'd better think about getting a new insurance agent," she confided to herself in the rearview mirror.

She backed out of the parking space and nosed her car onto the highway. Had she made a real mess of things by confronting Bert? Probably, she thought. But she wasn't going to stop now. Bert knew something for sure, and by rattling his cage, maybe she could get some results.

Now, though, she had another cage to rattle.

Eleven

Tullahoma High School was only a five-minute drive from Bert Vines's insurance office. Wanda Nell parked in a space marked for visitors, locked her car, then walked up the steps to the main entrance.

Inside, she went immediately to the office and stood waiting for nearly five minutes until the school receptionist finished what was obviously a personal phone call.

"Can I help you?" The woman stared at Wanda Nell in an unfriendly fashion. Wanda Nell remembered her from a confrontation they'd had back in the spring, and it appeared the woman remembered her, too.

"I need to see Coach Simpson, if he's available," Wanda Nell said, keeping her tone polite. "It's urgent."

Lips pressed together in a firm line, the receptionist didn't respond for a moment. "Let me see if he's in class right now," she said grudgingly.

"Thank you," Wanda Nell said. "I'd appreciate that."

The woman turned back to her computer, punched a few keys, then studied the screen. "You're in luck," she said, though it was obvious she was disappointed. "Coach Simpson has a free period right now."

"Where do you think I can find him?"

The woman shrugged. "Probably in his office in the fieldhouse," she said. "You know where that is?"

Wanda Nell nodded.

"Hold on," the receptionist said as Wanda Nell turned away. "You need a pass, or else the security guard might throw you off campus."

She handed Wanda Nell a laminated card with a small clamp attached, and Wanda Nell affixed it to her blouse. The word VISITOR was clearly visible.

"Just bring it back here when you're ready to leave," the receptionist instructed. Wanda Nell nodded.

The shortest way to the fieldhouse took Wanda Nell through the high school's main building. The halls were empty of people, and Wanda Nell hurried down the hall, the rubber soles of her shoes squeaking occasionally on the highly polished linoleum.

She came out the back end of the building and blinked at the bright sunshine. Shielding her eyes with her hand, she looked across an open space toward the fieldhouse about fifty yards away.

She ignored the sidewalk connecting the two buildings and instead walked through the grass in a more direct route to the front door of the fieldhouse. Stepping inside, she noticed the faint odor of stale sweat at once.

The door to the coach's office, a few feet down the hall, was closed. As Wanda Nell stepped closer to it, she could hear odd scuffling sounds coming from within. Peering through the inset opaque pane, she could see only blurs on the other side. She rapped on the door and called out, "Coach Simpson." She tried turning the knob, but the door was locked.

The scuffling sounds stopped abruptly. After a moment, a voice called out, "Just a minute."

Wanda Nell had a very good idea what had been going

on in the coach's office, and it was confirmed a couple of minutes later when the lock snicked open and the door swept inwards abruptly.

A beautiful blonde girl—seventeen or eighteen, Wanda Nell judged—pushed her way out. Wanda Nell moved aside, noting the girl's red cheeks and slightly disheveled hair.

"Good morning, Coach Simpson," Wanda Nell said, moving into the office.

Scott Simpson, once the star quarterback at Tullahoma High School, and afterwards an All-American at Mississippi State, stood behind his desk. His face was slightly red, and one hand raked over the short black hair on his head. He had put on quite a bit of weight since his glory days, Wanda Nell observed, but he was still pretty good looking. Certainly good looking enough to turn the head of a girl who was dumb enough to take up with a forty-year-old teacher.

"I'm not sure if you remember me," Wanda Nell continued when Simpson failed to respond to her greeting, "but we went to school here together. I think you were a year behind me, though."

"You married Bobby Ray Culpepper, didn't you?" Simpson's voice was hoarse. He cleared his throat. "Wanda Nell, right?"

"That's right," Wanda Nell said, advancing further into the office.

"I can't talk long," Simpson said. "I've got another student due in any minute for another counseling session. What can I do for you?"

Wanda Nell just looked at him a moment. Surely he didn't think she was going to buy that baloney about a counseling session. As she stared at him, he flushed beet red. He reached into his back pocket and pulled out a can of tobacco. Opening it, he pinched some between his fingers and thrust the stuff into his mouth.

Wanda Nell didn't comment as he put the tobacco into his pocket again. She thought it was a disgusting habit, but she wasn't here to talk to him about that, either. But she was glad she had a little leverage with him, because of the little scenario she had interrupted.

She sat down in one of the chairs in front of his desk, and after a brief hesitation, Simpson also sat down. He stared uneasily at her, working the tobacco in his mouth.

"If you remember who I am," Wanda Nell said, "then you probably remember my brother, too. Rusty Rosamond." She watched his face.

He paled a little, but didn't respond for a moment. "Yeah, I think I remember him. Skinny little red-headed kid, right?"

Wanda Nell nodded. "That's him."

"What's he doing these days?" Simpson tried to look as if he really cared about the answer.

Smiling, Wanda Nell said, "You mean he didn't bring you up to date the other day when he was here?"

Now Simpson really went pale. He reached for a Styrofoam cup sitting on his desk and spit into it. He set the cup down again. "What do you mean?"

"I know he came to see you," Wanda Nell said. "I just don't know what it was he wanted from you."

"If he did come here, and I ain't saying he did," Simpson said, trying to remain impassive, "I don't see where it's any business of yours."

"It is my business," Wanda Nell said, "because he's my brother and he's disappeared. I think somebody kidnapped him, and I want to know why."

Simpson couldn't hide the shock that her words gave him. He swallowed convulsively, and for a moment, Wanda

Nell thought he had downed his tobacco. He was looking a little green around the gills.

"Kidnapped? Are you serious?"

Wanda Nell nodded. Simpson's eyes strayed to the telephone.

"And I'm sure you heard about Reggie Campbell's murder."

"Yeah," Simpson said. "But it ain't got nothing to do with me."

"It strikes me as kinda odd," Wanda Nell said, her voice neutral, "Reggie Campbell being murdered, and then my brother disappearing like that. Now, I know my brother didn't kill anybody, so maybe whoever killed Reggie is worried about what my brother knows about it. After all, he was talking to Reggie, and he was talking to you." She leaned forward. "Now I just want to know what about."

Simpson stared at her like she was a snake about to strike. He licked his lips, obviously searching for some kind of response. He might have been a quarterback and a star athlete, Wanda Nell thought, but he didn't have brains for much besides football. That much she remembered about him.

While she was waiting for an answer, Wanda Nell let her eyes wander around the room for a moment. They fell on the shallow wastebasket at the side of Simpson's desk near where she sat. As she noted the contents, she smiled grimly.

Suddenly she bent forward and grabbed the wastebasket. She made a show of peering down into it. "My goodness," she said in mock horror, her nose wrinkling in disgust, "how on earth did *this* get into your trash can?"

There was no way she was going to touch it and dangle it in front of Simpson, but he surely knew what she was talking about. For a moment, Wanda Nell thought he was going to faint.

He made a sudden move, reaching for the wastebasket, but Wanda Nell pulled it back out of his reach.

"I bet the principal would just *love* to know what his students are getting up to," Wanda Nell said.

Simpson made another move for the wastebasket, but once again Wanda Nell held it out of reach. "I wouldn't keep doing that if I was you," she advised him sweetly. "I'd hate to have to go to the principal and tell him one of his teachers was attacking me. Then the whole story would have to come out, wouldn't it?"

Simpson swore at her, and Wanda Nell was tempted to get up and march straight for the principal's office, wastebasket in hand. But she sat still and waited for him to shut up.

"Now, you listen here," she said when he fell silent, "that girl's probably over sixteen, so it wouldn't be statutory rape, but you'd still be in a hell of a mess if somebody finds out what you're doing here. Am I right?"

Simpson nodded, his eyes wary.

"I think it's disgusting," Wanda Nell continued, "but right now I'm more worried about my brother. You tell me what you know, and I won't say anything about this." She held up the wastebasket again. "But you damn well better stop it, or you're going to be a in a whole heap of trouble."

"What do you want to know?" Simpson asked. If he could have come over that desk and strangled her with his bare hands, he would have. Wanda Nell could see it in his face. Though he frightened her, she made an effort to appear unfazed.

"I want to know what you and Rusty were arguing about."

Simpson shifted in his chair. He picked up his cup again and spit into it. Holding the cup, he stared down into it. "Just some old business, something that happened a long time ago."

"What was it?" Wanda Nell demanded, losing patience.

"I can't tell you," Simpson said stubbornly. "I don't care what you say, I'm not going to tell you."

"I know it's something involving you and Bert Vines and probably Reggie Campbell." Wanda Nell thought it was worth a try.

Simpson stiffened perceptibly. "Maybe you're right," he said after a brief, strained pause. "But I can't tell you anything, no matter what you do."

She'd thought she had enough leverage to make him talk, but it wasn't working. He was obviously more afraid of whoever he was protecting than he was of her.

Who could it be? Surely not Bert Vines?

Why would he be afraid of Bert?

Because Bert had killed Reggie Campbell?

"I don't know who it is you're trying to protect," Wanda Nell said at last. "But I can promise you this, if something happens to my brother because of all this, I'll talk to whoever I have to talk to. You're not going to get away with it, one way or another."

Simpson sat stone-faced.

Suddenly it went all over Wanda Nell, and her temper hit white hot. Before she even realized what she was doing, she threw the wastebasket at Simpson's head. He ducked, and the wastebasket clattered against the wall behind his desk. The impact dislodged several of the pictures hanging there, and they crashed to the floor.

Simpson stood up. "I think you better get the hell out of my office."

Wanda Nell stood up and leaned forward over his desk. She wasn't going to let him think he intimidated her, not one bit. "Don't you forget what I said. I don't care who I have to talk to, even if it's the governor himself. I'm going to find my brother, and he damn well better be okay."

She whirled around and marched out of the office. She

slammed the door behind her so hard she thought for a moment the glass would shatter. It didn't, and Wanda Nell was half disappointed.

Her fury carried her at a rapid pace all the way back to the school office, where she tossed her visitor's badge down on the counter. The receptionist took one look at her face and didn't say a word.

Out on the front steps of the school, Wanda Nell stopped to catch her breath. Her chest was heaving, she was so wrought up. Slowly she descended the steps and walked to her car as she got her breathing under control.

In the car she sat for a moment, not seeing anything in front of her. Instead, she focused on an image of Scott Simpson.

He was afraid of something, or somebody. That much was clear. And it certainly wasn't her.

Whoever, or whatever, it was, Simpson obviously feared it enough that he was even willing to let Wanda Nell expose his sexual escapade with a student rather than tell her the truth.

Her hands gripping the steering wheel to help her stop her sudden shaking, Wanda Nell closed her eyes. She was more afraid than ever that her brother was either dead or soon would be.

She had rattled a cage all right. Now that she had done it, she was beginning to realize she should have thought this all through more carefully.

Instead she had bulldozed her way into a situation where she really didn't know very much. She had probably stirred up a real hornet's nest now, and no telling what could happen next.

Too late now, she thought. She put her key in the ignition and cranked the car. One more stop to make, and she'd better do it now, before she lost her nerve.

Twelve

Even after knowing the woman twenty-some-odd years, Wanda Nell still had trouble dealing with Lucretia Culpepper, her ex-mother-in-law. They had managed to get along a little better since the death of Bobby Ray Culpepper, Wanda Nell's ex-husband and Lucretia's son, but that was mostly on account of T.J. Old Mrs. Culpepper thought the sun rose and shone where her grandson was concerned, maybe because he was the spitting image of his father in his early twenties.

Lately, though, Mrs. Culpepper had become increasingly critical of T.J., mostly because he refused to date the young women Mrs. Culpepper was always pushing in front of him. Though T.J. had come out to his mother and his sisters and a few friends, he had yet to tell his grandmother that he was gay. He was living in her house, helping take care of her, so T.J. kept putting off telling his grandmother the truth about himself. He was afraid she would react badly, and he worried about upsetting her too much.

Wanda Nell had given T.J. a good talking-to about being up front with his grandmother, but he just kept saying he would do it as soon as the right time presented itself. Wanda Nell kept assuring him that his grandmother adored him, and though she might be shocked at first, she would soon come around.

Old Mrs. Culpepper was pretty sharp, at least when she wasn't hitting the Jack Daniel's too hard, and Wanda Nell halfway suspected the old woman knew perfectly well T.J. wasn't interested in girls. She was probably pushing the girls at him for some strange reason of her own. Maybe because she was downright mean sometimes.

Wanda Nell pulled up in front of the antebellum mansion on Main Street that generations of Culpeppers had called home. A strange car at least twenty years old sat in the driveway, and Wanda Nell remained in her car for a few minutes, trying to decide whether to go in or just go home. If Mrs. Culpepper had company, Wanda Nell might not be able to get her to talk about the Campbell family, the reason for her visit.

Finally deciding she might as well go in, Wanda Nell got out of her car and proceeded up the walk to the front door. She rang the bell, then peered through the beveled glass on one side of the door. After a moment, she could see a blur approaching her, and she stood back. The door swung open, and Wanda Nell stared into a face that was vaguely familiar.

"Howdy, there," the woman said, her voice high-pitched and nasal. "You come to see Lucretia?"

Wanda Nell eyed her, trying to tie down the elusive memory. The woman in front of her, about her own height, could have been anywhere from forty to sixty. Mousy brown hair, lightly sprinkled with gray, framed a round, florid face. A dusting of brown hair spread across her top lip, and a couple of long hairs jutted out from her chin. Fascinated, Wanda Nell for a moment found herself unable to tear her eyes away from the chin hair.

"You deaf or something?"

Startled, Wanda Nell found her voice. "No, sorry, I guess I was just thinking about something. Yes, I'm here to see Miz Culpepper. I'm Wanda Nell Culpepper." She paused a moment as recognition dawned in the other woman's eyes. "Haven't I met you before?"

"Well, shore enough you have, honey," the woman said, standing back and motioning Wanda Nell into the hall. "I'm Lucretia's cousin, Belle Meriwether. It's been a long time since I seen you, so I don't mind much you not remembering who I am."

Wanda Nell caught a faint whiff of violets as she stepped past Belle Meriwether into the hall. Despite the lack of attention to her face, Belle was neatly attired in a cotton dress that had probably been new around 1955. "Now, you just come on in here with me and Lucretia," Belle said, leading the way into the front parlor. "I drove over this morning from Coffeeville to visit, seeing as how me and Lucretia ain't had a good visit in a couple of years."

Wanda Nell followed Belle into the parlor where they found Mrs. Culpepper seated in her customary place. Wanda Nell examined her as closely as she dared for signs that the old woman had been drinking, and she was relieved to find none. Mrs. Culpepper's eyes were clear and bright, and she was clean and dressed smartly, her hair showing signs of a very recent trip to the beauty shop.

"Lucretia honey, look who stopped by to see you," Belle announced. She plopped herself down on the sofa near her cousin.

"Afternoon, Miz Culpepper," Wanda Nell said.

Mrs. Culpepper looked up at her former daughter-in-law. "And what brings you here, Wanda Nell? You don't usually turn up here unless you're invited to, and even then you hardly come." She waved a hand toward a chair. "Might as well sit down, seeing as you're here."

"Thank you," Wanda Nell said. She took the seat indicated and set her purse on the floor beside her. "How have you been, Miz Culpepper? You're looking mighty well today."

"Thank you," the old woman said tartly. "I'm glad you approve. I wasn't really expecting all this company today. First, Belle here turning up out the blue, and now you. I guess it's lucky I decided when I got up this morning that I was going to dress for company. My nose was itching when I got up, and for once my nose was right. Company did come."

"Now ain't that a funny thing," Belle said. "You know, my nose itches like that whenever somebody's going to show up at my door. I mean, every day, just before the mail carrier makes it to my front door, I start feeling like I'm going to sneeze. And then a minute or two later, there he is at my door. Isn't that something?" She turned toward Wanda Nell, an expectant look on her face.

"You're probably just allergic to that old cat of yours," Mrs. Culpepper said before Wanda Nell could respond. "I keep telling you you ought to get rid of that nasty thing. What you want with a cat in the house, I'll never know. My mother never would allow a cat in the house, or a dog either."

"Your mama was the most house-proud woman I ever did know," Belle said, turning back to her cousin. "Even when she got to where she couldn't walk around the house and do anything, she made sure that colored girl of hers cleaned everything real nice all the time. You could just about eat off the floor in her house."

"Why on earth would anybody want to eat off the floor?" Mrs. Culpepper's voice dripped acid. "That's about the stupidest thing I ever heard, Belle, but coming from you, I guess I shouldn't be surprised. Your mama didn't know how to keep house to save her life."

"Well, that sure is true, Lucretia," Belle said, wagging her head up and down. Wanda Nell would have been furious if someone had insulted her and her mother like that, but Belle appeared to be pretty thick-skinned. "My mama was a saint, and lord knows she had to be, what with my daddy running around on her the way he did, but she didn't know much about keeping a clean house. Maybe that was why Daddy was the way he was." She shook her head dolefully. "I reckon I learned everything I know about keeping house from your mama, Lucretia, God bless her."

"Would you like some iced tea, Wanda Nell?" Mrs. Culpepper stared hard at her, and Wanda Nell realized she had better say she did.

"That sure would be nice, Miz Culpepper," Wanda Nell said, and the old woman nodded her approval.

"Belle, you get on out to the kitchen and fix Wanda Nell some iced tea." Mrs. Culpepper waved her hand at her cousin.

"I'd be glad to," Belle said, getting to her feet. "Would you like some, too?"

"Might as well," Mrs. Culpepper said. "Now, take your time. Don't hurry. I'm sure Wanda Nell will manage till you come back with it."

"Won't be a minute," Belle said, ambling out of the parlor.

Mrs. Culpepper sat back in her chair with a deep sigh. "Lord, that woman could talk the horns off a billy goat. It wouldn't be so bad if she actually had something to say, but she just goes on and on about nothing."

"I remember her now," Wanda Nell said, and indeed she did. In particular she remembered one Christmas when T.J. and Miranda were small, Belle had come to stay for the holidays with her cousin. Belle had cornered her in the kitchen on Christmas Day and subjected her to a history of her family and how many of them seemed to die around holidays. Wanda Nell had dearly wanted to see another of them expire, and right then, before she finally managed to get away from Belle.

· "She'll be back way too soon," Mrs. Culpepper said, "so you'd best get on with telling me why you're here and what you want. If it's money for something, you can forget that. I don't have any extra to spend after buying T.J. that truck of his."

The old woman delighted in making her lose her temper, Wanda Nell knew, and she was bound and determined not to do it, no matter how sorely tried she was. She smiled sweetly, "Now, Miz Culpepper, I don't need any money. I just wanted to talk to you for a few minutes."

"About what?"

"You know everybody worth knowing in Tullahoma," Wanda Nell said, "and I thought you could maybe help me with a little information." She paused for a moment to gauge the old woman's reaction.

Mrs. Culpepper snorted. "You can butter me up all you want to, Wanda Nell, but you might as well save your breath. Just get to the point."

Her right hand curling into a ball in her lap, Wanda Nell smiled at Mrs. Culpepper. "Did you hear about the murder?"

Mrs. Culpepper sat forward in her chair, her eyes suddenly alight with interest. "Are you talking about Reggie Campbell? Of course I heard about it. By now I'm sure everyone in town has heard about it."

"Probably," Wanda Nell said. "What have you heard? I mean, have you heard anybody talking about who did it?"

"That boy was no good," Mrs. Culpepper said. "I've known his poor mother just about all my life, and how she came to raise a boy like that, I'll never know. She's a good Christian woman, and that Reggie was nothing but a heathen."

Wanda Nell nodded encouragement, but Mrs. Culpepper scarcely needed it. "I can think of about five men, right off the bat, who could have killed him, and nobody would blame them. The way that Reggie treated women, it's a wonder somebody hadn't killed him long before now."

"Like who?" Wanda Nell asked. She realized her mistake, though, as soon as she spoke.

"Why do you want to know?" Mrs. Culpepper said. "Nobody needs to drag the names of the poor women through the mud, and I can't see it's any business of yours."

Wanda Nell despised the suddenly pious tone of the old woman's voice. If anyone else had asked her, the witch would have been talking a mile a minute.

"I'm trying to keep an innocent man from being blamed for it," Wanda Nell said.

"Who?"

"My brother."

"What's he doing back in town?" Mrs. Culpepper frowned. "Nobody told me about that."

Wanda Nell was relieved to hear it. If Mrs. Culpepper hadn't heard that Rusty could be involved, it meant the sheriff's department was probably keeping an open mind and their mouths shut.

"He came back for a visit," Wanda Nell said, "and one of the people he was visiting with was Reggie Campbell."

"And now somebody thinks maybe he did it," Mrs. Culpepper stated.

Wanda Nell nodded reluctantly.

"Why would he kill somebody he hasn't seen in years? I thought your brother hadn't been around Tullahoma for a long time."

"He hasn't been," Wanda Nell said, "but he just came back for a visit."

"It seems mighty odd, your brother comes back for the first time in a long time, and suddenly somebody murders Reggie Campbell." Mrs. Culpepper regarded her maliciously.

"My brother didn't kill anybody," Wanda Nell said, hoping her voice carried conviction. "But he may need help proving it." She didn't want to tell the old woman that Rusty had disappeared, but there might not be any way around it.

"Seems to me that maybe your brother used to run around with Reggie Campbell a long time ago."

Wanda Nell shrugged. "I don't know. I don't really remember Rusty being friends with him. Reggie was in the same class in school, but that's about all."

"I'm sure I heard something," Mrs. Culpepper said stubbornly. "I can't think what it is at the moment, but it'll come back to me at some point."

"I'd appreciate hearing it, whatever it is," Wanda Nell said. She paused a moment. She had debated this next move, but she didn't have much choice. "Have you ever heard anything about Bert Vines, you know, the insurance man, or Scott Simpson, the football coach at the high school?"

Mrs. Culpepper didn't reply for a moment. "I remember Bobby Ray didn't have much use for them, back when he was in high school. He used to laugh and say they weren't nearly as tough as they thought they were." She paused. "But maybe he was talking about Tony Campbell, Reggie's brother. Seems to me that Tony got into trouble a time or two."

Wanda Nell waited.

Mrs. Culpepper nodded. "Tony got a couple of girls in trouble when he was in high school, at least that's what

I heard, but he sure didn't marry either one of them. I guess they must have had it taken care of somehow." She wrinkled her nose in disgust. "And now Tony's married a girl just about young enough to be his own daughter. That's disgusting. I wouldn't let a daughter of mine marry a man like that."

"Well, you never had a daughter, now did you, Lucretia?" Belle came waddling back into the parlor, carrying a tray with a pitcher of iced tea and three glasses. She set it down on the table next to Mrs. Culpepper's chair. "I guess you could call Wanda Nell here your daughter, because she was married to your son. But then she divorced him, didn't she? So I guess she's not like your daughter after all."

"What are you going on about now?" Mrs. Culpepper scowled up at Belle. "Just pour out the tea and stop babbling. Wanda Nell is the mother of my three grandchildren, as you very well know. She and Bobby Ray may have gotten a divorce, but I reckon she's still a member of the family in a way."

Wanda Nell sat open-mouthed. Satan ought to be selling ice cubes about now. That was the only explanation she could come up with to explain what Mrs. Culpepper had just said.

"Are you trying to catch a fly?" Mrs. Culpepper turned her scowl on Wanda Nell. "Close your mouth, girl, you look plumb stupid sitting there. Somebody might mistake you for Belle if you're not careful."

Belle handed Wanda Nell a glass of tea, giggling. "Now, Lucretia, the way you do talk. Nobody could ever mistake Wanda Nell for me. She's blond, and she sure is pretty. You just take a real good look at her."

Blushing, Wanda Nell sipped at her tea as the other two women bickered back and forth for a moment. As she listened, she was struck by an idea that might help T.J. solve his worries about his grandmother. She'd have to think about it a bit more, but as she watched Mrs. Culpepper and Belle, she became more and more convinced it might work.

Finally Mrs. Culpepper turned her attention back to Wanda Nell. "Now, what were we talking about? Oh yes, the Campbells."

"Can you think of anything else?" Wanda Nell kept her question vague.

Mrs. Culpepper shook her head. "Not at the moment, but I'll keep mulling it over. Maybe something else will come to me."

Wanda Nell stood up, tea glass in hand. As she gave the nearly empty glass to Belle, she heard the muted tones of her cell phone ringing in her purse. "Excuse me," she said, and she reached hastily for her purse.

"I've been thinking about getting me one of them cell phones," Belle said as she watched Wanda Nell open hers up to answer it. "Aren't they just the cutest things?"

Mrs. Culpepper snorted loudly. "What would a fool like you need with a cell phone? You'd never figure out how to work it, for one thing."

Wanda Nell tuned them out as she answered the call. It was coming from her home phone, and as always when she got a call from home, she felt a little flutter of worry in her stomach.

"Hello," she said.

Before she could say another word, Miranda's voice spoke frantically in her ear. "Mama, somebody's trying to get in the trailer!"

Thirteen

Wanda Nell stopped breathing. Miranda's terrified words echoed in her brain.

She found her voice. "Miranda. Listen to me, I want you to scream as loud as you can. Do it!"

Wanda Nell heard a sudden intake of breath on the other end of the line. Then she jerked the cell phone away from her ear as Miranda's scream tore at her eardrum.

"Lord have mercy!" Belle almost jumped off the sofa.

"What's going on?" Mrs. Culpepper demanded at the same time.

Wanda Nell waved a hand at them, and they subsided.

The screams stopped, and Wanda Nell put the cell phone to her ear. "Miranda, can you hear me?"

"Yes, Mama," Miranda whispered into the phone.

"Can you hear anything now?"

There was a brief pause before Miranda answered. "I heard a car door slam, and now there's a car driving away."

Wanda Nell went almost limp with relief. Miranda's screams had scared off whoever it was trying to get in. "Listen, honey," Wanda Nell said. "I want you to hang up

right now, then call 911. I'm on the way home right now.
Got that?"

At Miranda's assurance, Wanda Nell ended the call.
She grabbed up her purse and gabbled a quick explana-
tion at the two women. "Call me as soon as you get home,
Wanda Nell," Mrs. Culpepper instructed.

Belle Meriwether was going on and on about something, but Wanda Nell didn't pay any attention. She was
out the front door and down the walk to her car as fast as
she could go. She wasn't sure later whether she had even
closed Mrs. Culpepper's front door behind her.

She took a shortcut through the east side of town to get
out to the highway, and from there it was only three minutes to the lakeshore road out to the trailer park. Eleven
minutes after she had left Mrs. Culpepper's house, Wanda
Nell arrived home. They were eleven of the longest minutes of her life.

Wanda Nell barely stepped inside the trailer before
she heard the sound of a siren approaching. "Miranda,
it's me," she yelled. "Where are you?"

Miranda came running out of the back of the trailer,
Lavon clutched in her arms. She was crying, tears stream-
ing down her face, and Lavon was wailing loudly, frightened by all the noise. Wanda Nell threw her arms around
Miranda and hugged her and the baby tightly to her.

"It's okay now, honey," Wanda Nell said. "I'm home.
It's okay." She said the words over and over, and Miranda's sobbing slowed.

"Ma'am, what's going on here?"

At the sound of a man's voice behind her, Wanda Nell
reluctantly released Miranda and Lavon, turning to face
the sheriff's deputy who stood in the doorway.

"Thanks for getting here so quickly, Deputy," Wanda
Nell said. She stopped for a deep, calming breath. "My
daughter called me and said someone was trying to break

into the trailer. I told her to scream real loud and then to call 911. I got here as fast as I could."

"Let me just have a look around outside," the deputy said. "Y'all just take it easy. Everything is going to be okay now."

He vanished.

Wanda Nell ignored the open door and guided Miranda and Lavon to the couch. Miranda had stopped crying, but Lavon was still sniveling. Wanda Nell pulled him into her arms and rocked him gently back and forth until he quieted.

"Tell me what happened," she said softly.

"Lavon and me was taking a nap, Mama," Miranda said. "We was lying down on my bed, and I had just gotten him off to sleep when I started hearing a funny sound outside. I thought maybe I'd heard a car drive up, but I didn't pay no attention to it. I thought it was just one of the neighbors coming home or something." She paused for a breath.

Wanda Nell nodded encouragement, and Miranda continued. "It was real quiet, and then I heard something like somebody jiggling the doorknob. I kept the door locked after you left, just like you always tell me, Mama."

"Good," Wanda Nell said fervently.

"I waited a second, and then I could hear a scraping kind of sound, and that's when I called you."

"Did they get the door open?"

Miranda shook her head. "I don't think so. Then, when you told me to start screaming, I did. And poor Lavon was so shook up he just laid there for a minute or two."

"You heard a car drive away," Wanda Nell said. "Did you hear any more noises at the door?"

"Nope," Miranda said. "I think I scared off whoever it was, Mama."

"Ma'am." The deputy reappeared in the doorway, then

stepped inside. "I didn't see anything outside. Whoever it was is long gone by now."

"Tell the deputy what you told me, honey," Wanda Nell said, and Miranda repeated her story.

The deputy listened, then excused himself for a moment. He squatted on the stoop with the door halfway open, and Wanda Nell could see him examining the doorknob.

When he came back in he was frowning. "Well, ma'am, there sure looks like somebody was messing with your door. I can see what looks like some fresh scratches around the lock, so I reckon somebody was trying to break in here." He pulled out a notebook. "I'll report it, but I don't think there's much we can do. Probably somebody thinking they could break into a trailer or two because it didn't look like nobody was home."

"Maybe," Wanda Nell said. She didn't think this was a random break-in, but she doubted she could convince the deputy of that, at least not without a long and involved explanation. She peered at his name tag. "Will you do me a favor, Deputy Garrett?"

"If I can," he said.

Wanda Nell gave him her name and the other information he wanted, then she said, "If you'll make sure you report this to Chief Deputy Johnson, I'd sure appreciate it."

Deputy Garrett was obviously curious, but Wanda Nell merely said, "I know he'll be interested to hear about this. If you'll be sure to tell him."

Wanda Nell could easily have called Elmer Lee herself, but she didn't want to have to deal with him right now.

"Yes, ma'am," Garrett said. "I'm going to check around the trailer park, see if anybody heard or saw something. But I think y'all can relax now. I doubt whoever it was will be back." Tipping his hat to her, he left.

Wanda Nell wasn't so certain they'd seen the last of

the would-be burglar, but she didn't want to alarm Miranda unnecessarily.

"What are they going to do, Mama?" Miranda asked.

Wanda Nell sighed. "Probably nothing. There's not much they can do. Especially since you didn't see anybody, or see the car. Maybe if somebody else in the trailer park did, they'll have something to go on. But I doubt it."

"Does this have something to do with Uncle Rusty?"

"I don't know, honey," Wanda Nell said. "I'd be willing to bet it does, but I don't know why somebody would be trying to break in here. What could they possibly want?"

"Maybe they thought Uncle Rusty hid something here, you know, like the time those men came in here and tied me and Juliet up with duct tape because they thought Daddy hid something here." Miranda's eyes widened as she talked, and Wanda Nell was afraid she was going to start crying again. Just thinking about that episode gave Wanda Nell nightmares.

"Could be," Wanda Nell said, her tone brisk. "But we're not going to worry about that right now. Rusty was hardly here long enough to hide anything. If he did hide something, he probably left it over at Mayrene's. But if your screaming scared them off, then maybe they won't come back as long as they think somebody's at home."

"I don't want to stay home by myself any more," Miranda said. "I don't want to be here with just me and Lavon and somebody trying to break in, Mama."

"I know, honey," Wanda Nell said. "We'll have to think of something, but I don't know what." Right about now, if she could have gotten her hands on him, Wanda Nell would gladly have wrung her brother's neck. It was because of him, she was sure, that all of this was happening. "If Mayrene can't come and stay with you, I'm sure T.J. will, so don't you worry about it. I'll make sure somebody's with you."

Mayrene would be home around five, and she wouldn't mind staying with the girls overnight. She had done it before, and as long as she had her shotgun with her, she wasn't afraid of anything or anyone. Ordinarily Wanda Nell wasn't too keen on having a loaded gun in the trailer with her daughters and her grandson, but these were special circumstances.

Maybe the girls and Lavon would be okay until Mayrene got home from work. Wanda Nell wouldn't be leaving until four, when the bus dropped Juliet off, so that left just an hour when they'd be on their own.

She gave Lavon back to Miranda and went into the kitchen to use the phone. She punched in the number of the beauty shop where Mayrene worked. After a brief chat with the girl who answered the phone and scheduled appointments, she asked for Mayrene. Her foot tapped restlessly on the floor until her friend came on the line.

"What's up, girl?" Mayrene's cheerful voice boomed in her ear.

Wanda Nell explained what had happened as quickly as she could, and Mayrene didn't say a word until she had finished.

"They sure as hell better not come around *my* trailer trying to break in," Mayrene said, "or they're going to get their backsides blasted off." She muttered a few words under her breath. "Now don't you worry, honey, I'll look after the girls and Lavon tonight. You go on to work and don't even think about it. You know they'll be safe with me."

"I know," Wanda Nell said. Mayrene was capable of defending herself and the kids, she knew that. "But do you want me to ask T.J. to come over, too?"

"You can if you want to," Mayrene said, "but we'll be all right. You going to leave at four for work?"

"Yeah."

Mayrene was silent a moment. "I was just checking the book," she said. "I can get out of here at three. I've got Dixie Abernathy coming in at three-thirty, but she won't mind coming tomorrow instead. I'll tell her it's a family emergency."

"Are you sure?"

Mayrene assured her it was no problem and said she'd be there as soon as she could. Wanda Nell hung up the phone, greatly relieved.

Glancing at the clock, Wanda Nell wasn't surprised to see that it was almost noon. She went back into the living room to ask whether Miranda was hungry. She was starving, and she was going to fix something for lunch.

While Wanda Nell made some sandwiches, Miranda fed Lavon his lunch. Miranda spoke to her a time or two, and Wanda Nell responded, but her mind was intent on mulling over everything she had learned that morning and the implications of the attempted break-in.

She would love to think that Reggie Campbell's death had nothing to do with Rusty's sudden reappearance in Tullahoma, but it would be too much of a coincidence if the two events weren't related. Especially since, she reflected, Rusty had obviously riled up both Bert Vines and Scott Simpson over something. And, she reasoned, whatever that something was, it probably was connected to Reggie Campbell's death.

But how?

What the heck was it that linked her brother with these men?

The most terrifying question, and the one that kept coming back to her again and again, was whether her brother was still alive.

If he was still alive, where the heck was he? Was he hiding out somewhere?

Or had someone kidnapped him? Why on earth would someone kidnap him?

And what was someone looking for in her trailer?

Another thought struck her, and she got up and reached for the phone again. Hitting the redial button, she waited. She said hello again and asked for Mayrene, not bothering with any chitchat this time.

"Anything wrong?" Mayrene asked when she picked up the phone.

"I forgot to ask you something," Wanda Nell said. "Sorry to bother you again."

"What is it?"

"Will you look around your place and see if maybe Rusty left something behind? I have no idea what they're looking for, but I bet they didn't know Rusty was staying with you. So whatever it is could be at your place."

"Yeah, I thought about that," Mayrene said. "And don't worry, I'm going to have me a real good look-see soon as I get the chance. If I find anything, I'll call you right away."

Wanda Nell thanked her and hung up the phone. If there was anything to find next door, Mayrene would find it. Wanda Nell fervently hoped Mayrene would find something, because maybe it would help them understand what was going on.

After reassuring Miranda that she and Juliet and Lavon would be okay tonight while she was at work, Wanda Nell decided to try to take a nap. She was tired, and her head was aching slightly. If she didn't get a little sleep, she'd never make it through her two shifts tonight.

Miranda promised to be sure she was up by three-thirty, and Wanda Nell left her and Lavon watching TV in the living room.

In her bedroom, Wanda Nell slipped out of her clothes

and crawled into bed. At first she thought she would never be able to drop off. She was too tired, and her mind was too occupied with worries. She made an effort to relax, and soon she dropped off to sleep.

She came to sometime later, feeling wet lips on her face. Startled, she opened her eyes to find Lavon sitting on the bed beside her. He giggled and kissed her again. Smiling, she sat up in bed and pulled him into her lap for a cuddle.

A glance at the clock told her it was three-twenty-seven. "Okay, you little monkey," she told Lavon, setting him on the bed beside her, "it's time for your old grandma to get up and go to work. Though your old grandma would much rather stay here and play with you." He was so adorable sitting there on the bed, his trusting little face staring up at her.

"Gamma stay," Lavon said, or at least that was what it sounded like to Wanda Nell. She smiled and ruffled his hair. He kept chanting the words over and over.

"Miranda," she called. "Can you come get Lavon? I need to get dressed."

Miranda appeared a moment later and retrieved the baby. "He wanted to wake you up, Mama."

"Well, it sure was nice to have a handsome boy give me a kiss to wake me up," Wanda Nell said. "Made me feel almost like a princess in a fairy tale." Lavon giggled and finally stopped chanting. He let his mother lead him out of the room.

Wanda Nell was dressed and ready to go a few minutes before four. Juliet had arrived home barely five minutes before that, and Miranda was telling her what had happened when Wanda Nell walked into the living room. Mayrene popped her head in the door right then, and she reassured Wanda Nell that she had everything under control.

Not for the first time, Wanda Nell wished she didn't have to go off in the evenings and leave her children like this. There was no use in complaining, though. She had her jobs to do, and that was that. Sighing, she put her car into gear and drove off.

Monday nights were usually slow around the Kountry Kitchen, and tonight was no exception. Wanda Nell had a chat with her boss, Melvin Arbuckle, and confided in him all of what had happened since Saturday night.

"I'm sure sorry all this is happening, Wanda Nell," he said. "That brother of yours sure has caused a big mess. I hope they get it all sorted out soon. I know Elmer Lee will do his best."

"Yeah, I guess so," Wanda Nell said. "I just keep hoping he could do it a lot faster." She went to check on one of her tables.

The night seemed to drag by, but finally it was closing time. A few minutes after ten Wanda Nell walked outside with Ruby and Melvin and headed for her car at the side of the building where they all parked.

As Wanda Nell approached her car she had the vague feeling that something was slightly odd. She stopped and stared at her car in the dim glow of the street lights.

Then she realized what was wrong.

Her two back tires had been slashed.

Fourteen

"Melvin!" Wanda Nell screamed the name.

A door slammed, and moments later Melvin Arbuckle ran up beside her.

"What's wrong, Wanda Nell?"

"Look." She pointed at her tires.

Melvin swore. "What kind of bastard would do something like that?"

"I can think of two, right off the bat," Wanda Nell said, her tone grim.

"You mean Bert Vines or the football coach?"

"Yeah," Wanda Nell said. "Bert for sure knows what kind of car I drive, and he could have told Simpson. Either one of them could have done this."

"Why?"

"As a warning not to meddle," Wanda Nell said. "Bert was trying to threaten me this morning without coming out and saying anything real specific. Just like the other night when he was here." She reached into her purse and pulled out her cell phone. Punching a button, she waited impatiently for it to come on. When it was ready, she called the sheriff's department and reported the incident.

"Where did this occur, ma'am?" the dispatcher asked. Wanda Nell told him.

"Ma'am, that's something you should be calling the police department about," the dispatcher said. "You're in town, and they're the ones that need to respond on this."

"I realize that," Wanda Nell said, though in her haste to call someone, she really hadn't thought it through. "But this is related to a case the sheriff's department is already working on. That's why I need to get in touch with Deputy Johnson. He'll know all about it."

The dispatcher sighed. "All right, ma'am. You just sit tight, and I'll see if I can get ahold of Deputy Johnson."

Canned music started playing in Wanda Nell's ear. "They've got me on hold," she explained to Melvin.

"You want me to go in and call somebody at Budget Mart while we're waiting?" Melvin asked. "'Cause it sure don't look like you're going to make it to work on time."

Wanda Nell rubbed her forehead with her free hand. Her head was really starting to ache. "Yeah, if you don't mind, Melvin. Tell them I'll get there as soon as I can." She waited while Melvin pulled a pen and a piece of paper from one of his pockets, then dictated the number. As Melvin loped off back to the front door of the restaurant, the music in Wanda Nell's ear ceased and a voice came on the line.

"Wanda Nell, that you?"

"Yeah, Elmer Lee, it's me," she said, for once grateful to hear his voice.

"What's going on now?"

Quickly she explained about her tires being slashed.

"All right, just hang on," Elmer Lee said. "I'm on my way."

Wanda Nell clicked her cell phone off, feeling slightly guilty. Elmer Lee had sounded pretty tired, and now he wasn't going to be getting to bed anytime soon.

Melvin came back a couple of minutes later to report that her boss at Budget Mart understood about the situation. She was to come in when she could.

About ten minutes after that, Elmer Lee pulled up, and he and another deputy got out of the car. Wanda Nell recognized the lanky form of Deputy Garrett.

Other than nodding their heads at Wanda Nell and Melvin, neither deputy said anything at first. They both examined Wanda Nell's back tires carefully. Elmer Lee used a powerful flashlight, and Wanda Nell flinched at the sight of the harshly exposed slashes.

"You got any idea why somebody would want to do this?" Elmer Lee clicked off the flashlight and stood up. He regarded Wanda Nell suspiciously.

This was the part Wanda Nell had been dreading. Elmer Lee was going to hit the roof when she told him what she had been doing.

"I guess because I was talking to a couple of people today about my brother and the murder," Wanda Nell said.

"What people?" Elmer Lee cut in before she could continue her explanation.

"I was getting to that," Wanda Nell said crossly. "Just hang on a minute." She paused for a breath. "I went to see Bert Vines this morning. You know I told you I overheard him and Rusty having an argument, and then he showed up here the other night, quizzing me about Rusty. I wanted to ask him about all that."

"Did he tell you anything?"

"No, he didn't," Wanda Nell said, "but he made some vague threats."

"He threatened you? Bert Vines?" Elmer Lee was patently incredulous.

"Yeah, he did," Wanda Nell said. "It wasn't real obvious, but he hinted around about my insurance on the trailer not being enough if something bad happened. How would you interpret that?"

Elmer Lee shrugged. "Maybe he was just trying to sell you more insurance."

"Oh, come on," Melvin said impatiently. "You ain't that stupid, Elmer Lee. You know perfectly well what Bert was getting at when he said that to Wanda Nell."

"Maybe," Elmer Lee said, "but if I was you, buddy boy, I wouldn't talk about nobody being stupid. You understand that?"

Melvin didn't respond. Instead, he pulled a pack of cigarettes from his pocket, shook one out, and lit it. Wanda Nell sniffed hungrily at the smoke. Now was one of those times she definitely wished she hadn't quit smoking.

"Okay, Bert Vines was one person you talked to," Elmer Lee said, focusing his attention back on Wanda Nell. "Who was the other one? You said a couple."

"Scott Simpson, the football coach at the high school."

"I know who he is," Elmer Lee said. "Why on earth was you talking to him?"

"Because somebody overheard him having an argument with Rusty."

"And what did the coach have to say when you asked him about it?"

"He wouldn't tell me anything neither," Wanda Nell said. "But it was real obvious to me that he did know something, but that he was holding back. I think he's real scared of somebody, otherwise he would've talked to me."

"Otherwise why? Why would he have talked to you?"

Elmer Lee was a lot quicker than she had thought, Wanda Nell realized with dismay. She shouldn't have said it like that. She expelled a breath. "I caught him in what I'd guess you call a compromising position, and

I told him I might get him in trouble for it if he didn't talk to me."

"If he was doing something illegal, Wanda Nell, then you better start talking to me right this minute."

Elmer Lee was getting more annoyed with her by the second, and Wanda Nell didn't see any way out of the situation, other than to tell Elmer Lee exactly what she had seen. Otherwise he probably wouldn't believe her about how scared Simpson was.

Tersely she reported what she had seen. Elmer Lee didn't say a word until she had finished. "You have any idea who the girl was?" he asked.

"No," Wanda Nell said, "though I think she probably was seventeen or eighteen."

"She might be legal," Elmer Lee said, "but that still don't make it right. He ain't got no business fooling around with students like that. He must be crazy."

"What are you going to do about it?" Wanda Nell asked.

"Never you mind," Elmer Lee said. "I'll take care of it. But going back to what you said. He was more scared of somebody else than he was of you telling on him about the girl. That's what you're saying?"

"Yeah," Wanda Nell said.

"There's something really bad going on here," Elmer Lee said, "and I don't like it. But I'm for damn sure going to figure it out."

He turned to Garrett, who had been busy jotting things down in a notebook the whole time the others had been talking. "You got everything down?"

"Yes, sir," Garrett answered.

"Okay, Wanda Nell," Elmer Lee said. "I'm going to be looking into this, and we'll communicate with the PD about it, but I doubt we'll know for sure who did this. In the meantime, you can go on and get your tires fixed, and if the insurance company hassles you about any of this, you let me know."

"Thanks, I will," Wanda Nell said. There were times when she actually almost liked Elmer Lee, and this was one of them.

"I'll help Wanda Nell with her car," Melvin said. He flicked his cigarette butt away. "Come on, I think I know where we can get you a couple of tires tonight."

He led Wanda Nell to his pickup while the two deputies got back in their car and drove off.

One of Melvin's buddies owned a tire place, and Melvin persuaded him to get out of bed and come sell Wanda Nell a couple of tires. Melvin even talked him into giving Wanda Nell a really low price, and Wanda Nell was very grateful. This kind of unplanned expense always worried her, and she needed every break she could get.

The man even offered to come and change the tires for her, but Melvin assured him that wasn't necessary. They loaded the tires in Melvin's truck and headed back to the Kountry Kitchen.

It took Melvin about twenty minutes to get the two new tires installed. Wanda Nell stood by, ready to help, but Melvin insisted on doing it himself. "No use you getting all greasy when you got to go to work," he said between grunts.

"You're a good friend, Melvin," Wanda Nell said. He was wiping his hands on an old rag from the toolbox on his truck. "I can't tell you how much I appreciate this."

"You just try to be careful," Melvin said. "I don't want to have to do this again for you anytime soon." He grinned.

"I hope you don't have to, or nobody else either," Wanda Nell said. "They better leave me and my family the hell alone."

Melvin took a quick look under the hood to make sure whoever had done the slashing hadn't messed with anything else. He also got down under the car with his flashlight and checked things. "Looks all right to me," he finally pronounced. "Should be safe to drive."

Wanda Nell gave him a quick hug, then jumped into her car and headed off to work. By the time she arrived it was a quarter to midnight. She explained to her boss what had happened, then endured questions from some of her coworkers, but as soon as she could, she got to work and concentrated on that. She didn't want to think about any of this for a while.

When Wanda Nell's shift ended at six the next morning, she was exhausted and ready to get home to bed. She followed several coworkers out into the parking lot, suddenly apprehensive that something else might have happened to her car.

It appeared untouched, and wearily she climbed inside, cranked it, and started for home. The sun was just beginning to rise as she turned into the entrance to the Kozy Kove Trailer Park. Yawning, she inserted her key into the lock on the front door and twisted it.

There were sounds of activity inside as she entered. She could hear the shower running in her bathroom. That meant Juliet was up and getting ready for school. From the kitchen she could hear someone moving around.

Dropping her purse on the coffee table, Wanda Nell went into the kitchen. Mayrene was at the stove, scrambling some eggs. Wanda Nell sniffed the air appreciatively. She was actually hungry.

"Morning," Wanda Nell said.

Mayrene turned with a smile. "Good morning, honey," she said. "I figured you might be ready for something to eat when you got home."

"I am," Wanda Nell said, "though I thought I was going

straight to bed. Instead, I'm starving." She went to the cabinet and found a mug. She poured herself some coffee from the pot Mayrene had made.

"You just sit right down there, and this'll be ready in a minute."

Gratefully Wanda Nell sat down at the table and sipped at her coffee. She shouldn't be drinking caffeine right before she intended on going to bed, but she was tired enough that maybe she'd go to sleep anyway.

"It's decaf," Mayrene told her as she set a plate of steaming eggs and toast on the table in front of her.

"Thanks," Wanda Nell said. "I was thinking I shouldn't be drinking caffeine right now, anyway." She picked up a fork and started eating.

Mayrene poured herself a cup of coffee and sat down at the table with her own plate.

Between mouthfuls Wanda Nell told Mayrene about her slashed tires.

"Those bastards," Mayrene said, her face grim. "I'd like to get my hands on them for about five minutes."

"I wish you could, too," Wanda Nell said, grinning. "But I reckon I'll leave it up to Elmer Lee for once."

Mayrene sniffed. She didn't think much of Elmer Lee.

"How was everything here last night?" Wanda Nell munched on a piece of toast. "Did you find anything Rusty might have left behind?"

Mayrene had a sheepish look on her face. "I'm sorry, honey, I never got around to looking. Miranda was real nervous about me not being in the trailer with them, and I thought maybe I'd go over when they all fell asleep and look around." She grinned. "But I fell asleep on the couch. I was tireder than I thought I was, I guess."

Wanda Nell was disappointed, but she didn't want to let Mayrene see that. "That's okay, Mayrene. I sure appreciate you coming over and staying with the girls. If they wanted you to stay with them, I sure don't blame them. I'd have been nervous myself."

"Well, I'll try to have a little look around before I go to work," Mayrene said. She picked up her empty plate and took it to the sink. She came back to the table for Wanda Nell's plate and put it in the sink, too.

Wiping her hands on a cloth, Mayrene said, "Now, if it's okay with you, I'm going to head home and start getting ready for work. You call me if you need anything, you hear?"

"I will," Wanda Nell promised. She thanked her friend again, but Mayrene waved her off.

As the door closed behind Mayrene, Juliet came into the kitchen for some breakfast. Wanda Nell spent time talking with her, deciding for the moment not to burden her with the story of the slashed tires. Miranda came in with Lavon, and Wanda Nell listened to the girls and Lavon chatter about various things.

With Juliet off to school and Miranda set to give Lavon a bath, Wanda Nell went to bed. She climbed gratefully between the cool sheets, and almost before her head touched the pillow, she was sound asleep. For once she was too tired even to let her worries keep her awake.

At three o'clock, Wanda Nell's alarm had barely gone off when the phone started ringing. Yawning, Wanda Nell sat up and threw back the covers. She went into the bathroom and washed her face.

Miranda burst into the bathroom, waving the phone. "Mama, it's for you. It's Mayrene, and she sounds real excited." She handed the receiver to her mother.

"Mayrene, what's going on?"

"I been waiting till you got up to call," Mayrene said, the excitement obvious in her voice. "You ain't going to believe this, girl, but there's been another murder."

"Who?" Wanda Nell felt the bottom drop out of her

stomach. It couldn't be Rusty, she told herself quickly. If it had been, Mayrene wouldn't have called her this way. She took a steadying breath.

"The football coach," Mayrene said. "Somebody blew his head off last night."

Fifteen

Wanda Nell turned and leaned against the sink. Her knees felt weak. "Oh my Lord. When did you hear about it?"

"About three hours ago," Mayrene answered. "Like I said, I was waiting till I knew you'd be up before I called. From what I heard, when he didn't show up at school this morning, they went looking for him. And that's when they found him, right there in his own living room." Her voice dropped to a whisper. "And the way I heard it, most of his head was gone."

"What is it, Mama? What happened?" Miranda stood in the doorway, her face alight with curiosity.

Wanda Nell was still trying to take it in. She was doing her best not to visualize Scott Simpson with his head blown off. Instead, she focused on her brother. Was he involved in this? Had he been murdered, too? Was his body somewhere just waiting to be found?

She felt like she wanted to throw up, but she made an effort to steady herself. She told Miranda what had happened, leaving out Mayrene's graphic description, and Miranda's eyes grew large.

"Wanda Nell. Are you talking to me?"

"Sorry, I was just telling Miranda what you told me," she said. "I'm trying to take it all in. This is awful. But I'm surprised they didn't find him before this morning. Surely one of his neighbors must have heard the shot that killed him." She pushed away from the sink and motioned for Miranda to precede her into the bedroom.

"He don't live in town," Mayrene said. "Guess I should say he didn't, now. Anyway, he lived out in the country, and his nearest neighbor wasn't very close. Besides, I guess whoever did it could have used some kind of silencer, like they do on TV all the time."

"Maybe so," Wanda Nell said. "Well, thanks for letting me know. I'd better wake up and start getting ready for work."

"If you want, I can stay with the girls again tonight," Mayrene said. "But I can't take off early this time, though. You think they'll be okay until I get there, about five-thirty maybe?"

"If you could stay with them again, I'd sure appreciate it," Wanda Nell said. "I hate the thought of them being here without somebody. I'll call T.J. and see if he can't come out for a little while."

Miranda poked her mother's arm. "T.J.'s already here, Mama. He wants to talk to you."

"Oh, Miranda is telling me T.J. is here already," Wanda Nell said into the phone. "I'll check with him, but I'm sure he'll stay, one way or another."

She and Mayrene said good-bye, then Wanda Nell clicked off the phone. She handed it to Miranda, saying, "Tell T.J. I'll be ready to talk to him in a few minutes. I've got to shower first and get dressed for work."

"Okay, Mama," Miranda said. She disappeared down the hall.

While she showered and then dressed, Wanda Nell

thought hard about the second murder and what it meant. She had to believe that her brother was still alive and that he wasn't the killer. If she started doubting him now, she just couldn't handle all this.

But none of this would have happened if he hadn't come back to Tullahoma, intent on seeing to this business of his. She had to find out what it was before anybody else got hurt, especially before someone harmed her, or the girls and the baby, or even T.J.

Her son was sitting on the couch playing with Lavon, when she walked into the living room some twenty minutes later.

"Hey, Mama," T.J. said, standing up with the baby in his arms. Lavon seemed fascinated by the diamond stud in T.J.'s left earlobe, and T.J. had to keep those busy little hands from pulling too hard on his ear.

Wanda Nell hugged him, then took the baby into her own arms. She kissed his cheeks, and he started talking to her. She listened for a minute or two, talking with him when he seemed to expect an answer. Then she set him down on the floor, and he wandered off, looking for a toy to play with.

Wanda Nell sat down on the couch with her son. "What's up, honey? Miranda said you wanted to talk to me."

"I do, Mama, but I'm a little worried about all this stuff that's happening. You want me to stay with the girls tonight while you're at work?"

"If you could stay with them till Mayrene gets home, about five-thirty she said, I'd appreciate it. After that, they'll be okay. Mayrene will look after them."

"Her and that shotgun of hers." T.J. grinned, and Wanda Nell's heart turned over as it often did at such moments. He looked so much like his daddy had at that age, about twenty-three. "I don't mind staying all night if you want me to."

"Maybe tomorrow night," Wanda Nell said. "That way Mayrene can have a break. As long as this mess is going on, I don't like to leave the girls alone here, and I can't take off work right now."

"Don't worry about it," T.J. said. "We're not going to let anything happen to them. Miranda told me about somebody trying to break in while she was napping with Lavon."

Wanda Nell shivered. "I can't stand thinking about that, not with everything else that's happened. But maybe they'll leave us alone, especially if they see somebody's always here, watching the place."

"I think the sheriff's department is keeping an eye out, too," T.J. said. "I saw one of their cruisers sitting out there on the road when I drove in, and I bet he's still out there."

"Well, bless Elmer Lee's stony little heart," Wanda Nell said, surprised. "I'll have to thank him."

"You ask me, he's kind of soft on you, Mama," T.J. said teasingly. "Maybe Jack has some competition."

Wanda Nell rolled her eyes. "He can tolerate me, but that's about it." Secretly, though, she wondered if T.J. wasn't right. She still remembered that odd scene between her and Elmer Lee after Bobby Ray's funeral. Right now, she preferred not to think about it.

"Tell me what you wanted to talk about," she said instead.

T.J. breathed deeply, then faced his mother squarely. "I came to a decision, Mama. I'm going to talk to Grandmother tonight and tell her the truth."

Wanda Nell blinked. She'd been after him for quite some time to do this, and now that he said he was going to, she was surprised.

"Are you sure you're ready, honey?"

T.J. nodded. "Yeah, I'm tired of pretending with her. I know it's not fair to her, and even if she wants to take back the truck she gave me and everything else, well, I'll just have to see what happens. Besides, Tuck really wants me to move in with him, and I want to, Mama. I really do. I want to be with him, and it's hard, me still living with Grandmother."

Wanda Nell was impressed. "Sounds like you've really made up your mind this time, sweetie, and I'm glad you're going to do it. It's better to be honest with her, and maybe she'll take it better than you think she will."

T.J. shrugged. "You never can tell with her. But I feel bad about leaving her alone in that old house by herself if she kicks me out."

"I have an idea about that," Wanda Nell said, smiling. "I'm sure you've met her cousin Belle."

Rolling his eyes, T.J. said, "I sure have. She's going to be staying with Grandmother for a few days. I never met a woman who could talk more about nothing than Cousin Belle. I swear, that woman's tongue must be loose at both ends, the way she talks."

Wanda Nell laughed. "I wouldn't be surprised, believe me. I think she may be just what your grandmother needs, though. When I was there yesterday, your grandmother was fussing up a storm about Belle and the things she said, but I can tell you this: she sure was enjoying herself, and Belle didn't seem like it bothered her a bit, the way the old battle-ax talked to her."

"I wonder if Belle would go for it," T.J. said.

"I bet she will," Wanda Nell replied. "Seems to me she must be pretty lonely, too, living all by herself there in Coffeeville. Except for her cat, that is." She frowned. "I wonder if your grandmother will let her bring her cat. She was carrying on about it yesterday."

"She will," T.J. said, grinning. "Grandmother doesn't think anybody knows it, but she likes animals. She keeps putting out food in the back yard for this old tomcat that comes around. I just act like I don't know she's doing it. She may carry on about it, but I bet you her and that old cat of Belle's will be getting on just fine."

"Good. Then when you tell your grandmother about yourself and everything, you can maybe talk her into inviting Belle to live with her. I think Belle would do just fine, taking care of her and that big old house."

"Sounds like a good plan to me, and I know it'll make Tuck happy." T.J. beamed.

"He really does mean a lot to you, doesn't he?" Wanda Nell couldn't quite bring herself to use the word "love," because she was still trying to get used to the fact that her son was gay.

"I love him, Mama, and he loves me," T.J. said simply. "I can't believe how lucky I am, and sometimes it scares me."

"He's pretty dang lucky too, if you ask me," Wanda Nell said around the lump in her throat. "You think it's going to be okay, the two of you living together?"

T.J. shrugged. "We won't know till we try, but I think we'll be just fine. I'm not going to mess this up, I can promise you that."

"I'm not really worried about *you* messing it up, or him either," Wanda Nell said softly.

"You mean you're afraid other people won't like it, the two of us living together."

Wanda Nell nodded. She was so afraid someone would hurt them.

"We can't hide forever," T.J. said gently. He reached out and clasped her hands in his. "And if somebody don't like it, well, they're just going to have to get used to it." He gave her hands a final squeeze, then released them.

"Now you go on to work and don't worry about the girls. Me and Mayrene will take care of them."

Wanda Nell leaned forward and kissed his cheek. "Thank you, honey, I appreciate it."

Juliet came in just before she left, and Wanda Nell explained the arrangements for the evening. Juliet sighed. "I sure hate all this, Mama."

"I know, baby," Wanda Nell said, cupping her youngest child's chin in her hand. "I hate it, too, but until they catch the guy, I want y'all to be safe."

Locking the front door behind her, she got in her car and drove off to work. As she drove, she prayed silently that everyone would be safe tonight.

At the Kountry Kitchen, everyone was talking about the latest murder. Wanda Nell mostly listened without entering into any of the conversations as she waited on customers. She was relieved not to hear any mention of her brother's name. The less public talk there was about him, the better, as far as she was concerned.

Around eight-thirty, Wanda Nell was at the counter, filling up Junior Farley's glass with tea, when the door opened, and Marty Shaw walked in.

She had known Marty since they were both kids. His father, the sheriff, and her father had once been good friends, and she and Rusty had played sometimes with Marty and his older sister, Becky. After her daddy and the sheriff had a falling out, they didn't spend any time with the Shaw family. Marty had been a year behind her in school, so she saw him around school all the time, but neither of them went out of their way to speak to the other.

At first Wanda Nell didn't think much about Marty turning up at the Kountry Kitchen tonight. He came in from time to time, but with the kind of money he made running the biggest car dealership in town, he usually went somewhere more expensive. When Ruby Garner, who had gone over to the table to wait on Marty, came up to Wanda Nell, saying he had asked for her, she thought it was a bit odd.

"You don't mind?" Wanda Nell asked, frowning.

"Doesn't matter to me," Ruby said. She was very easygoing, and Wanda Nell really enjoyed working with her. "You're welcome to him."

Wanda Nell walked over to the table. "Hi, Marty. How are you doing?"

"Evening, Wanda Nell," he said. "Long time no see. How have you been?"

"Pretty good," Wanda Nell said. "How's your wife doing?" She had almost asked after his first wife, but she remembered in time that he had recently remarried. His new wife, Tiffany, was about twenty years younger than Marty.

"She's doing fine," Marty said, his face glowing for a moment. "I can't tell you how happy we are. It's a blessing to have a woman like her."

"That's good," Wanda Nell said. It really wasn't any of her business, but she didn't think much of a man his age who took up with a girl who had barely turned twenty. She started to ask after his parents, but he forestalled her.

"I hear your brother's in town," Marty said abruptly. "How's he doing?"

"Far as I know, he's just fine," Wanda Nell said, instantly on the alert. Why would Marty Shaw be interested in her brother? They hadn't had much to do with each other since they were both teenagers, so why this sudden curiosity? What the heck was Marty up to?

Did this mean he was somehow involved in this mess?

Sixteen

"Yeah, Rusty was here for a couple of days," Wanda Nell continued, trying to keep her tone as casual as possible. "But then he had to head back to Nashville." She wondered how Marty would react to the lie.

"That's too bad," Marty said easily. If he knew she was lying, he certainly didn't show it. Head bent, he scanned the menu. "I haven't seen him in a coon's age. Thought it might be fun to see him and see how he's been doing."

"Too bad you missed him," Wanda Nell agreed. "Maybe next time he comes to town, y'all can get together."

"You wouldn't happen to have his address in Nashville, would you?" Marty asked, dropping the menu on the table and glancing up at Wanda Nell. "I'm going up there on business soon, and if I have time, maybe I can look him up."

This was getting stranger by the moment, Wanda Nell reflected. "You know, I don't actually have his address," she said, offering him her best sheepish look. "It's kind of embarrassing to admit, but Rusty and I ain't been what you'd call close in a long time. He just don't confide in me the way he did when we were kids." *There*, she thought,

maybe that'll put an end to this foolishness, if Marty has
anything to do with it.

"That's too bad," Marty said, a sympathetic expression on his face. "I remember now how close y'all were when you were kids."

There was something in his tone that made her uneasy. She tensed slightly.

"I bet y'all used to tell each other everything," Marty went on. "Anytime one of you got in trouble, the other one was there to help out." He stared hard at her, any trace of sympathy gone, and she sensed a hidden meaning in his words.

"Yeah," she said, feeling suddenly nervous. She had to watch what she said very carefully, and she wasn't even sure why. "We were, when we were kids. But you know how it is with teenagers, everything changes. Suddenly you don't want to talk to your big sister any more." She watched him relax as she said those last words.

"And then when Daddy died," she continued, "well, things really changed. Mama had a real hard time with Rusty after that, and I had my own troubles to worry about." She knew perfectly well Marty would know what she was talking about. Her and Bobby Ray Culpepper getting married had caused a scandal.

Marty nodded. "The people around this town sure do like to talk behind your back," he said, the bitterness evident in his voice. "Everybody's always minding everybody else's business. I don't like that, do you?"

Wanda Nell shook her head.

"People need to stay out of my business," Marty said. He stared straight at Wanda Nell.

She shrugged as if what he said meant nothing to her. "Yeah, I know what you mean. Now, what can I get you?" She had her pen poised over the order pad, ready to write.

Marty didn't respond for a moment. He just looked at

her. Then he ordered country-fried steak, mashed potatoes, green beans, and iced tea.

"Coming right up," Wanda Nell said. She walked away
to the kitchen to turn in his order.

The rest of the time Marty was in the restaurant, he
made no further reference to their conversation. In fact,
he had very little to say to Wanda Nell the few times she
approached his table. He didn't seem to be eating all that
much either. He just picked at his food. She breathed a
big sigh of relief when he paid his bill and left, but she
grimaced when she saw the meager tip he had left her.

"Cheap jerk," she muttered as she tucked the dollar
bill into her pocket. The next time she had to buy a car,
she sure wouldn't be buying one from him.

Business was so slow after that, they actually were
closed and heading out the door by nine-forty-five. Wanda
Nell made it to Budget Mart early for her shift, so she sat
in the break room for a while and put up her feet until it
was time to start work.

She pulled out her cell phone and called home. *Might
as well check in with Mayrene while I have a few minutes.*

"Everything's real quiet, honey," Mayrene said. "Juliet
and Lavon are both tucked up in bed, and me and Miranda are watching an old movie."

"Any word from Elmer Lee? Or anything else?"
Wanda Nell tensed as she waited for the answer.

"No, not a word," Mayrene said. "I sure wish I had
better news for you."

They chatted a little bit longer, then Wanda Nell ended
the call and put her phone away. Knowing that Mayrene
was there with the girls and the baby reassured her.

All that night as she busily restocked shelves, she kept
mulling over Marty Shaw's visit to the Kountry Kitchen.
There were too many questions buzzing around in her
brain.

If Marty was involved in whatever was going on, what was his connection with Bert Vines and the two dead men? That was something she had to find out.

If Marty was connected to those guys, how come he was asking her about getting in touch with Rusty? Shouldn't he know that Rusty was missing? Or was he just being really devious?

But then, maybe Rusty hadn't been kidnapped after all. Maybe he was hiding out somewhere and just wanted everyone to think he had been kidnapped.

That might explain part of why Marty was so anxious to get information from her. They were all looking for Rusty, and no doubt they were hoping to get ahold of whatever it was he had. Wanda Nell was convinced Rusty had something, probably something that meant trouble for Bert and Marty. But what could it be?

Was Rusty safe wherever he was? Wanda Nell wanted very much to believe he was still alive. Whether he had been kidnapped or whether he had hidden himself away didn't matter so much as long as he was alive.

She was completely drained, her head pounding, by the time her shift ended that morning. Wearily she climbed in her car and drove home, blinking into the rising sun.

At home she stayed up long enough to see Juliet off to school and to sit at the table while Miranda and Lavon had breakfast. Desperately worried though she was, she needed sleep. She knew she should be doing something to find Rusty, but if she collapsed from exhaustion she wouldn't be doing anybody any good at all. So she crawled into bed and was soon asleep.

When the alarm went off that afternoon, she woke up to hear loud voices coming from the living room. She lay there for a moment, yawning, trying to wake up. As soon as she was alert enough to recognize one of the voices, all she wanted to do was pull the covers over her head and stay there. That wouldn't help matters, though. Instead she got up, washed her face and brushed her hair, then dressed quickly.

In the living room she found Miranda arguing with her grandmother. Belle Meriwether, apparently oblivious as usual to the acrimony around her, had Lavon on her knee, bouncing him up and down. Lavon was giggling and having a good time, thankfully as unaware as Belle of the argument going on.

"Good afternoon," Wanda Nell said, raising her voice to be heard over Mrs. Culpepper's strident tones. "This is an unexpected pleasure, Miz Culpepper, Belle. What brings y'all here this afternoon?"

Startled, Mrs. Culpepper broke off in midsentence. She turned slightly to glare at Wanda Nell. "It's about time you got up, Wanda Nell. What do you mean sleeping all day? No telling what goes on around here while you're sound asleep."

"This is about the only time I get to sleep," Wanda Nell said, her tone sharp. "You know very well I work all night at Budget Mart. When else am I supposed to sleep?"

"I sure would hate having my days and nights mixed up like that," Belle said, still bouncing the baby on her knee. "I don't know how you do it, Wanda Nell, I really don't. I think I'd be real confused all the time, doing things at the wrong time of day. I guess you probably take a bath in the afternoon before you go to that restaurant, don't you?"

Without waiting for an answer, and barely pausing for a breath, Belle rambled on. "I like taking my bath in the morning when I get up. That way I feel like I'm starting the day off right, but I guess for you, your day really starts in the afternoon, doesn't it? I mean, that's when you get up, after all, and that's like me getting up after sleeping all night." She beamed at everyone and, mercifully, didn't keep talking.

"Nobody cares when you take a bath," Mrs. Culpepper said, "and what that has to do with anything, I don't have the foggiest notion. No wonder you're confused all the time, Belle."

Wanda Nell exchanged amused glances with Miranda, who was struggling not to laugh even as she glared at her grandmother.

"I'm sorry, Wanda Nell," Mrs. Culpepper said, her tone making her sound anything but contrite, "I forgot about you working all night at that place. Although why you want to work somewhere like that, I don't know. I don't think it's really suitable, but then, you never think about how I feel."

Wanda Nell started counting to ten, but she only made it as far as three when she couldn't hold back any longer. "I don't work there just because I'm bored and can't find anything else to do." She was getting really steamed. "I like to eat, and so do my daughters and my grandson. *And* we like to have a roof over our heads, *and* clothes to wear. Simple little things like that, and *somebody* has to earn the money for them."

"Well, you could give up this old trailer anytime you want to," Mrs. Culpepper said, unruffled by the venom in Wanda Nell's voice, "because the Lord knows I've got more than enough room in my house for all of you. Why you don't come and move in with me, I just don't know. Then you wouldn't have to work so hard, now would you? You certainly wouldn't have to waste money on this trailer." She sniffed loudly.

Wanda Nell stared open-mouthed at the old battle-ax. Had she suddenly and completely lost her mind? Only a few months ago Mrs. Culpepper had threatened to go to court to take Juliet and Miranda away from her, and now she was inviting them all to live with her? She resisted the urge to pinch herself to make sure she was awake.

Before Wanda Nell could respond to Mrs. Culpepper, Belle started talking again. "Why, Lucretia, what a lovely idea! Wouldn't it be wonderful to have this darling baby in the house all the time, and his beautiful mama? I tell you, Wanda Nell, Miranda is such a pretty girl. She reminds me of Lucretia when she was younger. You're just the spitting image of your grandmother at that age."

Neither Belle nor Mrs. Culpepper saw the horrified look on Miranda's face, Wanda Nell noted.

"Considering that you're nearly twenty years younger than I am," Mrs. Culpepper said acidly, "I think it must be some kind of miracle that you can sit there and say that, Belle. What kind of fools do you take us for? Look like me, indeed." She made an odd sound, but despite her protest, she appeared rather pleased by the comparison. Wanda Nell had to suppress a smile, though Miranda was still grimacing.

"Now, Lucretia, I know perfectly well how old you are, and how old I am," Belle said in a reasonable tone. "I was actually pretty good at math in school, and I even thought about going to college and learning to be an accountant, but my daddy didn't think girls ought to go to college." She turned a wistful face to Wanda Nell. "Isn't that incredibly old-fashioned? I sure wish I could have gone to college." She sighed. "But even though you are so much older than me, cousin, I have seen pictures of you. You know that. And I know how beautiful you were when you were Miranda's age."

Maybe caffeine would help, Wanda Nell thought vaguely. Or maybe sending Belle to Whitfield, the state mental hospital, for a few weeks.

"I did have my share of beaus at that age," Mrs. Culpepper said complacently. "But once I met Thaddeus

Culpepper, I never looked at another man. No, there was never anyone else for me after that."

Too bad the old man didn't feel the same way, Wanda Nell thought. Old Judge Culpepper had been a legendary womanizer, and remembering that, Wanda Nell couldn't help having some sympathy for his long-suffering wife.

She hated to break up this mellow mood, but she wanted to know what had been going on before she got up. "Seems like y'all must have been discussing something before I got up. What was it?"

Miranda, who had mostly been quiet since Wanda Nell walked into the room, opened her mouth to speak, but Mrs. Culpepper got in first.

"We were just discussing the news T.J. shared with me last night," she said. Her face reddened a bit. "I thought at first he was playing some kind of terrible joke, just to get back at me for introducing him to all those lovely girls. He's a very handsome young man, and he comes from a good family. At least, on his father's side, he does."

Wanda Nell rolled her eyes at that. She had heard it all before, and there was no point in getting annoyed about it now, not when there were plenty of other things to deal with.

"But I realized T.J. wasn't joking," Mrs. Culpepper said, ignoring the hissing sounds issuing from Miranda's direction. "He was very serious. And I have to say, if he is going to be *that way*, at least he had the good sense to pick someone from a good family with some money." She shook her head. "Although I do have to wonder what young Mr. Tucker's family really thinks about all of this, and about the two of them living together like man and wife."

Miranda, who adored her big brother, was nearly spitting with anger. "T.J.'s got the right to live with whoever he wants to, and it don't matter who that is. Nobody cares if you get embarrassed. It ain't none of your business. All you should care about is if T.J.'s happy, and I can tell you he is. So you just shut up about it."

Wanda Nell was secretly pleased that Miranda had spoken up for her brother, and especially to her grandmother, who usually intimidated her into speechlessness. Even so, she felt Miranda had gone a bit too far.

"Miranda's right, Miz Culpepper," Wanda Nell said, "though I think she should have said it a bit more politely. T.J. loves you, and he's not doing anything to hurt you on purpose. He just has to be who he is, that's all. We love him, and we need to stand by him."

"I didn't come over here today to be attacked by my so-called family," Mrs. Culpepper said, very much upon her dignity. "And did I say one single word about being embarrassed?"

"That's right, Lucretia," Belle chimed in. "You didn't really say you're embarrassed, though I remember you saying to me last night, after T.J. left to go home with that nice Mr. Tucker, that you weren't sure you would dare show up for church once word got around. But I surely don't see that that should keep you from going to church, I really don't. If the people at your church don't understand the meaning of compassion and charity, well, then they'd better start taking that up with the Lord. Maybe they're the ones who ought to be embarrassed about showing their faces in church."

Wanda Nell decided that, no matter what Belle said for the rest of her life, she would love her always for that little speech. She rubbed away a few tears with the back of her hand.

For once in her life, Mrs. Culpepper had been struck speechless. She stared at Belle, her face turning a deep red. Wanda Nell was afraid for a moment the old woman was going to have a stroke and die right there. When she didn't, Wanda Nell breathed a sigh of relief.

"For once in your life, you actually said something that made sense, Belle," Mrs. Culpepper said. Her voice at its acid best, she continued, "And don't think just because I've invited you to come live with me now that T.J.'s moving out, that I'm going to stand for any more of you being so uppity with me." Stiffly, she stood up from her chair. "Come along now, it's time for us to go home." She moved slowly toward the door.

Belle handed Lavon to his mother but sat for a moment staring at Mrs. Culpepper's back. "I'm not being uppity with you, Lucretia, truly I'm not. But I have to say what I think. That's how I've always been, and you know that. I just speak my mind, and that's that."

Mrs. Culpepper snorted. "In that case, you shouldn't be saying much of anything." She stalked on to the door. Saying goodbye to Wanda Nell and Miranda, she opened the door and disappeared outside, leaving it ajar.

Belle stood up. "Now y'all don't pay too much attention to Lucretia. Her bark is a lot worse than her bite, I can tell you. After all, I've known her fifty-something years. She means well, she just don't know how to show it most of the time."

Impulsively Wanda Nell hugged her. "I think it's a good thing, you moving in with her and looking after her."

Obviously pleased by the hug, Belle beamed at her. "I think so, too. It'll sure be nice for me to get out of my tiny little house, and being around y'all is sure going to be fun, too." She turned to Miranda. "Anytime you need somebody to look after that precious baby of yours, you just bring him on over to me. Even being an old spinster woman, I know about looking after babies."

From the gleam in Miranda's eyes, Wanda Nell knew it wouldn't be long before Lavon was spending a lot of time in the old house on Main Street.

Miranda went to the door with Belle and stood there

watching as the two women drove off in Mrs. Culpepper's old Cadillac. Then she shut the door and faced her mother.

"She sure is a nice old lady, isn't she, Mama?" Miranda giggled. "You could have knocked me over with a feather, the way she told Grandmother off like that. I thought Grandmother was going to explode right there in that chair."

"It's a miracle to me she didn't," Wanda Nell said wryly. She debated whether to bring up the subject of Belle looking after Lavon, but she decided for the moment to let it be.

"Why don't you put Lavon down for his nap now, honey? I've got some things I need to do, and I may have to leave in just a minute."

Miranda made a pouting face, but otherwise she didn't argue. Scooping Lavon up in her arms, she carried him off to their room.

Wanda Nell had been thinking about what she might do next in her quest for information, and she had decided to follow up an earlier idea. She went to the phone in the kitchen and called Melvin Arbuckle at the restaurant.

"Melvin, it's me, Wanda Nell," she said when he answered the phone after a few rings.

"Hey, Wanda Nell, what's up?"

She could tell from his voice that things must be pretty quiet at the moment. He sounded relaxed. She had been hoping to catch him in a good mood.

"You think it might be okay for me to be little late tonight?"

"How late?"

"Oh, maybe an hour," Wanda Nell said. "Not much more than that, anyway."

"I guess that would be okay," Melvin said, obviously reluctant. "You mind me asking why you need to be late?"

"Oh, just something I need to take care of," Wanda Nell said. "Somebody I need to talk to, if they're available. If they're not, then I'll be in on time."

"Well, okay," Melvin said, "but if you're going around poking your nose into something, you be careful."

"I will," Wanda Nell promised. She hung up the phone, then pulled her phone book from the drawer.

Turning the pages, she found the one she needed. She ran her finger down the column until it came to the name she was looking for. Picking up the phone, she peered down at the number, then punched it in.

Fingers crossed, she waited for someone to answer.

Seventeen

"Hello."

"Hello," Wanda Nell said, "is this Miss Carpenter?"

"It is," a strong, slightly husky voice assured her. "And I see by my caller ID that you're W. N. Culpepper. Would that be Wanda Nell Culpepper, by any chance?"

"Yes, ma'am, it sure is," Wanda Nell said, surprised. "Do you remember me?"

"Of course," Miss Carpenter said. "A teacher never forgets students like you."

Wanda Nell hoped she meant that as a compliment, but considering what had happened to her during her senior year at Tullahoma County High School, she wasn't sure. One teacher had called her a tramp to her face, and Wanda Nell had never forgotten the humiliation of that moment. Miss Carpenter had never treated her like that, though.

"I'm real sorry to bother you like this, Miss Carpenter," Wanda Nell said, trying not to rush her words in her anxiety, "but I need some help with some information. I figured you'd know better than just about anybody, but if you don't want to talk about it, then I'll understand."

"First it might help if I knew what it is you want to know," Miss Carpenter said tartly, though not unkindly.

"Oh, of course," Wanda Nell said, "but I was kind of hoping I could talk to you in person. If you don't mind, that is. This all has to do with my brother. You remember him? Rusty Rosamond?"

"I do," Miss Carpenter said. "If he's in trouble, or you're in some kind of trouble, I'd like to help, Wanda Nell. I can meet you in town, if you like, or you can come to my house, whichever is easier."

"If you don't mind me coming to your house, that might be best," Wanda Nell said, feeling greatly relieved. "Could I come right now? I know I'm asking a lot, but it's pretty urgent."

"You've certainly piqued my curiosity." Miss Carpenter quickly gave Wanda Nell directions. "From Tullahoma it's only about fifteen or twenty minutes."

"Thank you," Wanda Nell said. "I'm on my way." As she hung up the phone, she started repeating the directions to herself. Miss Carpenter lived about fifteen miles east of Tullahoma, in a little community called Pleasant Springs. It wasn't much more than a church, a country store, and a post office, but there were a number of small farms around it. Miss Carpenter lived not too far from the church.

Wanda Nell scribbled a quick note to Miranda, then grabbed her purse and keys and headed out the door.

The trailer park and the lake nearby were on the east side of Tullahoma, and Wanda Nell covered the distance to Pleasant Springs in about twelve minutes. She nipped around a school bus as she neared the turnoff toward Miss Carpenter's house. Following the sign which directed her toward Cadaretta, she turned right. She passed an old church on her left, not far after turning, and then about half mile later, the road curved sharply to the left and headed uphill.

At the top of the hill, on the right, a driveway led her up a slight rise to a large, two-story frame house. White with dark green trim, the house was framed by neatly arranged flower beds, a few trees, and a recently clipped lawn. Wanda Nell parked her car on a gravel drive at the front, got out, and proceeded up the walk to the front door.

Glancing at her watch to check the time before she rang the bell, she noted that it was about two minutes after four. With any luck, she might actually be back in town and at work without being more than a few minutes late.

The door swung open, and a face Wanda Nell remembered with a great deal of respect and affection peered out at her.

"Wanda Nell," Miss Carpenter said, swinging the door wide and stepping back. "Come on in. It's a great pleasure to see you, even under what must be distressing circumstances."

"I know this is an imposition," Wanda Nell said as she walked into the hallway. "I really appreciate you taking the time to talk to me like this, Miss Carpenter."

"I like helping people with their problems," her hostess said. "And I like to think that I'm very good at it, so don't you worry about imposing on me. Let's go into the parlor and have a talk about what's bothering you." She led the way from the hall into a room on the left.

Wanda Nell stopped for a moment on the threshold of the room and tried not to gasp. There must have been a fortune in antiques in the room. They rivaled the furnishings in the old Culpepper mansion on Main Street, and that house was about a century older than this one.

As she moved to the sofa where Miss Carpenter had indicated she should sit, Wanda Nell felt like she had walked onto a stage set for *Gone with the Wind*. She perched nervously on the edge of the sofa, covered in a rich wine-colored brocade, and looked at her hostess.

"How about some iced tea?" Miss Carpenter, with a wave of her hand, indicated a tray resting on a table beside her chair.

"Thank you," Wanda Nell said. "My throat is kind of dry."

"It's already sweetened," Miss Carpenter said as she poured out two glasses. "I just can't break myself of the habit of making it that way, although I know a lot of people these days prefer to sweeten it themselves." She passed a glass to her guest.

Wanda Nell sipped her tea, then smiled blissfully. "It reminds me of the iced tea my mama used to make. It sure is good, and just what I needed."

"Good," Miss Carpenter said. Tea glass in hand, she sat with her head slightly cocked, examining Wanda Nell.

Wanda Nell returned the frank appraisal, noting that, though Miss Carpenter's once-dark locks were now completely gray, she still had a youthful look about her. She must be about sixty-five by now, Wanda Nell reckoned. She had forgotten how tall Miss Carpenter was, at least six feet. Wanda Nell, who was not short herself, had always had to look up at her.

"Well, Miss Carpenter," Wanda Nell began.

Her hostess waved a hand in the air. "Call me, Ernie, Wanda Nell. You're not in my classroom any longer, and I prefer my friends to call me that."

Reddening slightly at the compliment, Wanda Nell said, "Thank you, Ernie." Boy, did that sound strange coming from her mouth. What would her mother think about her talking to one of her former teachers this way? She shrugged that off. "You said you remembered my brother, Rusty."

Ernie nodded. "Quite well. He was a good boy up until he hit high school, I believe. By the time he was in my senior English class, he had quite a reputation for being a troublemaker."

"Yes, ma'am," Wanda Nell said. "When our daddy died, I guess our family kind of went to pieces." She blushed. "I guess you can remember what happened to me."

Ernie smiled slightly. "Yes, I do, and I'm afraid that what happened to you is something I saw happen very often over the forty years I taught." She reached over and patted Wanda Nell's knee. "I was very sorry to hear about Bobby Ray's murder. I know how distressing all that was for you and your family."

"Thank you," Wanda Nell said. "It was rough, but we got through it. I'm afraid something like that may be happening again, and I need help."

Ernie regarded her quizzically. "Does this have anything to do with the two violent deaths in Tullahoma the last couple of days? Is your brother involved somehow?"

Wanda Nell nodded. Quickly she began to relate to her former teacher all that she knew and suspected about her brother and the men involved.

Quietly sipping her tea, Ernie waited until she had finished before speaking. "How do you think I can help you, Wanda Nell?"

"I'm hoping you can help me figure out what the connection is between my brother, the two dead men, Marty Shaw, and Bert Vines. And maybe Tony Campbell, for all I know." Wanda Nell just threw in the last name because he was the brother of one of the victims, plus she remembered that Tony and Marty had been good buddies for a long time. "Teachers always know a lot of what's going on at school, even if the students don't know they know it. And I thought maybe you would know something, or remember something, that could help me figure out what the heck my brother is trying to pull."

"Let's think about this for a moment," Ernie said. "Tony Campbell, Marty Shaw, Bert Vines, and Scott Simpson were all in the same class. A year behind you, as I recall."

Wanda Nell nodded.

Ernie continued. "Your brother Rusty and Reggie Campbell were a year behind them."

"I believe so," Wanda Nell said. "I mean, I know Rusty was two years behind me in school, and I'm pretty sure Reggie Campbell was in his class."

"I've been thinking about this ever since you called, I must confess," Ernie said. She set her empty glass on the tray, then leaned back in her chair. "I'll tell you what I remember, and we can go from there."

Wanda Nell nodded, waiting.

"Marty Shaw, Tony Campbell, Bert Vines, and Scott Simpson were all on the football team. They were all good friends, and they were seen around town a lot together. There was quite a bit of talk, from time to time, of some fairly wild parties. Drinking and so on."

Wanda Nell tried to keep from blushing. She had been with Bobby Ray to a few wild parties herself, and she didn't remember seeing those four boys at any of them. But then Bobby Ray hadn't particularly liked any of them. He had hung out with a different crowd.

"I believe Marty Shaw was the ringleader of the group," Ernie went on, "and that probably explains why none of them ever got in much trouble. Though I suspect they deserved to more than once."

"You mean because Marty's dad was the sheriff," Wanda Nell said, "and still is."

"Exactly," Ernie said. "I have a lot of respect for our sheriff for some of the good things he's done over the years. But like a lot of fathers he has turned a blind eye to his son's shenanigans." She smiled ruefully. "I believe Southern men see it as a mark of pride when their sons are rowdy hell-raisers. As long as they don't go too far, that is."

Thinking back about the old judge's reactions to some of Bobby Ray's escapades, Wanda Nell had to agree.

"Was there any particular incident," Wanda Nell said, "that might have been bad enough for them to be in real trouble?"

"Not that I recall." Ernie frowned. "That's not to say something *didn't* happen, but if it did, it was kept from public notice. The sheriff would have been able to suppress it, no doubt, especially if his son was involved."

"I've been thinking a lot about it," Wanda Nell said, "but, if you'll remember, mine and Rusty's daddy died the summer before I was a senior and Rusty was going to be a sophomore. After that, both Rusty and me ran a little wild, and Mama had her hands full with us." She shook her head. "And I was so wild for Bobby Ray then, I don't think I would have paid any attention if Martians had landed on the square."

Ernie grinned. "He was a handsome young devil, wasn't he? I can see where he might turn any girl's head, and in my experience, teenage girls aren't that hard to distract."

Wanda Nell didn't know whether to blush again or just smile. She settled for a brief grin.

"Now, back to business," Ernie said briskly. "I don't remember any particular incident that could explain all this. But I do remember a few things that are quite suggestive."

"Like what?" Wanda Nell asked when Ernie paused.

"I'm thinking about the way those four boys acted in school that fall, the fall after your father died. For one thing, I remember Bert Vines and Scott Simpson getting into fights with your brother on several occasions. In fact, one time they all got suspended for three days because of it."

Wanda Nell stared at her in astonishment. "You know, I had completely forgotten about that. By then I knew I was going to have a baby, and I was so terrified of telling Mama about it, I wasn't thinking about much else." She frowned. "I remember Mama having to go to school a couple of times and bring Rusty home, but I wasn't paying too much attention to Rusty and his problems then." She felt guilty all over again. Rusty might really have needed a sister to talk to, and she hadn't even cared enough to pay attention.

"Don't be too hard on yourself," Ernie said, her voice kind. "You were in a very difficult situation yourself, Wanda Nell, and at that age, you usually can't cope with anyone else's problems."

Wanda Nell appreciated her words, though they didn't lessen the burden of guilt she felt.

"Now, the odd thing about those fights," Ernie said, "was that, the spring before this all happened, I remember hearing talk about your brother and Reggie hanging around with the older boys. I know Reggie idolized his brother Tony, and he and your brother were trying as hard as they could to fit in with what they probably saw as the really cool crowd at school."

Wanda Nell shrugged. "I guess so, I just don't really remember much about it. That's what's so frustrating for me. I feel like I ought to know what's at the bottom of all this, but I don't. Rusty and I weren't having much to do with each other in those days. He didn't confide in me like he had before."

"That's only natural at that age," Ernie said. "Teenagers want to start separating themselves from their families, trying to find out who they really are apart from their family. And sometimes, sad to say, it gets them into trouble."

Thinking about the trouble both T.J. and Miranda had gotten into, Wanda Nell had to agree. At least T.J. was finally settling down. She hoped she wasn't in a nursing home before Miranda managed to do it.

"I wonder what kind of trouble it was," Wanda Nell said.

"At that age, and with boys, it could be several different things," Ernie said. "Especially if drinking or drugs, or both, are involved. It could have something to do with a girl, or a car." She frowned. "I believe there *was* some trouble with one or two of those boys over racing out on some of the back roads in the county."

"And if somebody got real badly hurt, and they tried to cover it up," Wanda Nell said, thinking aloud, "and all these years it *was* covered up. But here comes Rusty, all of sudden, threatening to make it public for some reason." She stopped.

"That's a possibility," Ernie said. "I should think that, whatever is behind these two deaths, it isn't petty. But think for a moment about the implications of what you just said, Wanda Nell. Do you really think your brother is blackmailing someone? Or several people, perhaps?"

Wanda Nell expelled a heavy breath. "I don't want to think so, but I just keep coming back to that same conclusion. I'm not sure what else it could be."

"If your brother is blackmailing someone, and I'm not saying he is, but if he is, then what does he want from the people he's blackmailing?"

Shrugging, Wanda Nell said, "I guess money. That's the most obvious thing, isn't it? Isn't that what blackmailers usually want?"

"Yes," Ernie said. "Does your brother appear to need money for something?"

"He does," Wanda Nell said, her heart aching. "He looks so tired and worn out, I almost didn't recognize him.

He's two years younger than me, but he looks about twenty years older. And he drives this beat-up old pickup that don't look like it'll make it to the next county, much less from here to Nashville."

"It does sound like he's having a rough time of it," Ernie said, her voice neutral. "In that case, it's easy to see where someone might be tempted to make use of an old secret."

"I hate to think of Rusty doing something like that, and on top of it, killing two men over it," Wanda Nell said. "I just can't believe he's killed anybody, and I don't want to believe he's blackmailing either."

"Simply because he might be blackmailing someone doesn't automatically make your brother a murderer," Ernie said. "Think about it for a moment. Why should he kill the goose that lays the golden egg, so to speak?"

"If they were refusing to pay up, he might get mad and kill them," Wanda Nell said.

"True," Ernie said. "But don't you think it's far more likely that someone else killed them to make sure they didn't talk? They could have been the weak links, and the killer was afraid they'd break under pressure."

"I hadn't really thought it all the way through like that," Wanda Nell said slowly. "But I think you're right. When I talked to Scott Simpson, it was real obvious to me that he was a lot more afraid of someone else than he was of me. Even if I had gone to the principal and told him what Simpson was up to in his office, he still wasn't going to talk to me."

"Then we are forced to conclude that something terrible must have happened in the past, involving the two dead men, Marty Shaw, and Bert Vines. And if those young men were involved, that means Tony Campbell probably was as well. Somehow your brother found out about it, or he may even have witnessed it."

"That makes sense," Wanda Nell said. Ernie had put it all into words for her, clearly and starkly.

"Another important question is, why did your brother wait all this time to do something about it? Why didn't he try blackmailing them sooner? Something sparked this, and if you can find out what it was, then you'll be able to understand better what drove your brother to it."

"If I could just get Bert or Marty to talk to me," Wanda Nell said. She shook her head. "What am I saying? One of them is probably the killer, or maybe even Tony Campbell. I haven't talked to him at all. They're not going to talk to me. But I've got to do something. I've got to find my brother."

She hadn't realized how upset she was becoming until she saw the look of compassion in Ernie's face. "I'm sorry," Wanda Nell said, leaning back on the sofa. "I just feel like I'm in a box, and every which way I turn, there's no way out."

"I understand," Ernie said, "and I wish there were more I could do for you, my dear. I'll put my mind to it, and if I can think of someone to uncover the cause of all this, I'll let you know." She paused for a moment, considering something. "I just wonder if it would do any good trying to talk to the sheriff. If he doesn't know what happened, he is the one person who might be able to get the truth out of his son."

"I don't know," Wanda Nell said. "He's been real nice to me since Daddy died, like when Bobby Ray was murdered. But I don't know if he'd talk to me about something like this, something his own son could be mixed up in. If Daddy was still alive, maybe he could talk to him. They were good friends once. . . ." Her voice trailed off as the implication sank in completely. "I don't know why I didn't see it before."

"See what?" Ernie prompted her.

"I bet this is why Daddy and the sheriff had a falling out," Wanda Nell said, her voice strained. "I never did know what happened between them, and Mama wouldn't say, even if she knew. And it was right after that that Daddy had his heart attack and died." She stared at Ernie, appalled.

"What is it, Wanda Nell?"

"Whatever it was, it killed my daddy."

Eighteen

"Killed your father?" Ernie asked, clearly puzzled by Wanda Nell's stark words. "How so?"

"Something must have upset Daddy pretty bad for him to have that massive heart attack." Wanda Nell was trying hard not to get upset and start crying. "And if Rusty was involved in something really bad, and it caused trouble between Daddy and the sheriff, well, I reckon it helped cause Daddy's heart attack."

"That's possible," Ernie said in a calm, even tone. "Try not to upset yourself, my dear. I know it must be very painful for you to have to think about all this now. Focus on the present, though."

"Yes, ma'am," Wanda Nell said, grateful for the concern. "If whatever happened really did cause the trouble between Daddy and Sheriff Shaw, then I guess I'm going to have to talk to the sheriff and see what he'll tell me." She paused, frowning. "Of course, maybe I've got this all wrong, and what happened between them has nothing to do with all this."

"That could very well be," Ernie said. "But I don't

think you can overlook the possibility that all of this is somehow linked." She stared thoughtfully at Wanda Nell. "I've known the sheriff a long time, my dear, and I'm wondering if you'll be able to get anything out of him. He is a man who is fiercely protective of his family, and if Marty is in any way involved, then he may do whatever he has to do for his son's sake."

"Meaning he's not going to be all that worried about my brother, if Marty's in on any of this," Wanda Nell said.

"Yes, I'm afraid so," Ernie said. "I'm sorry, Wanda Nell, but this does put you in a difficult position. It might even be a dangerous one."

"I know," Wanda Nell said. "But I don't like people threatening me or anybody in my family. I don't care who they are, sheriff or no sheriff."

"I admire your attitude," Ernie said, "and if there's anything I can do, you can count on me. In fact, if and when you do talk to the sheriff, you be sure and let him know that you've discussed all this with me."

"Are you sure?" Wanda Nell frowned. "I don't want to bring any trouble on you, in case this gets even uglier."

"I'm sure," Ernie said, her voice firm. "My family was the first to settle in this area back in 1831, except for Native Americans, of course. The Carpenter name is still respected, and if you let the sheriff know you have someone like me on your side, he's not going to ignore that easily."

Now Wanda Nell really did feel like she was going to cry. In her quest for information from her former teacher, she had never expected anything like this. "Thank you," she managed to say. She knew Ernie's word would carry a lot of weight, because Ernie wasn't exaggerating the family's prominence in Tullahoma County. "That means a lot to me, and I may need all the friends I can get before this whole mess is resolved somehow."

She stood up. "I think I've taken up enough of your time, and I've got to be getting back to town so I can go to work. I sure do appreciate all your help."

Ernie got up from her chair and escorted Wanda Nell to the door. "My dear, I'm happy to do whatever I can." She put a hand on Wanda Nell's arm as they paused before the door. "Please call me, and let me know how things are going. In the meantime, if I think of anything, or anyone, that can help, I'll let you know."

Wanda Nell pulled a scrap of paper and a pen from her purse and jotted down her cell number. She gave it to Ernie, explaining what it was. "Thank you," she said simply, then walked out the door to her car.

Glancing at her watch, she was surprised to see that the conversation with Ernie had taken only about thirty-five minutes. She should make it to work right on time, barring something unforeseen.

She backed the car around and headed down Ernie's drive to the highway. Pausing there, she looked both ways for oncoming traffic. Her view to the left was pretty good. She could see all the way back down to that sharp bend in the road. But on her right she could see for only about ten or fifteen yards. If a car came up fast from the right, she might be pulling out right in front of it. Also to her right, a gravel road branched off from the highway, forming the left side of a V. After a few feet the road was obscured by the heavy growth of trees and bushes on both sides, and she couldn't see very far down it. She hadn't paid it any attention before, but as she glanced at it, the sun glinted off something on that road just beyond the limits of clear sight.

Was there a car there? No other traffic was in sight at the moment, and though she probably had the right of way, Wanda Nell waited before pulling out on the highway, just in case.

No vehicle appeared, but whatever it was glinted in the sunlight again. Shrugging, Wanda Nell made another quick check before she accelerated left onto the road.

A moment later, out of habit, she glanced into the rearview mirror. There behind her about forty yards, seemingly from nowhere, was a black car.

That was odd. Where had the car come from? That side road? Had it been the sun glinting off something on the black car that she had seen?

Wanda Nell focused her attention on the road in front of her for a moment, belatedly remembering the dangerous curve she was approaching.

Safely around the curve, she looked into the rearview mirror again. The black car was still there, now about fifty yards behind her. She couldn't really see who was driving the car, but she thought it was a man.

Switching her glance between the road ahead and the car behind, Wanda Nell wondered why she suddenly felt so nervous.

The more she thought about it, though, she thought it was pretty strange, the way that car seemed to come out of nowhere. A vague memory stirred in her mind. Hadn't she seen that car somewhere recently? It looked like a Mercedes, and you didn't see too many of those around Tullahoma.

Was the driver of the Mercedes following her? And had he followed her on her trip out to Ernie's? She had been in such a rush to get there, concentrating on finding the place, she hadn't paid any attention to traffic on the road behind her.

She felt a chill down her spine. Why was she being followed, if she was?

Then she remembered where she had seen the Mercedes before. It belonged to Bert Vines.

That was pretty bold of him—following her in a car

that would be pretty easy to identify. But maybe he wasn't too worried about her knowing who was following her.

Then a more chilling thought struck her. Did he intend to do something besides just follow her to see where she was going?

Surely he wasn't going to try to run her off the road?

Without thinking about it she pressed her foot to the accelerator, and her little Chevy jumped forward.

Startled, she eased her foot off the accelerator a bit. Just ahead of her lay the intersection with the highway back to Tullahoma.

She slowed the car and came to a halt at the junction. To her right the highway crested the top of a hill. Glancing both ways, she pulled quickly onto the highway, turning left toward Tullahoma. Below her to the left was a country store.

Making a quick decision, she pulled into the parking lot of the store, watching her rearview mirror as she did so.

The Mercedes drove by, and Wanda Nell watched until it disappeared down the road.

Shaking slightly, she pulled her cell phone out of her purse and punched in a number.

"Law offices of Hamilton Tucker," T.J. said after about two rings. "How may I direct your call?"

"T.J., it's Mama," Wanda Nell said, barely letting him get out the standard greeting.

"Mama, what's wrong?" T.J. had instantly picked up on the tension in her voice.

Wanda Nell took a breath to steady herself. "I'm out in Pleasant Springs. I drove out here to talk to somebody, and I think I'm being followed."

"By who?"

"I think it's Bert Vines," she said. "It's a black Mercedes, and he's the only person I know of who's got one."

"Where are you now?"

"I'm at a store out here on the highway, just before you turn off on the Cadaretta road."

"You want me to come out there? I know where you're talking about."

"No, I think it'll be okay," Wanda Nell said, feeling calmer. "I don't think he's going to try to run me off the road or anything. I think maybe he was just watching to see where I was going."

"Where did you go?"

"I was talking to Miss Carpenter, the English teacher. You remember her from the high school?"

"I sure do," T.J. said, laughing a little. "She used to scare the bejeezus out of me. She was one tough lady."

"Yeah, she is that," Wanda Nell agreed, smiling. "I talked to her about the men involved in this mess, hoping she might know something or remember something that could help."

"Did she?"

"Sort of," Wanda Nell said. "I'll tell you more about it later."

"Okay," T.J. said. "But what are you going to do now?"

"I'm going to get back on the road, because I've got to get to work." She hesitated. "Would it be okay if I don't hang up? I'm going to put my phone down on the seat, and if for some reason I need help, I can talk to you right away."

"That's fine, Mama," T.J. said. "I'll hang on till you get to work."

"Okay," she said. "I'm going to put the phone down now and get back on the road." She laid the phone on the seat, put the car back into gear, and drove back onto the highway.

There was very little traffic on the road. In the first half mile Wanda Nell met only one truck heading in the other direction. When she passed a gravel road leading into woods on either side, she glanced into the rearview mirror. A black car was pulling onto the highway behind her.

Hand trembling slightly, she picked up her cell phone.

"T.J."

"I'm here, Mama."

"He's there."

"You want me to call the sheriff's department?"

"No, I don't think he's going to try anything," Wanda Nell said, with more confidence than she actually felt.

"Then you hightail it back to town, and don't mess around."

"I will," Wanda Nell said. "I'm going to put the phone down again." She did, checking the rearview mirror.

The Mercedes was hanging back. There was a long, flat stretch of road ahead of her and not another vehicle in sight. If Bert wanted to try something, now would be a good time.

Wanda Nell floored the accelerator, and her little car shuddered as it picked up speed. In a few seconds she was doing nearly eighty, and the Mercedes was quickly receding in her view. Wanda Nell focused her attention on the road ahead of her.

The next time she checked the rearview mirror, the Mercedes had closed the gap. The black car still hung back about four or five car lengths, and Wanda Nell figured she was probably right. Bert wasn't intending to try to run her off the road, but he sure wanted her to know he was there.

She eased off the accelerator slightly, bringing her speed down to about seventy. Then she had to bring it down even more, because there were two vehicles on the road a little way ahead of her.

Breathing more easily, Wanda Nell hoped that the trucks ahead of her were going all the way into Tullahoma. She drew close to the truck immediately in front of her and maintained a distance of about two car lengths between her car and the truck.

In a few minutes they reached the outskirts of Tulla-homa, and Wanda Nell began to breathe more easily. Bert's car was still there behind her, but he had never made a move to come any closer. As Wanda Nell reached the intersection where the Kountry Kitchen was located, she pulled into the turn lane and waited for the signal to change. Turning her head, she looked to her right. A couple of lanes over, Bert Vines also sat, waiting for the light.

He saw her looking at him, raised a hand in a quick wave, and smiled at her. Then the light changed and he drove off.

Suddenly almost shaking with rage, Wanda Nell was tempted to tear out after him and let him have it. How dare he follow her around like that?

The honk of a horn from a truck behind her brought Wanda Nell back to her senses. She glanced up at the light, saw the turn signal glowing green, and made her turn. She pulled her car into the parking lot at the Koun-try Kitchen and turned off the ignition.

Still angry, Wanda Nell picked up her phone. "T.J., honey, I'm here. I made it to work just fine."

"What about the car following you?"

"He stayed behind me the whole way," Wanda Nell said, doing her best to calm down, "and he never tried anything. I think he was just letting me know they're watching me."

"What for, do you think?"

"I think it's one of two things, probably," Wanda Nell said slowly, thinking aloud as she tried to work it out. "I think it may mean that nobody kidnapped Rusty, that he's hiding out somewhere on his own, and they think maybe I'll lead them to him before the sheriff's department finds him. That's one reason."

"I can see that," T.J. said, "though don't you think it's kind of strange that Uncle Rusty hasn't tried to get in touch with you? Seems to me he might want some help from his family if he's in real trouble."

Wanda Nell sighed. "Well, honey, that's the problem. I'm the last person Rusty might call on for help. He's real bitter towards me, and he didn't seem to want me to know what's going on."

"What happened between you two to cause all this?" Wanda Nell could hear some kind of clicking sound while T.J. talked. He must be working on the computer and talking to her at the same time.

"That's a long story, honey, and I don't have time to go into it right now," Wanda Nell said, "but if we ever find your uncle alive and all right, I'll tell you all about it. First we've got to find him."

"Okay," T.J. said. "But what about the other reason they're following you? Nobody's tried to get into the trailer again, have they?"

"No, thank the Lord, I don't think they have," Wanda Nell said, "but I know they're looking for something. I don't know what it is, but it's something to do with Rusty. And if they can't find him, I guess they're trying to find whatever it is, in case Rusty doesn't have it with him. Covering all their bases, maybe."

"Why isn't Elmer Lee doing something about all this?"

"I honestly think he's doing his best," Wanda Nell said, "but I think Elmer Lee may be in kind of a delicate situation here."

"How do you mean?" T.J. must have stopped what he was doing on the computer, because Wanda Nell couldn't hear any tapping now.

"Because of the sheriff," Wanda Nell said. "I think his son Marty is involved."

"That's not good," T.J. said.

"No, it's sure not," Wanda Nell agreed. "That makes everything harder, but I may just have to go to the sheriff myself and try to talk to him. We'll see." She paused for a moment. "Honey, will you make sure you tell Tuck about all this and bring him up to date? I haven't had a chance to talk to him."

"Will do, Mama," T.J. said. "I know he wants to do what he can to help."

"Thanks, honey," Wanda Nell said. "I'd better go before I use up all my minutes this month."

She clicked her phone off and dropped it into her purse. She checked her watch and was pleased to see that it was only five-fifteen. After all that had happened this afternoon, she thought being only fifteen minutes late to work wasn't too bad.

She had barely walked in the front door, however, before Melvin started waving at her from the kitchen door. Hurrying, she went around the counter and down the aisle to where he waited.

"Something wrong?" she asked, alarmed.

"There's somebody in my office wants to talk to you," Melvin said in an undertone. "You go on back and I'll stay out front."

Wanda Nell didn't stop to ask who it was. She hurried through the kitchen and down the hall to Melvin's tiny office near the back door.

She stepped into the room, then stopped, puzzled. There was no one in the office. She moved back into the hall and looked out the back door. No one there either.

Alarmed and annoyed at the same time, she went back out front to find Melvin.

Nineteen

Melvin was chatting with a customer at the cash register when Wanda Nell came through the kitchen door. She waited until Melvin had finished giving the man his change before approaching him and tapping him on the shoulder.

"What do you need, Wanda Nell?" Melvin said, frowning slightly.

"I need whoever it was supposed to be back there in your office waiting for me," she said, keeping her voice low.

Melvin's astonishment was plain on his face. "You mean she's not there?"

Wanda Nell shook her head. "Uh-uh, she's not. Who was it?"

"Some girl said she had a message for you. Showed up here about twenty minutes ago, and when I told her you weren't here, she looked upset. I told her she could wait for you, but she didn't want to wait out front here. Seemed kind of like she didn't want nobody to see her."

"You ever seen her before?"

"Naw, not that I can remember," Melvin said, "but she was real pretty, kinda Mexican-looking. You know, light brown skin, like coffee with a lot of milk in it. Dark, silky hair. She was real pretty, like I said."

"How old?" Wanda Nell was trying hard to remember ever meeting a girl like Melvin described. So far she was coming up blank.

"Maybe twenty or twenty-five," Melvin said after a moment's thought. "Hard to tell." He frowned. "One more thing, though. I said she was pretty, but she was way too thin. Didn't look or act like she felt too good."

"I have no idea who she is," Wanda Nell said. "She didn't give you a name or anything?"

"Nope," Melvin said. "It was all I could do to get her to wait for you back in my office. I swear I hadn't left her back there more than ten minutes before you got here. I never figured she'd just run off."

"Well, if it's important enough," Wanda Nell said, shrugging, "maybe she'll come back. In the meantime, guess I'd better get to work."

"If I see her, I'll let you know," Melvin said.

Wanda Nell realized she was still holding her purse, so she went back through the kitchen and down the hall to the cubbyhole that doubled as a storeroom and locker room for the employees. She stuck her purse on her shelf, and as she did, she had an idea.

She walked a little farther back to Melvin's office and stood inside the door, looking around.

If the girl had been too impatient, or too nervous, to wait, Wanda Nell reckoned, maybe she had left some kind of note.

She stepped into the office and moved toward Melvin's desk. Without disturbing any of the small piles of paper on the surface, she examined what was there.

Nothing that looked like a note for her, not anywhere in the office. She huffed in annoyance.

Why hadn't the girl waited? Was she frightened? Maybe that was it.

She had to be connected to the murders somehow, but what was the connection?

Was she a friend of Rusty's? Or was she connected to one of the other men?

Wanda Nell wanted to howl in frustration. She was sick of pedaling hard and not getting anywhere.

She uttered a loud groan, venting her feelings. Then she marched back down the hall, out through the kitchen doors, and to work.

She chatted a bit with Ruby Garner and Gladys Gordon in between waiting on the few tables she had. It looked to be a slow night, and Wanda Nell was trying her best to keep her mind off the mysterious girl.

Jack Pemberton turned up at seven, and Wanda Nell escorted him to a table in the back dining room. The rest of the room was vacant, and Jack pulled Wanda Nell into a corner, screened from the sight of anyone in the front dining area.

After a long and satisfying kiss, Wanda Nell reluctantly pulled away from him. "It sure is good to see you," she said, her voice husky.

"You, too," Jack said, smiling as he removed his steamed-up glasses and cleaned them with a handkerchief from his jeans pocket. "I've been missing you."

"I know," Wanda Nell said, "I've been missing you, too. All this craziness, not to mention work. I'm about sick to death of all of it."

"Poor baby," Jack said, putting his glasses back on. He pulled out a chair for Wanda Nell, then waited until she was sitting before he seated himself.

Wanda Nell smiled at his courtly manners. He treated her like a lady and made her feel cherished.

"I could just about wring your brother's neck," Jack

said, keeping his tone light, though Wanda Nell could see he was worried. "I hate it that he's got you involved in all this."

"What else is a family for?" Wanda Nell spoke lightly, too, but Jack knew her well enough by now to understand how she really felt.

"So what's been going on?" Jack asked. "We haven't had much time to talk."

"Hang on a second," Wanda Nell said, "I'll be right back, and I'll bring you some tea." She got up from the table and walked back into the front dining room.

She poured a glass of tea for Jack and one for herself. Telling Ruby she was going to take a short break, she asked if Ruby would look after her two tables for a little while. Ruby simply smiled and said, "You don't worry about a thing, Wanda Nell. I'll give a holler if we need you."

Ruby is such a good girl, Wanda Nell thought, not for the first time. *Sure wish I could trade Miranda for her*, she said to herself, then was ashamed.

She gave Jack his tea before sitting down with her own.

"Thanks," he said and raised his glass to her in salute.

Quickly she filled him in on all that had happened since they had last talked. He listened without comment, another quality that Wanda Nell appreciated deeply. Bobby Ray would have interrupted her every other sentence—one of the many reasons she had divorced him.

"One of these days I'd really like to meet Miss Carpenter," Jack said when Wanda Nell finished. "She retired the year before I came to Tullahoma. I've heard all kinds of stories about her, but I'm not sure I believe most of them."

"She's pretty amazing," Wanda Nell said, smiling. "I want you to meet her, too. I know you'll like her, and she'll like you."

"I like her just for the help she's given you," Jack said. "She sounds like a good person to have in your corner."

Wanda Nell nodded. "She sure is." Sighing, she continued, "I'm going to need her when I go talk to the sheriff."

"Are you really going to?"

"Yeah, I don't see that I have much choice," Wanda Nell said. "If Rusty doesn't turn up before tomorrow afternoon, I'm going over to the sheriff's department and insist on talking to him."

"I'll come with you," Jack said. "I can get away from school at three."

"Thank you, honey," Wanda Nell said, reaching out to touch his hand. "I sure appreciate that, but I think it's probably better for me to talk to him by myself."

"If you won't let me come with you," Jack said with a tinge of mingled anxiety and exasperation in his voice, "what about Tuck? Don't you think it would be a good idea to at least have a lawyer with you?"

"I don't know," Wanda Nell said. "I hadn't really thought about that." She paused for a moment. "I just don't know. I feel like I've got a better chance of getting the sheriff to talk to me if I go by myself."

"You always try to carry the burden alone," Jack said. He had spoken in a neutral tone, and Wanda Nell wasn't sure if he was criticizing her or simply stating a fact.

"I guess I just don't know any other way of getting things done," she said, deciding not to take it as criticism. "For a long time I haven't had anybody else to lean on except Mayrene, and it's hard learning to do anything else."

"I know, love, I know," Jack said, reaching out to take one of her hands. He cradled it in both of his. "You're so strong and so capable. You know, sometimes you scare me a little. I don't know if I can be strong enough for you." He shrugged.

"I don't have any complaints so far," Wanda Nell said, smiling, "but I don't think I can change a lot and suddenly turn into one of those women who can't do a thing for herself."

"Believe me, that's not what I want," Jack said. "I think you're just about perfect, anyway."

"'Just about,' huh?" Wanda Nell said teasingly. "And here I thought I was completely perfect."

"Well," Jack said, grinning.

Standing up, Wanda Nell said, "I think I better get you something to eat before we get any sillier. What are you in the mood for?"

"You mean something on the menu?" Jack was still grinning.

"Yes," Wanda Nell said, trying to look stern.

Jack made a sad face. "Then I guess I'll just have to settle for chicken-fried steak, as usual."

"Coming right up, though you're going to turn into chicken-fried steak one of these days, the way you eat it," Wanda Nell said teasingly. She went to the kitchen and turned in his order.

After that she stayed pretty busy, and soon the back dining room started filling up. She didn't have much time to chat with Jack, other than stopping by his table a couple of times to refill his tea.

When he was ready to go, he dropped a hefty tip on the table. Wanda Nell had fussed at him about that, but he smilingly refused to stop doing it. "Call me," he said as he walked by her on the way to the cash register.

"I will," Wanda Nell promised. She pocketed the tip, thinking she would use it to buy some nice, juicy steaks for next Sunday's dinner. Jack loved steak and swore she cooked it to perfection.

Wanda Nell took advantage of a short break around nine o'clock to call home. Mayrene answered the phone.

"Oh, everything's fine, honey," she assured Wanda Nell.

"Juliet is in her room and Lavon is in bed. Tuck and T.J. are here, and them and me and Miranda are watching a movie. You want to talk to one of the boys or Miranda?"

"No," Wanda Nell said, "I just wanted to check on y'all. Listen, Mayrene, some strange girl showed up here before I got to work this afternoon looking for me, but she ran off before I got here." She repeated Melvin's description of the girl. "She sound like anybody you know?"

"No, don't think so," Mayrene said after a moment's consideration. "Wonder what she wanted?"

"I was hoping she might turn up again tonight, but so far she hasn't shown," Wanda Nell said. "Sure is frustrating. Especially if it's something important."

"I reckon if it's important enough, she'll get in touch with you somehow," Mayrene said. "In the meantime don't you worry too much about it."

They both laughed at that, knowing Wanda Nell wouldn't do any such thing. Wanda Nell hung up the phone and went back to work. She kept worrying about who the girl was and what she wanted. This was going to drive her crazy until she could answer those questions.

At closing time, when the restaurant was finally clear of customers, Wanda Nell asked Ruby and Gladys to stay for a moment and talk to her. "I need to ask you both a question. I should have asked you before, but I didn't really like to with a lot of people around."

Ruby and Gladys looked at her questioningly.

"Y'all know I was running a little late this afternoon on getting to work," Wanda Nell began, and they both nodded. "Well, some girl showed up here a little before five looking for me. Did either one of you happen to see her?" She offered a brief description.

Gladys shook her head. "No, I sure didn't, Wanda Nell. Who was she?"

"That's what I'm trying to find out," Wanda Nell said. She turned to Ruby. "Did you see her?"

"I did, now that you mention it," Ruby said, nodding. "I only saw her for a minute, because I was busy with a couple of tables. But I think I know her."

"You do?" Wanda Nell almost shrieked in excitement.

Ruby nodded again. "I'm pretty sure. She was in one of my classes at the junior college last year." She paused, thinking. "I'm pretty sure her name is Lily, but for the life of me, I can't think of what her last name is."

Wanda Nell tried hard to conceal her disappointment. "Please try to remember, Ruby. This could be real important. She ran off before I got here, and I don't know what she wanted to talk to me about. I need to find her, just in case."

"I'm sorry, Wanda Nell," Ruby said, obviously distressed. "I just can't think of it. I'm sure I know her name, and maybe I can remember it if I think hard enough."

"I appreciate it, Ruby," Wanda Nell said, softening her voice. "Look, let me give you my phone number. If you remember the name, call me, no matter what time it is. Will you do that?" She reached into her purse for something to write on.

"Sure," Ruby said. "I'll look through some of my things at home. Maybe something will jog my memory. We had to do some team projects in that class, and I might have something with her name on it." She laughed in an embarrassed way. "I hold on to stuff and just never throw anything away. My mama is always fussing at me about it."

"I really appreciate it," Wanda Nell said, handing Ruby a slip of paper with her number on it. "I'm glad you hold on to things, if you can find that girl's name for me."

"I'll check as soon as I get home," Ruby promised. She gave Wanda Nell a hug.

"Thank you," Wanda Nell said, returning the hug. "Now, you and Gladys get on home. I'm coming right behind you. You ready to go?" She called out to Melvin as she walked out the door.

Melvin yelled for her to go on, and she went on to her car. Feeling grateful that she didn't have to face a night shift at Budget Mart, she drove home, hoping for a decent night's sleep. There were so many things weighing on her mind right now, she might never get to sleep, though. She would just have to take things as they came. *I'm doing everything I can*, she told herself. *And that's all I can do*.

Slightly cheered by these thoughts, she sustained the mood until she turned into the trailer park entrance. As her headlights swept the end of her trailer, she slammed on her brakes and stared.

Someone had spray-painted a message across the end of her trailer. Hands trembling on the steering wheel, Wanda Nell read the words, "NOSY = DEAD."

Twenty

For a moment Wanda Nell was terrified. She could hardly breathe.

Then she was angry—blazingly angry. "Bastards!"

Who they hell did they think they were? Spray-painting a threat on her home. She'd get them for this. She wasn't going to be intimidated by anyone.

Easing her foot off the brakes, Wanda Nell drove her car to the carport and parked it. Still shaking slightly, she got out of the car. For a moment she leaned against the car to steady herself. When she felt stronger and more in control, she climbed the steps to her front door and let herself in.

"Hey, honey," Mayrene said, looking up from the couch. "You'll never guess what the boys and me found after you called earlier."

Wanda Nell paid no attention to her words. "I've got to call the sheriff's department."

"Well, yeah," Mayrene said, frowning, "I think you should. But don't you want to know what we found first?"

Intent on getting to the phone in the kitchen, Wanda Nell didn't even hear her. She punched in the number, and when the dispatcher answered, she demanded to speak to Elmer Lee.

"Just a moment, ma'am," the dispatcher said. "I think he's still here."

When Elmer Lee came on the line, Wanda Nell said, "You need to get out here to the trailer park right now, Elmer Lee. I want you to see something."

She listened to him sputter at her about being too busy for any of her foolishness, but she cut him off. "You get yourself out here *right now*. Do you hear me?" She slammed the phone down. Her temper had flared again, and she was surprised she hadn't knocked the phone loose from the wall where it was mounted.

"Honey, what's going on?" Mayrene, watching from the other end of the kitchen, now came forward to put an arm around Wanda Nell's shoulders. "Calm down."

"Did you hear anything outside tonight?" Wanda Nell asked.

Obviously puzzled, Mayrene shook her head. "No, honey, we was all watching TV, and I reckon it was kinda loud. We didn't hear anything. What happened?"

Tersely, Wanda Nell explained what she had seen.

"Good Lord," Mayrene said. "I can't believe somebody had the gall to do that, and us just sitting here inside the whole time." She squeezed Wanda Nell hard against her. "You just wait. If I get ahold of the bastards who did this, honey, I'll take my shotgun to 'em."

Wanda Nell almost laughed at that. That shotgun was Mayrene's answer to everything. "Let's let the sheriff's department do their job first."

While they waited for Elmer Lee to turn up, Mayrene sat Wanda Nell down at the table and got her some water. "You want something to eat?"

Wanda Nell shook her head. "No, I'm fine. This water

is all I need." She drank down half the glass. "Are the girls already in bed?"

"Yeah," Mayrene said. "They went to bed about ten minutes before you got home."

"Good," Wanda Nell said. "I don't want them upset about all this. Maybe I can paint over it tonight after Elmer Lee's been here."

"I'll help you," Mayrene said.

"Thanks," Wanda Nell said, drinking the last of her water. "I think I've got enough paint left from that paint job I did last year."

Moments later, they both heard the sound of a car outside. They both got up, heading outside before Elmer Lee could reach the door.

"What's going on now, Wanda Nell?" Elmer Lee stopped about two feet away from her and stood, arms crossed, waiting.

He was peeved about something, and maybe it was her he was annoyed with. Right now, though, Wanda Nell didn't really care. "Somebody's threatening me again, Elmer Lee," she said. "Didn't you notice it when you drove up?"

"No, I didn't. What are you talking about?"

"Have you got a flashlight?"

Elmer Lee called to his subordinate, who brought him the requested light.

"Come around here," Wanda Nell said, turning and walking to the end of the trailer. "Just flash your light up there." She pointed.

Elmer Lee switched on the light and aimed the beam where Wanda Nell had indicated. The words stood out starkly against the pale blue of her trailer.

After a moment, Elmer Lee switched the light off. "So what have you been doing to make somebody threaten you?"

"Now look here, Elmer Lee," Mayrene said hotly, "Wanda Nell's the victim in this situation. Nobody's got the right to blame her. You need to be looking for the sonofabitch who spray-painted her trailer."

"I sure do appreciate you telling me how to do my job, Mayrene," Elmer Lee said, his face expressionless. "If it wasn't for you and Wanda Nell here, well, I reckon I wouldn't ever know what to do."

Mayrene took a step forward, her hand raised, but the deputy accompanying Elmer Lee suddenly moved up and blocked Mayrene from going any farther.

"Now let's all just calm down here," Wanda Nell said. "And you stop being a jackass." She looked straight at Elmer Lee as she said it.

"What's been going on, Wanda Nell?" Elmer Lee asked. "And don't give me any crap about you being an innocent victim here. I know you ain't killed anybody, but you must be doing something to stir up this kind of thing."

"Just talking to a few people," Wanda Nell said. "Anything wrong with that?" Without waiting for a response, she continued, "And some of them are coming to me."

"Like who?" Elmer Lee asked.

Wanda Nell lowered her voice. "Like Marty Shaw, for one."

Elmer Lee went completely still. Then he muttered a curse under his breath, but Wanda Nell heard what he said.

"Exactly," Wanda Nell said, with grim satisfaction. "He showed up at the Kountry Kitchen, asking me about Rusty and how he was doing. He even asked me for Rusty's phone number in Nashville. Said he was going to be up there on business, and he might look him up." She snorted in disgust. "You ever heard such a load of bull hockey in your life?" Beside her, Mayrene shifted from foot to foot, obviously uneasy.

Elmer Lee stared at her for a long moment. "I'm just going to say this once, Wanda Nell. And you'd better listen to me—for once in your life." He paused to be sure he had her attention. "Back off from this, and let me do my job. This is no time for you to be running around playing Nancy Drew."

Something in his tone chilled Wanda Nell. She could feel the flesh crawl along the back of her neck and shoulders. She stared back at him, trying to figure out why this was so disturbing to her. Then it hit her.

Elmer Lee was afraid.

Feeling she had to tread more carefully now, Wanda Nell said, "What are you going to do about this?" She pointed to the graffiti.

"We'll do what we can," Elmer Lee said, "but unless one of your neighbors saw something, I don't know that there's much we *can* do."

"Then while you're getting on with whatever it is you can do," Wanda Nell said, careful to keep the sarcasm from her voice, "I guess we'll go back inside."

"You do that," Elmer Lee said. He turned away to talk to his deputy.

Pulling Mayrene with her, Wanda Nell went back inside her trailer. She was disturbed by Elmer Lee's behavior, but she recognized the fact that she could do little, if anything, about it. But he wasn't going to stop her doing what she felt she had to do.

"Wanda Nell," Mayrene said, calling her back to the present. "You think you can deal with something else now? I found something I thought you should know about."

Grateful for a distraction, Wanda Nell said, "Sure." She sat down on the couch and motioned for Mayrene to join her. Reaching for the TV remote, she turned the volume down. "What is it?"

That was all the encouragement Mayrene needed.

"Well, T.J. and Tuck showed up here about six o'clock to have dinner with me and the girls. And you'll never guess, honey, but Tuck said he and T.J. was going to do the cooking. I like to have fell out of my chair. I had no idea that man could cook." She laughed. "He's gorgeous, makes a lot of money, and he can cook to boot. Too bad he don't play on my team, or I'd have him in my locker so fast he wouldn't know what hit him."

Wanda Nell usually didn't mind Mayrene's rambles, but tonight she was on edge. "So what did you find?"

Hearing the impatience in her friend's voice, Mayrene got on with what she had to say. "Like I said, T.J. and Tuck came over for dinner. I been meaning to search through my guest room ever since you and I talked about it, but I felt kind of funny about going through your brother's things. I mean, Lord knows I'm nosy enough for three people, but it just felt strange for me to be doing it."

"I understand," Wanda Nell said. "I should have come over there and done it with you, but I haven't had much time."

"No, I know that, honey," Mayrene said. "But with T.J. here tonight, I figured we ought to do it. So Tuck stayed at your place with the girls, and T.J. came over to my place with me. That was after you called me, what was it, nine o'clock? We started looking through everything in here, but there wasn't much to see." She sighed in annoyance. "Your brother travels light, and he didn't bring much with him."

"But you found something," Wanda Nell prompted her. Try as she might, she wasn't having much luck in hurrying Mayrene along.

"Yeah, we did," Mayrene said. "We were about to give up. I mean we had looked through everything twice, and even under the mattress. Nothing. Then T.J. got down on his hands and knees and looked under the bed and the night stand and everything." She chuckled. "I could have done it, but I'd have had a heck of a time getting back up. At first, T.J. didn't see anything, but then he found a scrap of paper that had slipped under the nightstand."

Wanda Nell was beginning to get aggravated. She loved Mayrene dearly, but if her friend didn't get to the point soon, she was going to scream.

"Anything on the paper?" she asked in a mild voice.

"Yeah," Mayrene said. She pulled a scrap of paper from the pocket of her pants and handed it to Wanda Nell.

She examined it. There were sets of numbers on the paper. Phone numbers by the looks of them. She turned to Mayrene for an explanation.

"A couple of them are toll-free numbers, and the other one had a 601 area code. Turns out it was a Jackson number. We called all three of them, honey, and you'll never guess what they were."

"What?" Wanda Nell almost shouted, she was so tired of this dragging on and on. "What were they?"

"All three of them was closed, it being so late, of course, but they all had recordings," Mayrene said, seemingly oblivious to her friend's impatience. "All of them are DNA testing places, honey. What do you think about that?"

Twenty-one

Whatever answer Wanda Nell had been expecting, it certainly wasn't that one. Why would Rusty need the numbers for DNA testing facilities?

"You understand what I'm saying?" Mayrene asked. "Wanda Nell?"

"Yeah, I understand," Wanda Nell answered. "Just stunned, I guess."

"I know," Mayrene said. "You reckon Rusty was going to have to take a paternity test or something like?"

"I don't know," Wanda Nell said. "I just don't know."

"You think you should let Elmer Lee know about this?" Mayrene asked.

Wanda Nell almost laughed. "Yeah, I guess so. Maybe he's still outside. We'd better get him in here if he is."

"I'll go," Mayrene said. "You just sit there and try to keep calm."

Wanda Nell sat with her eyes closed while she waited for Mayrene to return. She hoped Elmer Lee hadn't left yet, otherwise he was going to be really annoyed if he got called back here.

"Here he is," Mayrene said. Wanda Nell opened her

eyes and looked up to see Elmer Lee glaring down at her. He was definitely in an even worse mood than he was before.

"What is it?" Elmer Lee almost spit out the words.

"Mayrene found a piece of paper with some phone numbers on it in the room where Rusty was staying," Wanda Nell said. "I think you should check them out. Give it to him, Mayrene." She wasn't going to tell him that Mayrene had already called the numbers. He'd have to do it anyway.

Elmer Lee took the paper from Mayrene and squinted down at it. "What are these, phone numbers?"

"Sure looks like it," Mayrene said with a quick glance at Wanda Nell.

Elmer Lee swore under his breath as he tucked the paper into his pocket.

"You'd better check those numbers out," Wanda Nell said, then immediately wished she hadn't.

The look Elmer Lee gave her could have peeled the paint off her trailer, but she pretended like it didn't bother her. She did have the grace to mutter, "Sorry."

"You want to show me where you found this?" Elmer Lee turned to glare at Mayrene, who suddenly had a very startled look on her face.

"Oh my Lord," Mayrene said. "I plumb forgot. T.J. and Tuck are over at my place watching TV. They wanted to watch some special on PBS, and I sent 'em over there."

"Where's the car?" Wanda Nell asked. "I didn't see it when I drove up."

"It's over there with mine," Mayrene said. "Lord, Elmer Lee, come on with me next door." She glanced at Wanda Nell. "Honey, why don't you just sit here for a few minutes and rest."

"I think I will," Wanda Nell said. "I'm exhausted."

"Good night, then," Elmer Lee said. "You try to stay

out of trouble for an hour or two, okay? I can't be running out here every fifteen minutes."

Wanda Nell ignored that. She sat quietly with her eyes closed, even after she heard them shut the door behind them. She needed to unwind, or she was going to have a doozy of a headache before long.

She had been sitting there for maybe two minutes when the phone rang. Sighing with tiredness, Wanda Nell got up to answer it. Who would be calling her at this time of night? Most people knew she were either at work or in bed asleep by this time. She hoped it wasn't some boy calling Miranda.

Then her heart skipped a beat. Maybe it was Ruby. She had almost forgotten about Ruby's promise to search among her papers for that strange girl's last name. She grabbed the receiver. "Hello."

"Wanda Nell, it's Ruby."

Breathing a hearty sigh of relief, Wanda Nell said, "I'm so glad you called, Ruby. Have you got good news for me?"

"I sure do," Ruby said triumphantly. "As soon as I got home, I started looking through my old papers and things. And I found it. I had a copy of the team assignments we did for that class, and there was her name."

"What is it?" Wanda Nell could barely control her impatience.

"Lily Golliday," Ruby said. "As soon as I found it, I got out the phone book and looked. There's about twenty-three Gollidays listed in the book, but there's no Lily. I sure am sorry."

Wanda Nell's heart sank a little. She had thought as soon as she had the girl's last name, she could find her right away. Now she'd probably have to call every Golliday in the phone book until she found her.

"That's okay," Wanda Nell said. "The main thing is, I know her name now. I really appreciate you going home and looking it up for me."

"I'm glad I could," Ruby said. "Anything else I can do?"

"You don't remember anything else about her, do you?"

Ruby thought for a moment. "No, not really, except that she was always kind of shy. She seemed like a nice girl, but she hardly ever said a word in class." Ruby paused to clear her throat. "Maybe that was because she was what my mama would call 'high yellow'."

Wanda Nell hadn't heard that saying in a long time. "You mean she's mixed race."

"Yeah," Ruby said. "I noticed that the black students in the class didn't seem to want to have much to do with her, and neither did most of the white ones. I tried talking to her a couple times, but she just didn't want to talk to me."

"That's too bad," Wanda Nell said. "It sounds to me like she could have used a good friend like you, Ruby."

"I don't know what happened to her after that class," Ruby said. "I haven't had another class with her since then and I haven't seen her at all, until she showed up at the restaurant tonight."

"Well, thanks for everything," Wanda Nell said. "I'm going to try to find her tomorrow." She was a bit daunted by the thought of calling strangers up on the phone and asking if they knew this girl, but she didn't have much choice.

"You're welcome," Ruby said. "If you talk to her, tell her I said hello."

"I will," Wanda Nell promised. She hung up the phone, then she leaned against the counter for a few minutes, thinking about the new pieces of information she had.

A girl named Lily Golliday had come looking for her.

A girl of mixed race—she had actually suspected as much, based on Melvin's description of her. She sounded a lot like her own grandson, Lavon.

And Rusty had been carrying around the numbers for several DNA testing places with him. Did that mean maybe he was this girl's father, and he was going to take a paternity test? All at once, Rusty's odd comment about Lavon came back to her. He hadn't said anything nasty, the way Wanda Nell expected, when he found out Lavon was half black.

If he was the father of a mixed-race child himself, that might explain his attitude to Lavon.

But if that's all it was, why were Bert Vines and Marty Shaw involved? And Reggie and Tony Campbell and Scott Simpson? What about them?

Wanda Nell couldn't figure out an answer, but there was one thing that was certain. Something really nasty lay at the bottom of all this, and uncovering the truth was bound to cause a lot of trouble for someone. Maybe for everyone involved.

Wanda Nell sat down hard in one of the kitchen chairs. Suddenly she felt like everything was spinning out of control. She wanted to go back in time, before all this started. The way ahead was too dark, too frightening, and she didn't want to have to deal with it all.

Hands clasped tightly on the table in front of her, Wanda Nell closed her eyes and uttered a prayer. She asked for the strength to endure it all and the strength to keep her loved ones safe. She prayed also for her brother, that he would be found alive and well and that he wouldn't turn out to be a cold-blooded murderer.

Comforted now, and feeling stronger, Wanda Nell decided to go next door to see what was going on at Mayrene's.

Simply opening the door and walking in, Wanda Nell caught those inside by surprise.

Elmer Lee scowled when he saw her. He and his fellow officer occupied Mayrene's couch, and Mayrene, Tuck, and T.J. sat in chairs near them.

"I thought I told you stay out of this," Elmer Lee said.

Wanda Nell ignored that. There was no point in getting into another argument with him about it. She just looked at Elmer Lee. "What do you think of those numbers?"

"Right now I don't think anything," Elmer Lee said, glaring at her. "I'm going to take this back to the sheriff's department with me, and we'll work on it there. You can just forget about it for now. Let me get on with my job."

Wanda Nell had briefly considered telling him about Lily Golliday, knowing that Elmer Lee could probably find her faster than she could. But his attitude decided her. She would find the girl herself and talk to her first. No telling how Elmer Lee might treat her. She probably wouldn't even talk to him, but she might talk to another woman.

Elmer Lee stood up from the couch, heading for the door, and the other deputy followed him.

"Have you got any leads on my brother?" Wanda Nell asked.

His hand on the doorknob, Elmer Lee turned back to face her. "No, not a sign. Far as we can tell, he vanished into thin air. You heard anything from him?"

"No, nothing since that one phone call," she said. Taking a deep breath, she asked the question she had dreaded to put into words. "Do you think he's still alive?"

Elmer Lee's face softened for moment. "I don't know, Wanda Nell. I just don't know." His face hardened again. "But we've got to find him, one way or another."

Chilled, Wanda Nell could only nod. T.J. had quickly moved from his chair to stand beside his mother. He slipped an arm around her shoulders, and Wanda Nell was grateful for the warmth and support.

"He's got to be alive," she said. "And he's not a killer. I know he's not. He couldn't just kill two men in cold blood like that." T.J. squeezed her to him again, and she rested her head on his shoulder.

Elmer Lee cleared his throat. "Take this and go on out to the car," he instructed his subordinate, handing him the scrap of paper, safely sealed in a plastic bag.

The deputy nodded and did what Elmer Lee had ordered.

When the door had closed behind him, Elmer Lee faced Wanda Nell and said, "I reckon there's something I ought to tell you, Wanda Nell. I shouldn't be doing this, but you deserve to know."

Her stomach tensing into a knot, Wanda Nell said, "What?"

"Scott Simpson wasn't murdered," Elmer Lee replied.

"What do you mean?" Wanda Nell couldn't believe what she was hearing.

"It was suicide," Elmer Lee said. His eyes burned into hers. "He left a note. He said he couldn't live with himself. He didn't mention any names, but he made it clear somebody pushed him into it. Some woman, he said."

Elmer Lee didn't wait for a response. He opened the door, walked out, then slammed it behind him.

Wanda Nell, horror-stricken, could only stand and stare at the door.

Twenty-two

Mayrene was on her feet and out the door before Wanda Nell had time to register what was going on. She was still rooted to the floor with T.J.'s arm around her shoulders, trying to take in the implications of what Elmer Lee had said to her. Tuck came to stand with them on Wanda Nell's other side. Together the two men enveloped her in warmth.

Moments later, all three of them could hear the sound of voices raised in anger coming from outside. The argument continued for a couple minutes, but it ended with the sound of a car door slamming shut. An engine roared, tires squealed, and Mayrene bellowed.

After a brief interval, Mayrene came clomping back into the trailer. She had fire in her eyes, and her chest was heaving.

"What did you say to him?" T.J. asked.

Mayrene came forward and took Wanda Nell's arm. "You come on over here and sit down, honey. I can't believe that jackass said something like that to you. I stripped a few layers of hide off him, let me tell you. The nerve he had, to do something like that. I've got a good mind to call the sheriff myself and complain." She pulled Wanda Nell down on the sofa beside her and started patting one of Wanda Nell's hands.

T.J. sat on the other side of his mother. "Are you okay, Mama? Can I get you anything?" Tuck stood, arms folded across his chest, an angry look on his face.

"I'm okay," Wanda Nell said, but her voice carried no conviction. She was sick to her stomach. Elmer Lee had basically accused her of being responsible for Scott Simpson's suicide. If that was really true, how could she ever forgive herself?

"Now you listen here, Wanda Nell," Mayrene said, reading her friend's state of mind correctly. "Despite what that idiot Elmer Lee said to you, you're not to blame for that man killing himself. You said yourself that he was a lot more scared of somebody else than he was of you." Mayrene snorted in disgust. "Now if he was afraid of somebody else, why would he kill himself on account of you? That just don't make sense."

"She's right, Mama," T.J. said, his voice quiet but confident. "Coach Simpson was involved in whatever's going on with Uncle Rusty, and none of that's your fault. If it's anybody's fault, then it's Uncle Rusty's, in a way. He's the one who came back here and stirred things up."

"That's right," Mayrene chimed in. "Listen to T.J. I told Elmer Lee he was just being vindictive, saying that to you, and he didn't deny it. I asked him if he really thought that man was talking about you in his suicide note, and Elmer Lee couldn't look me in the face. Now, I don't think he was lying about some woman being mentioned in that note, but I'd be willing to bet you anything it wasn't you Simpson was talking about."

"They're right, Wanda Nell," Tuck said. "Elmer Lee was just lashing out at you. Don't let him get to you. But you can bet I'm going to have something to say to him about this."

"Thank you," Wanda Nell said. The more she thought about it all, the more she realized that probably all three of them were right. She hadn't driven Scott Simpson to kill himself. Whatever was going on with her brother and the other men was the root cause of Simpson's decision. Still, she felt shaky.

"But why would Elmer Lee say something like that to me?" Wanda Nell asked. "Does he really hate me that much?"

"He's scared about something," Mayrene said. "I don't know what it is, honey, but he ain't acting like himself. He's lashing out at you because he thinks he can get away with it." She laughed suddenly. "And let me tell you one other thing, and don't you slap me for saying it, but I think ol' Elmer Lee's sweet on you. He's got the hots for you, and he can't stand it."

When Wanda Nell failed to protest, both Mayrene and T.J. stared at her in surprise. Tuck just shook his head in wonder.

"You may be right," Wanda Nell said finally, refusing to look any one of them straight in the eye.

"He sure has got a funny way of showing it, if he does," T.J. said in disgust.

Mayrene laughed. "Don't you remember how it was when you was in the fifth or sixth grade, T.J.? If a boy likes a girl at that age, he's more likely to pull her hair or hit her on the arm than come out and tell her he likes her. Shoot, Elmer Lee's just a big old fifth-grader when it comes to women. He ain't never known what to do with a girl."

Wanda Nell was finally recovering her equilibrium. She had to laugh at what Mayrene was saying. Elmer Lee *was* like a big kid sometimes. He was attractive, in his way, but Wanda Nell never could feel that way about him. She wasn't attracted to him and wouldn't ever be.

Unfortunately for her, though, she was stuck with him.

"I can't see him as a stepdaddy," T.J. said jokingly.

Wanda Nell poked him in the side. "You don't have to worry about that, believe me. Not if he was the last man on the face of the Earth." She grimaced in distaste.

"Good," T.J. said. "I don't ever want to have to call *him* 'Daddy.'" He grimaced right back at his mother, and they both laughed. "And I don't think Tuck would much care to have him as a father-in-law." Tuck rolled his eyes, not saying a word. That made Wanda Nell laugh a little.

"Feeling better now?" Mayrene asked.

"Yeah, I guess," Wanda Nell said. "Though I sure wish Elmer Lee hadn't done that to me."

"He ain't getting away with it," Mayrene said, and Wanda Nell decided she wouldn't want to be Elmer Lee when Mayrene got hold of him again.

"Look, it's late," Wanda Nell said, standing up. "We need to be getting on home, and you need to be getting ready for bed. I know you must be worn out. I sure am." She bent and gave Mayrene a quick hug.

"I do need my beauty sleep," Mayrene said, laughing, "but for all the good it does me, I might as well not ever go to bed."

"Thanks for looking out for me," Wanda Nell said, pausing by the door. T.J. and Tuck were right behind her. "Good night."

"Night, y'all," Mayrene said.

The night air was cool, and Wanda Nell stood for a moment, breathing it in. She had a sudden desire to sit outside for a while and put off thinking about anything serious. How nice it would be just to sit there and look up at the sky. Beyond the faint light from the couple street lights at each end of the trailer park, she could see the stars overhead.

"You okay, Mama?" T.J. said, his voice low.

Wanda Nell sighed deeply. "I'm fine, honey," she said. She would have to stargaze some other time. "Let's go on in." She climbed the steps to her front door and opened it.

"Anything else we can do for you before we go home, Mama?" T.J. asked.

"Yeah, there is," she said, "if y'all don't mind waiting a few more minutes." She crossed to a chair near the couch and sat down.

"Course not," Tuck said. "What can we do?"

"I need help finding a girl," Wanda Nell said. "Her name is Lily Golliday." She told them about the girl's visit to the Kountry Kitchen and the way they had managed to identify who she was.

"And you have no idea why she wanted to talk to you?" Tuck asked.

Wanda Nell shook her head. "No idea at all. I don't know her. But all I can think, naturally, is that it has something to do with Rusty."

"And those phone numbers for DNA testing facilities," Tuck added. "That puts a really strange twist on everything."

"It sure does," Wanda Nell said. "I don't know what to think. But I've got to find that girl, and I've got to find Rusty."

"You've looked in the phone book," Tuck stated.

"I didn't, but Ruby did," Wanda Nell said. "There's a bunch of Gollidays listed, but not this girl, as far as Ruby could tell."

"I've had a couple of different men named Golliday as clients," Tuck said. "As far as I know, they weren't related, but I could be wrong. I could certainly get in touch with them in the morning and find out if they know this girl."

"I'd sure appreciate it," Wanda Nell said. "Otherwise, the only thing I can do is start calling people up and asking about her."

"That would probably work, too," T.J. said. "I can help you call, Mama. We can take the list and divide it if neither of those men Tuck knows can't help us."

"We can do that," Wanda Nell said, "though I'm not sure what people will think, some stranger calling up and looking for a girl."

"Some of them will probably be suspicious and not talk to you," Tuck said, "but others will talk. You'd be surprised how much people will tell you sometimes."

"We'll see," Wanda Nell said. "But there's one other thing you can do for me, besides call those men."

Tuck nodded. "Sure, what is it?"

"I've been thinking about where Rusty could be," Wanda Nell said. "I just have to believe that he's alive, and he's probably being kept somewhere."

Tuck started to say something, then evidently thought better of it.

"I know," Wanda Nell said. "I know he might not be alive, but I've just got this feeling he is." She paused for a moment, because she had to blink back sudden tears. "Anyway, I've been thinking about where he might be, like I said."

"Where do you think he could be?" T.J. asked.

"If somebody kidnapped him," Wanda Nell said, "it had to be Bert or Marty, probably. And I really doubt they would be keeping him in one of their houses. They've got to have some other place where they're hiding him. And I thought maybe you could find out where that could be."

T.J. turned to Tuck. "I could go over to the courthouse first thing in the morning and start looking through the property records."

"That's fine," Tuck said, "as long as what we're looking

for is in Tullahoma County. If it's not, then you'll have to get on the Internet and see what you can dig up. But we'll deal with that if we have to. We'll get the information, one way or another." He paused for a moment. "But say we do find that one of them has some property elsewhere, what are you going to do?"

"I'm going there to look for my brother," Wanda Nell said.

"That could be dangerous," Tuck said.

"I know," Wanda Nell replied, "but I don't see much else to do. Can you see me telling Elmer Lee he's got to go looking for Rusty at some place out in the country belonging to Bert Vines or Marty Shaw? He'd laugh his head off."

"Maybe," Tuck said. "But you've got to be really careful, Wanda Nell. We need to think about this and come up with a plan."

"We will," Wanda Nell said. She knew Tuck meant well, but he was a lawyer, after all, and he was a lot more cautious about things than she tended to be. When she saw something that needed to be done, she did it. Especially when there was as much at stake as there was here. This was her brother's life they were talking about, and she had to take action, even if it was drastic or dangerous.

Tuck didn't make any further issue of his point. He knew Wanda Nell well enough by now to know how stubborn she could be. He stood up. "Time for us to go home, T.J. We're both going to have very busy days tomorrow by the looks of things."

T.J. followed him to the door, and Wanda Nell came to see them out.

"Have you moved in yet?" Wanda Nell asked her son.

"Pretty much," T.J. said.

"And your grandmother's taking it okay?"

T.J. grinned. "Pretty good, surprisingly. But she and

Belle are getting on like a house on fire. Grandmother's having such a good time ordering Belle around and telling her to stop talking so much, I don't think she even misses me."

"Hallelujah," Wanda Nell said. She gave them each a kiss and a hug and locked the door behind them.

Before she went to her room, she turned off the TV set. Then she went to check on Miranda and Lavon. Both were sound asleep, and Wanda Nell stood in the doorway for a moment, watching them.

Quietly she moved back through the trailer to the other end where her bedroom and Juliet's were. Juliet's door stood slightly ajar, and Wanda Nell pushed it open a bit. Juliet too was sound asleep, her teddy bear Alexander keeping her company. If all the ruckus earlier had disturbed either of the girls or the baby, there was no sign of it now. Wanda Nell watched for a moment, reassured by the quiet breathing of her youngest child.

In her own room she slowly changed into a nightgown and cleaned the residue of her makeup from her face. Then, turning out the lights in bathroom and bedroom, she climbed into bed.

Though she was tired, she wasn't sure she would be able to sleep. Normally at this hour she would be at work at Budget Mart. Plus she had so much on her mind that sleep might not come easily.

Her thoughts turned to Scott Simpson. He was like a sore spot she couldn't help touching. In her mind she knew she wasn't directly responsible for his suicide, but her heart wasn't so sure. Maybe once this whole mess was straightened out—and it would be, she was determined about that—she could put this particular demon to rest. Once she understood everything that had happened, she could find some peace of mind.

She lay there a long time, her mind seething with facts

and ideas, what-ifs and maybes. Restlessly she turned first one way, then another, hoping sleep would come. "Dang," she said aloud a moment later, "I forgot to ask Elmer Lee if I could paint over that mess on the trailer." Deciding that could wait until morning, she tried once again to go to sleep. Finally, around three, she drifted off.

Twenty-three

Wanda Nell stirred uneasily as the sound of voices penetrated her light sleep. Bleary-eyed, she rolled over in bed and peered at the clock. The time was six-forty-three. For a moment, she couldn't remember what day it was, or whether it was morning or evening.

Then her mind began to clear, and she knew it was morning. She sat up on the side of the bed, yawning and stretching. She had slept poorly, her fitful dozing punctuated by disturbing dreams about her brother and the two dead men.

Wearily she got up from the bed and went to the bathroom. Her limbs were heavy and unresponsive, but she felt a bit more alert after splashing her face with cold water.

Her hair lay matted and sticky against her head. She would have to wash it when she showered. She tugged her brush through it and finally tamed it enough so that she no longer looked like a wild woman. She pulled on a bathrobe and tied it loosely around her.

In the kitchen, Juliet was rinsing her bowl in the sink, and Miranda was scrambling some eggs. Lavon, at the sight of his grandmother, picked up his sippy cup and started banging it on the tray of his highchair, claiming her attention.

Everything seemed so normal at the moment, and Wanda Nell was grateful for that.

She kissed both of Lavon's cheeks and rubbed his head. He chattered away to her, but she listened with only half an ear. He often required no response, being happy simply to talk.

"Mama, are you feeling okay?" Juliet asked with concern. "Didn't you go to work last night?"

"No, honey, I didn't. I'm sorry, I just forgot to tell you I traded a couple of shifts with one of the other girls at work. I'm going to be off tonight, too." Wanda Nell peered at the coffee pot, pleased to see that Miranda had made coffee already. She poured herself a cup and sat down at the table near Lavon. "Thanks for making coffee, Miranda."

"You're welcome. Would you like some eggs, Mama?" Miranda asked. "You can have some of these, and I'll scramble me some more." She separated the cooked eggs onto two plates, a small portion on one and a larger portion on the other. She left them both on the counter near the stove, letting the eggs cool before she gave Lavon his plate.

"No, thank you, sweetie," Wanda Nell said. "I'll have to be up for a while before I feel like eating anything. You go ahead and have your breakfast."

"Okay," Miranda said, "but I can fix you some later if you want." She pulled two pieces of browned bread from the toaster and buttered them lavishly. She cut half of one of the slices into small pieces for Lavon, added them to his plate, then set the plate on his tray. He wasted no time sticking his fingers into the egg and stuffing bits of it into his mouth.

"Mama," Juliet said, "before I forget it, Mayrene left you a note. She wasn't sure when you'd be up." She pushed a folded piece of paper across the table to her mother.

Curious, Wanda Nell picked up the paper and unfolded it. "W.N.," she read, "I took care of that little paint job for you. Talk to you later, M." Smiling, Wanda Nell stuck the note in the pocket of her bathrobe. Mayrene was a friend in a million, and she'd have to do something special to thank her, particularly because the girls seemed completely unaware of what had been painted on the trailer.

"I've got to go," Juliet said, pushing away from the table. "The school bus will be here any minute."

She gave her mother a quick hug, patted Lavon on the head, and waved bye to Miranda.

"Have a good day," Wanda Nell called.

"What are you going to do today, Mama?" Miranda asked. She looked down at her plate. "If you're not going to need the car, and if you wouldn't mind looking after Lavon for a little while, I need to go into town for something." She stuck a forkful of egg into her mouth before lifting her face to check her mother's reaction.

Wanda Nell hated to disappoint her, but there was just no way around it. There was no telling what she might have to do today, or where she might have to go, and she couldn't be without a car.

"I'm sorry, honey," Wanda Nell said gently, reaching out a hand to her daughter. "I just can't today. I may need it all day long, I just don't know. Is it something you could do tomorrow maybe?"

"I guess so," Miranda said, her face turning sulky. "I don't know why I even bothered to ask." She laid her fork on the table beside her plate and picked up the piece of toast. Tearing it into strips, she dropped them onto the plate. "I hate this. Why don't you just put a chain on me and leave me here."

Wanda Nell was irritated by the anger in Miranda's voice. "I know you get tired of having to stay here and look after Lavon," she said, trying not to speak in the same tone Miranda had used. "But you're his mama, and you have to take care of him. When you get a job, we can look into day care for him, because then you'll be able to afford it. And having a job to go to will get you out of the house and give you something to look forward to."

"Yeah, like work is something I'm really gonna look *forward* to," Miranda muttered.

That did it. Wanda Nell's temper flared. "When are you going to understand that you just can't sit there on your rear end all day long and expect everyone else to take care of you? I was barely a year older than you are now when I had T.J., and I didn't go running around and having fun all the time, expecting my mama or anybody else to take care of him. I know it's hard, but you've just got to do it." She almost added, *You made the bed, and now you've got to lie in it,* but she held back.

Miranda's defiance wilted in the face of her mother's little sermon. Her lip trembled, but she didn't say anything for a moment. Instead, she picked up her fork and ate a bit more of her scrambled eggs.

Wanda Nell sipped her coffee and kept an eye on Lavon, in case he started throwing eggs on the floor. He liked doing that, but for the moment he seemed to be happy enough with eating them. He wasn't paying any attention to the grown-ups, Wanda Nell was glad to see.

"I kinda wanted the car today so I could go look for a job," Miranda said in a tone dripping with self-righteousness. "But I guess it'll have to wait."

"I'm sorry, honey," Wanda Nell said, still exasperated with the girl. She had clearly been doing her best to manipulate her mother. "I didn't mean to come down so hard on you. You should have said that's why you wanted the car today." She wasn't completely sure she believed Miranda, but there was no point in arguing about it now. "As soon as this mess is straightened out, I'll make sure you have the car so you can look for a job. Okay?"

Miranda nodded. She got up from the table and took her plate to the sink. For once, instead of leaving it there for someone else to deal with, she rinsed it and stuck it in the dishwasher.

"I'll be back in a minute," Miranda said. "I'm going to the bathroom." She walked out of the kitchen.

Wanda Nell got up and poured herself more coffee. She was getting restless. Maybe it was the combination of the caffeine and a bad night, and arguing with Miranda sure didn't help. She needed to be doing something, but what?

It was too early to start calling people and asking them about Lily Golliday. Besides, she might as well wait until she heard from Tuck. If either of the Golliday men he knew had some knowledge of Lily, there was no use in her jumping the gun.

Same thing with T.J. and the property search. She wasn't sure what time the courthouse opened, but she doubted it was before eight o'clock. Then there was no telling how long it might be before T.J. could find anything.

So what could she do?

She thought about her plan to confront the sheriff and question him about all this. Would that do any good?

What if it did harm? What if the sheriff knew all about this and was helping his son cover it all up? If she went barging into his office making accusations, she might make things a lot worse for Rusty and for the rest of her family.

She had always thought of the sheriff as a pretty decent man, and her daddy had once thought that himself. But then they had had a falling out, and shortly afterward her daddy died. Wanda Nell had a gut feeling that whatever had soured the friendship between her daddy and the sheriff lay at the bottom of this current mess.

If only her parents were still alive, she could have asked them. She was sure her mother had known what happened, but her mama had never confided in her about it.

It was no wonder, Wanda Nell thought, looking back. At the time, toward the end of her junior year in high school, she had been so wild for Bobby Ray she wasn't paying attention to anything or anybody else. It got so bad that, as soon as school was out for the summer, her parents had packed her up and sent her off to stay with her mama's cousins in Little Rock, Arkansas. They were hoping if they kept her away from Bobby Ray long enough, she would get over it and get back to normal.

She had barely been in Little Rock for two months, though, when the news came that her daddy was in the hospital. She got back to Tullahoma one afternoon in late July, and her daddy had died that night in the hospital.

After that, everything went to hell in a handbasket, as her grandmother used to say.

They were all distraught over her daddy's death. She had sought comfort with Bobby Ray, oblivious to her family's needs. It wasn't long before she discovered she was pregnant. Rusty had grown more and more distant, but Wanda Nell was too preoccupied to notice or even care that much. She had claimed most of their mother's attention until well after the wedding and the birth of T.J.

Miranda comes by it honestly, she told herself. *But I had to learn responsibility, and so does she.*

When Miranda came back into the kitchen a few moments later, she no longer had a petulant look on her face. She didn't say anything to her mother, and Wanda Nell decided not to prolong their previous conversation. Instead, she said, "Honey, I'm going to jump in the shower.

I need to wash my hair this morning, and then I may have to go into town. Will you listen for the phone? I may get a call, and it could be important."

Miranda heaved a sigh. "Sure, Mama."

"Thanks, honey," Wanda Nell said. When she got up from the table, she made a point of going over to where Miranda stood by the sink and gave her a big hug. Miranda stiffened slightly, but then she hugged her mother back.

As she luxuriated in the hot water of the shower, Wanda Nell tried to clear her mind and relax a bit. The water comforted her, enveloping her in its warmth. If only she could stay in here for a month or two. She laughed at the notion, but she definitely felt much better as she toweled herself dry about ten minutes later.

Combing out her hair, then blow-drying it, she let her mind roam back to the problems at hand. She wished Tuck would hurry up and call. How nice it would be to find a shortcut to Lily Golliday, but if she had to sit down with the phone book and start calling every Golliday in it, she would do it.

Twenty minutes later, she had finished getting dressed. She was putting the final touches to her makeup when the phone rang. She went into the bedroom to answer it, but Miranda had already picked up in the kitchen.

"Oh, hi, Tuck," she heard Miranda say. "You want to talk to Mama?"

"I'm here, Miranda," Wanda Nell said. She heard a click as Miranda put down the receiver in the kitchen. "Tuck, you there?"

"I'm here, Wanda Nell," he said. "How are you this morning?"

"Tired and anxious," Wanda Nell said flatly. "But what else is new?"

"It's not like you to sound sorry for yourself," Tuck said in a light tone.

Wanda Nell sighed. "I know. I don't even know why I said that. Sometimes it just slips out."

"In a way, I take it as a kind of compliment," Tuck said, and Wanda Nell could hear the smile in his voice, "the fact that you feel comfortable enough with me to say something like that."

"Well, you are part of my family," Wanda Nell said. "I guess you could say you're my son-in-law. I'm not really sure what else to call you." The conversation had taken an odd turn, at least for her, and she was a little uncomfortable.

"That'll do just fine," Tuck said. "But I promise I won't start calling you mama, like T.J. does."

Wanda Nell had to bite back a retort. Tuck was only about ten years younger than she was, and that made him about eight years older than T.J. who had recently turned twenty-three.

"The reason I called," Tuck continued, after a brief pause, "is that I spoke to both of those men I was telling you about last night."

"Any luck?"

"In a way," Tuck said. "Neither one of them actually knew the young woman, but they both gave me the name of an elderly woman in the community who might be able to help you."

"At least that's something," Wanda Nell said. "If it keeps me from calling everybody in the phone book, I'd be happy."

"Have you got something handy to write with?"

"Hang on a second," she said. She pulled out the drawer of her bedside table and scrambled inside for a scrap of paper. She found an old eyebrow pencil, and then she was ready to write. "Got it. Go ahead."

"Her name is Mrs. Hattie Conley," Tuck said, and then he read out the phone number.

Wanda Nell read it all back to him.

"That's it," he said. "From what Jasper Golliday told me—he's the one who apparently knows her the best— she'll be happy to talk to you. She's quite elderly, but she's sharp as a tack, and she knows everybody. Plus she knows who everybody's related to, and everything else besides."

"Sounds like Miz Culpepper," Wanda Nell commented a bit acidly.

Tuck laughed into the phone. "In a way, but from what Jasper said, Mrs. Conley is a lot sweeter."

"Wouldn't be difficult," Wanda Nell muttered.

"What was that?" Tuck asked, though from his tone, Wanda Nell was convinced he had heard her.

"Never you mind," Wanda Nell said. "Thanks for this information. I'm going to call her right now." She glanced at the bedside clock. It was a little after seven-thirty. Surely Mrs. Conley would be up and about by now.

"Good luck," Tuck said. "And call me if you need anything else. T.J. will be heading over to the courthouse in about an hour to start that property search. As soon as we find anything—if we find anything—one of us will call you."

"Thanks," Wanda Nell said. She put the phone back on the hook.

She waited a moment, then picked up the phone and punched in the number Tuck had given her.

After about six rings, someone answered. "Hello."

"Good morning," Wanda Nell said, sitting down on the edge of the bed. "I hope I'm not calling too early in the morning. Is this Miz Hattie Conley?"

"Chile, you ain't calling too early for me," the woman said, chuckling. "I don't sleep much anymore, and it be all I can do to keep myself in the bed past five o'clock most mornings. Who did you say this was?"

"I'm sorry," Wanda Nell replied. "I didn't say yet. Miz Conley, my name is Wanda Nell Culpepper. I got your name and phone number from Mr. Jasper Golliday, because he thought you might be able to help me out."

"Why, honey, I'm too old to work anymore," the old voice said with a hint of laughter. "I don't know what Jasper be giving my name out for. He done know I be too old."

Wanda Nell had a sneaking suspicion that Mrs. Conley was teasing her. "Actually, it wasn't work I needed, ma'am. I actually need some help in finding a girl I think might be in trouble. Mr. Golliday said you would probably know who she is and how to find her."

For a moment Mrs. Conley was so quiet Wanda Nell was afraid she had fallen asleep or put the phone down.

"Did you say you was a Culpepper?"

"Yes, ma'am," Wanda Nell said. Should she explain her relationship to the Culpepper family?

Before she could say anything else, Mrs. Conley spoke again. "Then I reckon you must be the girl that was married to the old judge's son. The one that got hisself kilt a few months ago. That be right?"

"Yes, ma'am, that was my ex-husband."

"That sure was a sorry business," Mrs. Conley said. "I been knowing the judge and his wife for a long time. My cousin Charlesetta used to work for Miz Culpepper."

"How is Charlesetta doing?" Wanda Nell remembered Mrs. Culepper's elderly maid with great affection. Charlesetta had always treated her nicely, unlike her employer.

"She be doing just fine, particularly now she don't have to be going up and down them stairs seventeen times a day." Mrs. Conley laughed. "Charlesetta done told me that Miz Culpepper tried to keep her hopping all the time."

"I'm glad Charlesetta is doing fine," Wanda Nell said. "I don't know how she put up with Miz Culpepper for so long, either. I'm sure Charlesetta would vouch for me, Miz Conley, if you want to ask her before talking to me."

"Land sakes, chile, I don't need to ask Charlesetta about you," Miz Conley said, her voice warm and friendly. "I know you come from good people. But I tell you what, it sure would ease my mind if I could talk to you in person. I just hate talking over this here telephone. Would you mind coming to see me?"

Wanda Nell had to smile at the question. Mrs. Conley sounded almost like a child asking for a present. "I'd love to come see you, Miz Conley. You tell me where you live, and I'll drive on over."

"That sure sound good, chile," Mrs. Conley said. She gave Wanda Nell the address and told her how to find the house. She lived a few miles east of Tullahoma in a small black community that had sprung up in the 1970s.

"I know just where that is," Wanda Nell said. "How about if I come in about thirty or forty minutes?"

"You just come on when you can," Mrs. Conley said. "I ain't going nowhere." She chuckled again, and Wanda Nell said good-bye.

It would have been a lot easier if Mrs. Conley had given her the information over the phone, but Wanda Nell didn't begrudge the old lady her wish for a face-to-face talk.

She headed for the kitchen to tell Miranda where she was going, but halfway there she realized she had a problem. She couldn't leave Miranda and Lavon here by themselves, just in case someone made another attempt to break into the trailer or do further damage than just spray-painting hateful graffiti. Mayrene was at work, and Wanda Nell didn't want to ask T.J. to come, because he was working on something important.

Wanda Nell sighed. She had no choice. She would just have to take Miranda and the baby to visit Mrs. Culpepper, and if Miranda balked at that, then they could go with her to Mrs. Conley's house. This was going to be a difficult morning.

Twenty-four

Miranda surprisingly made no fuss about taking Lavon to visit his great-grandmother. After Wanda Nell had ascertained that Mrs. Culpepper was going to be at home that morning and wouldn't mind if Miranda and Lavon came over for a while, she hurried Miranda along.

While Miranda dressed herself and the baby, Wanda Nell gathered into the diaper bag the various things that Miranda would need for even a short stay at Mrs. Culpepper's. They were ready to leave twenty minutes later.

On the drive into town, with Lavon secured in his car seat in the back, Wanda Nell explained to her daughter where she was going and why.

"If that old lady tells you how to find this girl," Miranda said, "are you going to try to talk to her right away?"

"Yeah," Wanda Nell said. "I think I'd better. We've got no time to waste. We've got to find your uncle and make sure he's okay."

As she drove, Wanda Nell kept checking the rearview mirror. She kept expecting to see a black Mercedes somewhere behind her, but it wasn't there this morning. The only vehicle behind her at the moment was a Ford pickup, but there were lots of those around. She relaxed and concentrated on driving.

"I don't mind staying with Grandmother," Miranda said. "She's not so bad. Sometimes she watches Lavon and lets me take her car and go to the store for her."

"I didn't know that," Wanda Nell said, though she wasn't surprised. No wonder Miranda hadn't balked at spending time with Mrs. Culpepper this morning. "Just be careful you don't leave Lavon with her for too long."

"I know, Mama," Miranda said. "And I always check to see if she's been drinking. I wouldn't leave Lavon with her if I thought she wasn't going to look after him."

"I'm glad, honey," Wanda Nell said. She didn't add that she was surprised Miranda had even thought about it. Perhaps Miranda was more responsible about some things than she realized. "At least now, with your grandmother's cousin staying with her, there'll be someone to look after your grandmother *and* Lavon."

"That Belle lady is something else," Miranda said. "She'll talk your ears off if you let her."

"She means well," Wanda Nell said. She had turned onto Main Street moments before, and they were soon approaching the Culpepper house. Wanda Nell pulled into the driveway and parked. Miranda freed Lavon from his car seat, and Wanda Nell gathered up the diaper bag and Miranda's purse.

Wanda Nell expressed her gratitude to Belle, who answered the door, but she quickly made her excuses. She had to get away before Belle engaged her in conversation. Luckily for her, Belle was so busy helping Miranda with Lavon she paid little attention to Wanda Nell.

"I'll be back as soon as I can," Wanda Nell said. She almost ran down the walk to her car and hopped into it.

As she drove back the way she had just come, Wanda

Nell mulled over how much of the story she should tell Mrs. Conley. She wanted the old lady's help, and she didn't feel like lying to her. On the other hand, though, she didn't want to get bogged down in a lot of detail if she could help it. Time was of the essence.

Glancing into the rearview mirror, Wanda Nell noticed a couple of pickups behind her on the two-lane highway. The one closest to her, about three car lengths behind, was not the truck she had seen earlier. The second pickup, another three or four car lengths behind, could be the one that had followed her into Tullahoma. She hadn't noticed it following her down Main Street, but she hadn't really been looking either.

She wasn't completely sure the second pickup was the same one. It was far enough back that she couldn't really make out the details. It was a Ford, she was pretty sure. But she couldn't remember the color of truck she'd seen on the way to Mrs. Culpepper's.

Her stomach beginning to knot up, Wanda Nell concentrated on watching for the road to Mrs. Conley's house. It should be coming up in a minute or so.

When she reached the turn, Wanda Nell had to stop for oncoming traffic. Her turn signal clicked, and she glanced into the mirror again. The two trucks were still there, but the second one was hanging back a bit.

Would it follow her when she turned? What would she do it if did?

She certainly didn't want to bring any trouble on poor old Mrs. Conley, but if someone was following her, they might try to find out from the old lady what Wanda Nell had wanted from her.

The oncoming traffic passed, and Wanda Nell made her left turn. She started counting the houses as she followed the winding road up the hill. Mrs. Conley's house was the fifth one on the right, about a quarter of a mile from the highway.

She peeked into the rearview mirror, and then she breathed more easily. The truck hadn't followed her, as far as she could see.

Just ahead was Mrs. Conley's driveway. Wanda Nell turned into it and parked. She sat in the car a moment, collecting her thoughts. Then, picking up her purse and taking her keys, she got out of the car and walked to the front door.

Wanda Nell knocked and waited. She glanced around the neatly kept front yard, with its precisely laid-out flower beds and three pecan trees off to one side. The small house itself was freshly painted, a cheerful yellow with black trim.

The door swung open, and Wanda Nell turned to smile at Hattie Conley. Looking at her, Wanda Nell wasn't sure of her age, though she suspected Mrs. Conley must be around eighty-five. She was nearly as tall as Wanda Nell, and she wore a gaily colored dress and comfortable slippers.

"You must be Miz Culpepper," Mrs. Conley said. "You just come right on in here, chile, and let's have us a talk."

"Thank you for taking the time to talk to me," Wanda Nell said, following her hostess into a parlor so clean it made her think guiltily of all the cleaning she needed to do at home.

Mrs. Conley seated herself in a rocking chair and motioned for Wanda Nell to sit on the couch near her. She started to rock gently. "It's nice to have some company," Mrs. Conley said, "and if I can help you, I'll be right glad to do it."

"This is a lovely room," Wanda Nell said, casting an

admiring glance around it. "I wish I could keep my house this neat and clean."

Mrs. Conley laughed. "Chile, I wish I could, too! My granddaughter comes over here three times a week, and she cleans so much I swear dirt is scared to death of coming in this house. She won't let me do a thing." Then she winked at Wanda Nell. "You can see I'm so old and helpless I just can't lift a finger for myself."

Wanda Nell couldn't help laughing with her. Despite her age, Mrs. Conley appeared spry and energetic. But she clearly enjoyed the attention she and her house received from her granddaughter.

"Now what can I do for you, chile?" Mrs. Conley said. "You said you was looking for some girl."

"Yes, ma'am," Wanda Nell said. "I know her name, but I don't know her. I know it sounds strange, but this girl came looking for me, and she ran off before I could talk to her. I think she may be in trouble, and I want to help her." She paused for a moment. "Plus I think it has something to do with some trouble my brother's in, and I want to help him, too."

"What kind of trouble?" Mrs. Conley said, continuing to rock. Her eyes never left Wanda Nell's face.

"Murder," Wanda Nell said bluntly. "Have you heard about the two murders in town?" At the moment, she didn't see any reason to call Simpson's death a suicide. That would require too much explanation.

"I sure have," Mrs. Conley said, nodding. "Terrible thing, two young men like that. Are you saying this girl knows something about these killings?"

"Maybe," Wanda Nell said.

"And your brother? What's he got to do with all this? What's his name?"

"His name is Rusty Rosamond, and he knew both of the men back in high school."

"I see," Mrs. Conley said. "And you afraid your brother killed these men?"

"No," Wanda Nell said. "I don't think he did. But other people think so. My brother has disappeared, and I'm desperate to find him. I want to prove he's innocent."

"What's this girl gonna know about all that? What's her name?"

"Her name is Lily Golliday," Wanda Nell said. "I'm not sure what she knows. But she must know something. Else why would she come looking for me, a total stranger? There's got to be a connection somewhere."

"Lily Golliday," Mrs. Conley said. She turned her eyes away from Wanda Nell and looked out the window. "I know that girl."

"You do?" Wanda Nell said. "Can you tell me how to find her? Do you know where she lives?"

Still looking out the window, Mrs. Conley said, "That girl has had one sorrowful life, Miz Culpepper. Her mama's been bad on the drugs most of her life, and Lily ain't had nobody else. Her grandmama and her granddaddy died when she was just a baby, and they didn't have no more children besides her mama."

"That's awful," Wanda Nell said. She knew the words were inadequate, but there was nothing else to say.

"They's a bunch of Gollidays around," Mrs. Conley said, "but Lily's mama, she don't have nothing to do with any of 'em. She keep to herself, and Lily that way, too." She shook her dolefully. "Yes, ma'am, they's both powerful sad."

"I don't want to cause them any trouble," Wanda Nell said gently, "but I have to talk to Lily. Maybe I can help her somehow. If she wanted to talk to me, it must be something important."

"I know, chile, I know," Mrs. Conley said. "I'll tell you where they live. But Lily's mama, Lavinia, she be kinda mean when she on them drugs, so you be careful when you go around to see Lily."

"I will, I promise," Wanda Nell said, though her heart sank at the thought of having to confront Lavinia Golliday if she was strung out on drugs of some kind. But she had no choice. She had to talk to Lily.

Mrs. Conley gave her directions, and Wanda Nell jotted them down on a piece of paper she pulled from her purse. "I don't know if they got a telephone now or not. Lavinia don't work much, and I don't know if she be getting much welfare now. And Lily don't work either. I don't know how they gets by, I surely don't. The Lord, He be looking after them somehow."

"Miz Conley, I don't know how to thank you," Wanda Nell said.

"You just come back and see me," Mrs. Conley said, "and tell me all about it. I be praying for you and your brother." She held out a hand to Wanda Nell.

"Thank you," Wanda Nell said, grasping the hand. She took comfort from the warmth and strength of it. If she were still alive, her grandmother Rosamond would be about Mrs. Conley's age.

Still holding the old lady's hand, Wanda Nell leaned forward. "Just in case, Miz Conley, I think I'd better warn you about something. Somebody's been following me around, watching where I go." She paused. "I'm not sure if they followed me here this morning, but I don't want them to do anything to you."

Mrs. Conley laughed. "Chile, if some fool shows up here asking about you, I'm just gonna tell 'em you was looking for a girl to help out your mama-in-law. That's all they need to know, and the Lord will forgive me for lying, I know."

Wanda Nell said a couple of prayers herself as she backed her car out of Mrs. Conley's driveway a few minutes later. She'd never forgive herself if she had brought harm on that sweet old lady. If anybody did hurt her, Wanda Nell swore she'd hunt the bastard down herself.

Wanda Nell had gone about a mile on the highway back to Tullahoma when she spotted a Ford pickup about fifty yards behind her.

Was she being paranoid? It sure looked like the pickup she had seen earlier, but maybe she was just imagining things.

She couldn't take any chances though. She didn't want anybody following her when she went to talk to Lily Golliday. She just had a hunch that she didn't want to lead anyone to the girl.

She could be completely wrong, and Lily Golliday could be working hand-in-hand with Bert Vines or Marty Shaw. But somehow she didn't think so.

How was she going to get away from the person following her?

As she drove into Tullahoma, she worked out a plan to elude her pursuer. With her right hand she fished her cell phone out of her purse.

She hit the speed-dial number for Tuck's law offices. After two rings, his secretary answered. She was new, a replacement for Mayrene's cousin who had quit to get married. "Hi, Judy," Wanda Nell said. "This is Wanda Nell Culpepper. Can I speak to T.J. or Tuck?"

"Hi, Wanda Nell," Judith said, her voice annoyingly chipper. "I'm sorry, but T.J.'s over at the courthouse. Mr. Tucker is in, though. Let me put you through."

Sending up a silent prayer of thanks that he was in the office, Wanda Nell waited for Tuck to pick up.

As soon as he said hello, she started talking, not giving him much chance to speak.

"Tuck, I need a favor, real quick. I need to borrow a car. Does T.J. have his truck at the office?"

"Yes," Tuck said. "We drove in separately this morning."

"Do you have a key to the truck?"

"Yes. Why?"

"Can you go and move it around the back of your building and wait there for me? I should be along in about five minutes. I'll explain when I get there."

"I'll do it right now."

Wanda Nell ended the call. Thank the Lord Tuck didn't waste time on questions. She stuck her phone back in her purse.

She drove quickly but carefully downtown to the building on the square where Tuck had his office. She parked in a spot across the square from the building and got out of her car. Making herself walk at a normal pace, she crossed the street and entered the building.

Once inside, she stepped to the side of the glass door and peered out. A Ford pickup was circling the square, and as she watched, the driver parked it across the square from where she had parked her car.

A man got out of the pickup, but he was too far away for Wanda Nell to see who he was. She didn't wait to see where he was going. She turned and sprinted down the hall. She knew there was a way out to the back of the building, and she wanted to find it quickly.

The hall dead-ended in a dentist's office, and Wanda Nell stopped and looked both ways down the intersecting hallway. To her left she spotted a red exit sign. She ran toward it.

One more turn and she had reached the back door. She pushed it open.

Tuck stood in the alleyway near T.J.'s truck. Trying to catch her breath, Wanda Nell hurried up to him.

"What's going on?" Tuck asked.

"Someone's following me," Wanda Nell said, "and I don't want him to see where I'm going next."

"Where *are* you going?" Tuck handed her the keys to the truck. "Do you want me to go with you?"

Wanda Nell grasped the keys. "No, I think I'd better go by myself. As long as nobody's following me, I'll be okay."

"Where are you going?" Tuck repeated his question.

"I'm going to talk to Lily Golliday," Wanda Nell said, opening the door of the truck. She climbed inside and shut the door behind her. "Miz Conley told me where to find her. I'll call you as soon as I've talked to her."

"Be careful," Tuck said. "Are you sure you don't want someone to go with you?"

"I'm sure," Wanda Nell said, cranking the truck. "You go on back inside, and try not to let anyone see you going back up to your office."

Tuck grinned. "Agent Tucker at your service, ma'am. I'll be invisible."

Wanda Nell rolled her eyes at him, but he had already headed for the door. She put the truck in gear and accelerated down the alley to the street. From here it should take her only about ten minutes to get to Lily Golliday's house.

She turned down a street away from the square and checked the rearview mirror.

No sign of the Ford truck behind her.

She sped on her way, feeling proud of herself for putting one over on her pursuer. Now she just had to hope her luck was holding, and that Lily Golliday was home and would talk to her.

Twenty-five

The closer Wanda Nell came to her destination, the more run-down the houses appeared. There was little traffic on the streets, but here and there elderly black folk sat on porches or on stoops. Their heads turned as Wanda Nell drove by, and Wanda Nell felt increasingly uncomfortable and out of place.

She tried to shake those feelings off, but the sensation of entering another world persisted. She could easily have driven out of the present day back into the 1950s.

At last she reached the street where Mrs. Conley had told her she would find the Golliday house. She turned down it and counted until she reached the fifth house on the right. Wanda Nell pulled T.J.'s truck up in front of it and sat staring at the house in dismay.

The tar-paper-and-tin-roof building, probably no bigger than four rooms, hunched in a tangle of weeds and debris like a drunken spinster in a threadbare dress. As she got out of the truck and walked slowly up the path through the weeds, Wanda Nell feared that knocking on the door might cause the whole structure to topple over.

The screen door hung slightly loose, and Wanda Nell

pulled it open. She knocked on the wooden door, then glanced at her knuckles. Flecks of paint dusted her fingers, and she wiped them against her jeans.

"Who is it? What you want?" The door opened just enough to let Wanda Nell glimpse one wary green eye through the slit.

"My name is Wanda Nell Culpepper, and I'm looking for Lily Golliday," Wanda Nell said, trying to keep her voice steady. She wanted to sound friendly and confident, but the surroundings unnerved her. "Mrs. Hattie Conley told me I could find her here."

The eye blinked several times, but the door wasn't moving. Then, suddenly, the door swung open, and the person holding it stepped back into shadow.

"Come on in," she said.

Wanda Nell stepped into the house. As the door swung shut behind her, she took her first full breath. She almost gagged. The air was fetid, reeking of stale smoke and several other odors Wanda Nell didn't care too much to identify.

Breathing as shallowly as she could, Wanda Nell followed the woman into the room into which the front door opened. There was very little furniture, an old, stained couch that sagged in several places, and a couple of metal chairs with vinyl seats. A battered TV sat on a low table across from the couch, and the only light, hampered by the unchecked shrubs and trees outside, emanated from the windows on two sides of the room.

As the woman turned, Wanda Nell got her first good look at her face. This had to be Lily Golliday. She was every bit as pretty as Melvin had described her. She might even be beautiful, but weariness and something else Wanda Nell couldn't define had marked her face. The skin around her startlingly green eyes was puffy, and she moved listlessly, as if every step required an effort.

Lily Golliday slumped down on the couch and waved a languid hand at one of the chairs. "Please sit down."

"Thank you," Wanda Nell said. The girl's voice had a pleasing tone to it, but she uttered even those three words with an obvious effort.

On closer scrutiny, Wanda Nell decided Lily was probably closer to twenty-five than twenty. Melvin hadn't been certain, but perhaps she hadn't been so tired and washed-out looking when he saw her. Her skin was more gray than pale brown today.

Lily leaned back on the couch and regarded Wanda Nell with half-closed eyes.

"You came looking for me at the Kountry Kitchen," Wanda Nell said. "What did you need to talk to me about?"

"How did you find me?" Lily asked. More than curiosity, there was a tinge of fear to the question.

"One of the girls I work with, Ruby Garner, saw you. She remembered you from a class she had with you at the junior college."

Lily didn't respond for a moment. "Yeah, I wanted to talk to you," she finally said.

"Is it something to do with my brother?" Wanda Nell felt oddly protective toward this girl. There was something about Lily's obvious unease and her appearance that aroused Wanda Nell's maternal instincts. Was the poor girl here by herself? Then Wanda Nell remembered what Hattie Conley had said about Lily's mother, that she was bad on drugs.

"Yeah," Lily said. "I been trying to find him."

"Why?" Wanda Nell asked. "I don't mean to sound rude, but how do you know my brother? I'm trying to find him, too."

Lily stared at her for a moment before turning her head aside. Her gaze fixed on something Wanda Nell couldn't see, she said, "I need to find him. I need some help."

"I can see that," Wanda Nell said gently. She had to be careful and not lose her temper with this girl. "But why my brother?"

"Do you know where he is?" Lily asked.

Why won't she answer my question? Wanda Nell thought. She could think of several possible answers, none of which pleased her.

"I don't know where he is," Wanda Nell said. "He's been missing a few days, and the sheriff's department is looking for him. He's a possible witness in a murder case." That seemed a safe way to put it. "I'm afraid he could be in trouble, and I want to find him and make sure he's safe."

When Lily didn't respond, she went on, "You see, I'm afraid he may have been kidnapped. We may be running out of time, and if we don't find him soon, I just don't know what might happen."

"He *was* kidnapped," Lily said, "but he's not anymore."

"How do you know that?" Wanda Nell demanded.

Lily's face was sullen as she replied. "Because I talked to him a couple days ago. I ain't heard from him since, though. That's why I come looking for you. He told me if I needed help to come to you."

"Then why didn't you wait until I got to work so we could talk?" Wanda Nell asked. This girl was confusing the heck out of her. She didn't know what to make of her, but despite her increasing irritation, she felt sorry for Lily.

"I didn't feel good," Lily said, "and I had to get some-body to give me a ride over there. She couldn't wait till you got there, so I just came on home with her. I ain't felt good enough since then to try to get a ride back over to the Kountry Kitchen."

"Well, I'm here now," Wanda Nell said. "We'll try to

figure out what to do. First, though," she continued, her tone firm, "tell me what you know about my brother being kidnapped, and how come he's not still kidnapped."

"He told me about it," Lily said.

"So you've seen him? Or did you just talk to him on the phone?"

"Ain't got no phone," Lily said. "He come by here a couple days ago."

"Where had he been before that?"

Lily shrugged. "He said a couple guys had run his truck off the road, and they made him go with them. They was keeping him at somebody's house, but he was able to get away from them."

"And he came here?"

Lily nodded.

"And they didn't follow him here?"

"No," Lily said, "he was real careful about that. He didn't want nobody connecting me and him and my mama."

"Where is your mother?" Wanda Nell asked.

"Where she always is," Lily said in a tone of contempt mingled with resignation. "She's out looking for money for drugs."

Wanda Nell didn't offer any comment. Frankly, she had no idea what to say. Instead, she pressed on with her questions. "What about Rusty, then? Where did he go when he left here?"

"I don't know exactly where he is," Lily said, frowning. "He just said he knew someplace safe to hide out while he figured out what to do. He said nobody would know about it, except you."

Wanda Nell was puzzled. Where on earth was Rusty talking about? What safe place did they both know? There were times recently when she could have used it herself.

"How did he get there? Was he walking? The sheriff's department has his truck."

"He's got my mama's car," Lily said, "and she's real pissed about that." From the look of grim satisfaction on Lily's face, Wanda Nell figured that her mother's irritation pleased her.

"Why didn't he have you or your mama drive him to this safe place he told you about? He must have known you'd need the car." Wanda Nell was puzzled by her brother's actions.

Lily shrugged. "Him and Mama had an argument about it. Wasn't nothing to do with me. I ain't never seen him before this weekend. Mama don't let me drive the car, but sometimes I get the keys when she's passed out."

"Your mother's name is Lavinia?" Wanda Nell asked. Rusty must have known Lily's mother for some time, and she was beginning to suspect exactly what the connection between her brother and Lily was.

"Yes," Lily said. "People call her Veenie."

If Rusty had ever mentioned this woman in the past, Wanda Nell just didn't remember it.

"I don't reckon I know her," Wanda Nell said.

Lily shrugged. "No reason you should, 'less you keep up with the drug addicts around here."

Wanda Nell hoped none of her children ever referred to her in such a tone. She felt chilled.

She decided to probe deeper. "Lily, why are you staying here with your mother? It doesn't sound to me like you get along real well."

Lily laughed, a bitter sound. "You got that right. Only reason I'm here is 'cause I got nowhere else to go. I got evicted from my apartment. I couldn't work no more, and if I can't work, I can't pay the rent."

"I can see you're ill," Wanda Nell said. "You mind me asking what's wrong with you?"

"My kidneys," Lily said. She got up from the couch. "Excuse me a minute. I be right back." She shuffled from the room.

Wanda Nell sat in that depressing room and tried to remember to breathe through her mouth. After a minute or two, she heard the sound of a toilet flushing. Lily came slowly back into the room and dropped onto the couch.

"You said it's your kidneys," Wanda Nell said. "Can't you get some kind of treatment for them?"

Lily stared at her, and Wanda Nell felt foolish. Of course this girl didn't have the money for a doctor.

"How bad is it?" Wanda Nell said after a moment.

"Doctor says I'm gonna need a transplant. Not right this minute," Lily said, "but sometime soon. If I don't get it, I'll die."

Once again Wanda Nell's heart went out to the girl. Lily had said those last two words as calmly as if she were announcing that was going to take a walk.

"And there's no help for you at all?"

Again Lily stared at her. Then, relenting, she said, "I can go to the doctor 'cause I get Medicaid, but they ain't gonna be hurrying to find me a kidney. They got me on a list, but there ain't much use in that."

"What about your mother?" Wanda Nell asked. "Couldn't she donate one of her kidneys?"

Lily laughed. "You think she in shape to be giving me anything of hers? I'd be worse off than ever. You don't know how bad she be. It's a wonder she's even able to walk."

Dear Lord, Wanda Nell thought. No wonder Lily seemed so hopeless.

Rusty must be trying to blackmail these men into giving money for Lily's medical expenses. That made sense. He was trying to help this girl get treatment. The question was, why was he involved in this? What was his connection to Lily and her mother?

"So how does my brother figure into all this?" Wanda Nell asked. This time Lily had to answer her. No more evasions.

"I think he's my daddy," Lily said. She got up from the couch. "Excuse me. I be right back." Once again she shuffled out of the room.

Wanda Nell had the answer she had been looking for, one she had pretty much figured out for herself. She was appalled by the situation. If Rusty was this girl's daddy, how could he have abandoned her and her mother? He had a lot of explaining to do, and when she got her hands on him, she might just wring his neck first and talk afterward.

Twenty-six

When Lily returned from the bathroom and flopped down on the couch again, Wanda Nell said, "I think my brother's trying to help you. He may be your daddy. I just don't know. He's never said anything about it to me." *Not that he's talked to me about anything important in years*, she added silently.

"I'm going to find him," Wanda Nell said, "and we're going to get this mess straightened out. If he's your daddy, maybe he can donate a kidney. One way or the other, I'm going to see if we can't get you some help."

"Maybe you're my aunt," Lily said. She watched Wanda Nell warily.

Wanda Nell smiled. "Honey, I'd be proud to have a niece as beautiful as you are."

Lily startled her by breaking into loud sobs. Hurriedly Wanda Nell got up from her chair and moved to the couch beside Lily. Gathering the girl's frail body into her arms, she rocked her gently, as she would her grandson.

"Everything is going to be okay," Wanda Nell murmured over and over.

Lily's crying gradually lessened, and Wanda Nell held her until she had stopped. "I'm sorry," she said, her voice hoarse. She pulled gently away from Wanda Nell and leaned against the back of the couch.

"Don't you worry about it," Wanda Nell said. She had been thinking more about the possibility that Rusty was Lily's father. "Lily, how old are you?"

"Twenty-three."

"When were you born?"

Lily named the date, and Wanda Nell did some rapid calculations. "You weren't premature?"

Lily shook her head.

Wanda Nell expelled a shaky breath. Counting back nine months from the day Lily was born, Wanda Nell arrived at a time about three months before her father's death.

Rusty would barely have been fifteen when Lily was conceived, and if he had told his parents he had gotten a black girl pregnant, well, that would have been enough to trigger Mr. Rosamond's fatal heart attack.

But why had Mrs. Rosamond never said anything to Wanda Nell about any of this? Wanda Nell couldn't believe that her mother would simply turn her back on a grandchild, no matter what that child's heritage. There was still so much she didn't know, so maybe Mrs. Rosamond hadn't ignored Lily. Only Rusty knew the details, and the sooner she found him, the better.

"Lily, tell me again what Rusty said about his hiding place," Wanda Nell said.

Lily, who appeared to have fallen asleep, started and opened her eyes. "Huh? Oh, just what I told you before. He said he had someplace safe to stay, and you was the only one who'd know where it was."

Wanda Nell shook her head. What on earth could Rusty

be talking about? When their father died, Mrs. Rosamond had been unable to hold on to the house they were living in. There just wasn't enough money coming in, so they'd had to sell it. The same family who had bought it then still owned it, and Wanda Nell knew Rusty couldn't be hiding there.

So where?

Then it hit her.

The only possible place Rusty could be hiding was an old house in the woods on property that had once belonged to their maternal grandfather. He had been a farmer, and he died when Wanda Nell was about thirteen. His widow, his second wife, had sold the farm without giving her stepdaughter, Mrs. Rosamond, any say in the matter.

Before their grandfather's death, Wanda Nell and Rusty had visited often, and they had found many places to explore on the farm. One of them had been an old house out in the woods. Their grandfather said it had belonged to a family who owned the land before he did. It had an artesian spring near it, and though the house was suffering from neglect, it was still standing. Wanda Nell and Rusty had loved playing in it. If their parents had ever realized how much time the two children had spent there, they probably would have been horrified. Looking back now, Wanda Nell wondered how on earth she and her brother had escaped serious injury in the old place.

After the land had been sold, Wanda Nell and her family had periodically been back. There was an old gravel road on the boundary of the property that ran very near where the old house stood, and the new owners of the land didn't seem all that interested in tearing down the house or clearing the woods. Wanda Nell had even taken her kids there a few times on picnics, and no one had ever bothered them. The house had still been there about five years ago, and it must still be there. Otherwise Rusty would have found some other place to hide out.

"I do know where he is," Wanda Nell said. "I'm going to get him."

"What about those men that's looking for him?" Lily sat up in alarm. "He say they real dangerous."

"I know," Wanda Nell said. "One of them's a murderer, or maybe both of them. But they don't know where I am, and I'm not going to lead them to him. I'll get him away from there, and we can go to the sheriff."

Even as she said the words, Wanda Nell wondered if going to the sheriff would be the right thing to do. If Marty Shaw was implicated in this, how would the sheriff handle it? She would have to tread carefully.

"Lily, will you be okay a little while longer here by yourself?" Wanda Nell examined the girl with concern. "I can take you somewhere you'll be safe and somebody will look after you until I find Rusty." There was no telling how Mrs. Culpepper would react if Wanda Nell drove up with Lily, but she would trust Belle to look after her.

"No, I'll be okay," Lily said.

"Do you have something to eat?"

Lily nodded.

"Okay, then," Wanda Nell said, though she hated going off and leaving the girl, even for a little while. "As soon as I get my brother and find out what's going on, we're going to help you."

"Thank you," Lily said, her voice barely above a whisper.

Wanda Nell leaned forward and kissed the girl on the forehead. "You get some rest, and I'll be back soon."

She turned as she reached the front door and looked back. Lily had fallen asleep.

Wiping away some tears, Wanda Nell hurried to the truck. When she was inside, she realized she had left her purse in the truck the whole time, and her cell phone was in it. Thankful that no one had interfered with the truck, she pulled her cell phone out and checked it.

She had a message. She started the truck, then she called and checked her voice mail.

The message was from T.J., asking where she was and why she wasn't answering her phone. He went on to say that his search of records in the courthouse hadn't turned up anything. And would she please call right away?

Wanda Nell deleted the message, then hit the speed-dial number of Tuck's office. As she tried backing the truck around with one hand, Wanda Nell decided she ought to get herself one of those ear thingies so she could talk and drive with both hands at the same time.

T.J. answered the phone. "Mama, where the heck are you?"

"Honey, I don't have time to explain right now," Wanda Nell said. "Hold on a second." She put the phone down to finish turning the truck around. Once she was heading in the right direction, she picked up the phone again. "I've been talking to Lily Golliday, and now I'm going to get Rusty. I know where he is."

"You can't go by yourself," T.J. said, his voice sharp with concern. "Come get me, and let me go with you in case there's trouble."

"There won't be any trouble," Wanda Nell said. "Rusty is certainly not going to hurt me, and nobody else knows where I am. Nobody followed me here, so I'll be just fine."

T.J. sighed heavily into the phone. "I know it's no use arguing with you."

"Nope," Wanda Nell said. "But y'all be ready when I get back with Rusty. We're going to have to figure out what the heck to do with him. I'll call you when we're on the way."

"Okay," T.J. said. "I'll tell Tuck.".

"One more thing," Wanda Nell said. "That Ford truck I thought was following me. Can you go see if it's still out there parked across the square?"

From Tuck's office windows there was a clear view across the square, and if the truck was still there, T.J. would see it.

"Hang on," T.J. said. "I'll go check and be right back."

Wanda Nell concentrated on driving while she waited for T.J. She needed to get to the highway and head west a few miles.

T.J. came back on the line. "There's a Ford pickup parked across the square," he said. "And there's a guy sitting on one of the benches facing in this direction. I can't see who it is, though. You think it's the guy who was following you?"

"Probably," Wanda Nell said. She took great satisfaction from the thought that the guy had been sitting there all this time, waiting for her to come out of the building. He'd be waiting quite a long time.

"You be careful," T.J. said.

"I will. I'll have my phone with me, and if I need help I'll call." Quickly she told him where she was going, and before he could protest further, she ended the call.

She half-expected him to call her back and continue fussing at her, but he knew her too well. He might try to follow her, if he could remember how to find the place.

Well, if he did, he did. She'd deal with that if she had to. Right now she concentrated on threading her way through the streets to the highway.

Once she hit it she headed west, past the interchange with the interstate highway just west of Tullahoma. Her destination lay only about four miles west of this inter-section, and she watched the speedometer as she drew closer and closer to it.

Wanda Nell glanced into the rearview mirror a few times as a precaution, but she didn't note any suspicious vehicles. A couple other trucks and one car passed her, evidently impatient with her slower pace.

If she hadn't known where to look, she might have missed the road where she had to turn. She saw the faint tracks ahead and slowed down for the turn. She made a quick check for traffic in both directions, then turned left and was almost immediately swallowed up by the trees and bushes lining the old road.

Most of the gravel was gone now, leaving a deeply rutted dirt track nearly engulfed by the vegetation around it. Wanda Nell winced repeatedly as she heard the scrapes against the sides of the truck. She might owe T.J. for a paint job by the time this was over.

She traveled slowly for a mile and three quarters, watching for any landmarks she could remember. She thought the old house lay about two miles from the highway and about three hundred yards into the woods from the road.

Up ahead was a gnarled old tree she recognized. Its trunk grew straight for about two feet, then it angled sideways almost ninety degrees for about five feet before growing upright again. Judging by its size, the tree had to be well over a hundred years old, and Wanda Nell had always wondered what had made the tree grow in such a bizarre shape. With this tree as her guidepost, she could find the old house.

Wanda Nell peered ahead, hoping to see a spot large enough to allow her to turn the truck around and point it back out toward the highway. A few yards ahead there was a small clearing, and Wanda Nell drove toward it.

The canopy of leaves was thick here, keeping much of the sun from penetrating, and Wanda Nell switched on the headlights. She hated to do it, in case Rusty saw them and disappeared before she could find him. But she didn't have a lot of choice. She was afraid to turn the truck without some illumination.

As she was backing around in the clearing, the lights glinted off something through the trees. Wanda Nell paused in her maneuvers and stared into the gloom.

Sure enough, her lights had picked up either chrome or glass. As she kept looking, Wanda Nell gradually made out the outlines of a small car.

Her heart beating faster, Wanda Nell finished turning the truck. Once she had it positioned to her satisfaction, she switched the lights off. She checked the glove compartment for the flashlight she knew T.J. kept there and put it in her purse. She got out of the truck and locked it.

The car she had glimpsed must be the one Rusty had borrowed from Lily's mother. And that meant Rusty was somewhere nearby.

Wanda Nell examined the ground around her for a large, stout stick. She hated snakes, and she didn't want to go charging through the woods without some kind of weapon, just in case.

She found a sturdy limb, stripped off a few small branches and leaves, and tested it against the ground. It would do.

Shouldering her purse, she made for the gnarled tree. Once there, she paused to get her bearings. From here, a short walk should take her to the old house. She uttered a quick prayer for protection from snakes and anything else that might be lurking in the woods.

She set out, moving cautiously through the underbrush. The light was better here, and she shifted her gaze nervously back and forth from the ground in front of her to the woods ahead of her.

Her progress was slow, but she didn't want to risk falling and spraining an ankle, or worse, getting bitten by a snake.

After she had gone about two hundred yards by her es-
timation, Wanda Nell paid more attention to what lay
ahead of her. Praying that she hadn't lost her bearings
and was still heading in the right direction, Wanda Nell
forged ahead.

She pushed through a clump of trees dense with vines
and ferns and stepped into the edge of a small clearing.

There was the house, sixty feet ahead of her.

Wanda Nell paused to catch her breath and examine
the scene.

The house appeared much the same as the last time
she had seen it. The roof had a few holes in it, and the
porch sagged on one end. The windows had been broken
out long ago, and vines grew through them into the house.

Wanda Nell shivered. What a terrible place to have to
seek refuge. It had been exciting and full of adventure
when she and Rusty were kids, but now it looked awful.
Why would Rusty prefer to hide out here, rather than ask
for her help? He really must hate her to go to extremes
like this.

She pulled the flashlight from her purse and moved
cautiously ahead. She approached the front of the house
and stared at the rotting steps in dismay. How was she going to get up to the porch and the door without falling
through? How on earth had Rusty managed it?

Then she remembered that there were stone steps at
the back of the house. She circled around, switching on
her flashlight and pointing it toward the ground.

At the rear of the house, she found the steps. They
were overgrown with moss, but as Wanda Nell examined
them, she saw recent scuff marks in the moss. This had to
be how Rusty went in and out.

She went carefully up the steps and stepped onto the
back porch. It, too, sagged on either end, but in front of the
door it seemed solid enough when Wanda Nell tested it.

The door stood slightly ajar, and Wanda Nell pushed it farther open, wincing at the screech it made. She flashed the light inside and called out, "Rusty! Are you here?"

For a moment, she heard nothing. Then Rusty's voice called out to her, "Help me!"

Twenty-seven

"Rusty! Where are you?" Wanda Nell stood rooted to the spot. It was dark inside the old house, and the musty scents of decay and dampness crept into her nose.

"In here," Rusty called. "In the next room."

At least his voice sounded fairly strong, though tired. Wanda Nell expelled a sigh of relief as she moved carefully through what had once been the kitchen. The floor groaned but did not give way.

"Hurry up!"

"I'm coming," Wanda Nell yelled back. "Just hang on a minute. I'm trying to be careful."

She stepped into the doorway into the next room and paused. She cast the beam of the flashlight around, trying to find Rusty.

"Where the heck are you?"

"In here, dammit!"

Following the sound of his voice, Wanda Nell spotted where Rusty must be. Near the wall was a door that led into a closet, if Wanda Nell remembered correctly. She drew in a sharp breath as she steadied the light in that direction.

Part of the ceiling had collapsed, bringing with it a beam and other debris. That mass was lodged against the door of the closet, holding it shut. The beam lay at an angle, wedged in such a way that Rusty couldn't push the door open.

"Are you in the closet, Rusty? Are you hurt?" Wanda Nell stepped cautiously closer to the closet and the debris.

"Yes, I'm in here, where the heck do you think I am?" Rusty banged hard against the door. "I ain't hurt, but I been stuck in here for more'n a day, and I want the hell out of here."

Wanda Nell played the light against the door. It looked surprisingly sturdy. If it hadn't been it would have shattered from the impact of the beam falling against it.

"Let me see how I can get you out," Wanda Nell said. She stood and assessed the situation.

If Rusty had tried to break through the door, he would have run the risk of the beam pressing further against the door and pushing in on him as it fell.

"Well, hurry up," Rusty called, obviously exasperated. "I ain't sure how much longer the hinges of this door is gonna hold, and I could get mashed."

"I see that," Wanda Nell said. She moved right up to the pile of wood and dirt blocking the door. She put her hand against the beam and pushed. It moved ever so slightly. She flashed the light up and down the length of it. The other end rested solidly against the wall. Maybe if she got hold of it and pulled it toward her, she could dislodge it enough for Rusty to open the door safely.

"Does the door open in or out?"

"Out," Rusty said. "Toward you."

"Okay."

There was a fireplace to her left, and Wanda Nell scanned it. The mantel appeared solid enough, so she set her purse and the flashlight atop it, pointing the light toward the beam. Some light filtered in from outside, but it wasn't enough.

When she had the beam of light directed to her satisfaction, she called to her brother, "Now I'm going to try to pull this beam out of the way. Just hold tight."

"Be careful," Rusty said. "Won't do neither one of us any good if you get hurt."

Wanda Nell ignored that. She was pretty strong, and she did a fair amount of lifting heavy boxes at Budget Mart. The beam was pretty solid and no doubt quite heavy, but she thought she could manage to move it out of the way. If she couldn't she was either going to have to find some other way for Rusty to get out of the closet or she would have to call for help.

Where the beam rested against the closet door was chest high on Wanda Nell. She sidled up to it, squatted a little, then pushed up until she felt the beam touching against her right shoulder.

She brought her right arm up and tucked it carefully around the beam. Using her left hand to steady it, she pressed with her legs and stood up.

Straining with the effort, Wanda Nell pushed until she had loosened the beam from its wedged position. Grunting, she stepped slowly sideways. For one panicked moment, she thought the beam was slipping away before she was ready to release it. She grabbed on, though, and steadied it.

One step sideways, then another. From the beam of the flashlight Wanda Nell saw that one more step would bring her far enough away from the door so she could let the beam go.

Panting from the exertion, she readied herself. She let go of the beam with her right hand. Tensing slightly, she pushed with her left hand while rolling her right shoulder.

As the beam began to slip toward the floor, she jumped free of it.

With a loud crash the beam landed, and Wanda Nell felt the floor tremble with the impact. She was afraid for a moment that the floor would give way beneath her, but it held.

While she stood there trying to catch her breath, Rusty began pushing against the door. There was still debris against it on the floor, but without the beam locking it into place, Rusty was able to push the door open wide enough to escape. He slipped out and stepped carefully over all the mess until he was standing near his sister.

"Are you okay?" he asked.

Wanda Nell nodded. She flexed her right shoulder. "I'm probably going to be real sore for a couple of days, but I'm fine."

"Thank the Lord you found me," Rusty said. "Be back in a minute." He scrambled past her before she could say a word.

"What are you. . . ." Her voice trailed off as she realized where he was headed.

She retrieved her purse and the flashlight from the mantel and slowly made her way back through the house to the back steps. Standing there, she breathed the fresher air of the outdoors and wished she had some water or something to drink.

Rusty emerged from the woods a couple of minutes later, a slightly sheepish look on his face. He was grimy and exhausted-looking, but otherwise he seemed to have suffered no ill effects from his ordeal. One of his eyes was decorated with a yellowing bruise, but that looked as if it had happened before he got trapped in the closet.

"Sorry about that," he said as he walked up to the back steps. "I just hope that wasn't poison ivy I grabbed ahold of."

Wanda Nell had no comment for that. She started to sit down on the steps, but Rusty hustled her back inside the house.

"Come on back in here, just in case," he said.

"I don't think it's very safe," Wanda Nell said, exasperated. "Let's get out of here."

"No," Rusty said. He went back through the kitchen into the room where he had been trapped, and Wanda Nell followed him with great reluctance. He scrambled across the beam and climbed back into the closet. He came back with a flashlight, his cell phone, and a blanket. He spread the blanket on the floor near the door into the kitchen and motioned for Wanda Nell to sit down. She made herself as comfortable as she could on the floor. He made another trip to the closet and came back with two bottles of water and several candy bars.

Rusty sat down beside her. He handed one of the bottles to her, then opened his and drank almost the whole bottle. He offered her a candy bar but she declined. He opened one and wolfed it down.

Sipping at her water, Wanda Nell eyed her brother. Now that she had found him, what should she ask him first?

She decided on the obvious. "How did you get stuck in that closet?"

Rusty laughed bitterly. "Just my luck. I thought I heard somebody in the house, and I scooted into the closet with my blanket. I barely got the door shut, and that's when all that came crashing down." He waved a hand toward the beam. "I thought I might die in that closet. But I was hoping you might turn up."

"It's a good thing I came along when I did."

"I guess Lily must have found you."

Wanda Nell nodded. "I found her, just a little while ago. She came by the restaurant to talk to me, but she

disappeared before I got there. One of the other waitresses recognized her though, and I was able to track her
down."

"What did you think of her?" Rusty shifted back and
forth from one foot to another.

"She's a pretty girl," Wanda Nell said, "and it sounds
like she's in a real bad way. She needs help."

"She does," Rusty said.

"How do you know her?" Wanda Nell asked. "You've
got to start talking to me, Rusty. I want to know what's
going on, and why two men have died. It's all connected
somehow, and you're the only one who can tell me how."

"*Two* men?" Rusty was plainly startled. "Who else
died?"

"Scott Simpson committed suicide," Wanda Nell said.

Rusty swore violently.

"Look, come on back outside. Let's find somewhere to
sit. You've got to talk to me."

"Yeah, I know," Rusty said. "I can't do this on my own
anymore. But let's stay here. I don't want to be outside,
just in case."

She didn't try to argue with him. He had a mulish set
to his mouth. "Why didn't you call me?" Wanda Nell
asked instead, pointing to his phone.

"It's dead," he said. "I forgot to turn it off, and by the
time I realized it, it was too late. And I didn't have any
way to recharge it."

"Bad luck," Wanda Nell said.

"The only kind of luck I seem to have," Rusty said in a
tone of self-loathing. "I screw up everything. Look at the
mess I'm in now."

"Things are bad, I'm not going to lie about that," Wanda
Nell said. "But you don't have to do this alone, whatever it
is you're doing. If you're trying to help Lily, I'll help you.
And I know I can get other people to help, too."

"You'd do that?" Rusty shot her a sideways glance.

"You're family," Wanda Nell said. "Of course I'll help you. I don't believe you killed anybody."

"Thank you," Rusty said. He bumped his shoulder briefly against hers.

"But why the heck are you trying to blackmail Bert Vines and Marty Shaw? What did they ever do to you?"

Rusty drew away from her, the moment of closeness gone.

"It's a long story," Rusty said. "Are you sure you want to hear it?"

"Yes," Wanda Nell said, rapidly losing what little she had left of her patience. "It's about damn time. People have been following me, trying to break into my house, and I don't know what all. I want some answers, Rusty. We have got to put an end to this."

"Okay," he said. He leaned forward, propped his elbows on his knees and crossed his arms. "It all goes back to when I was a freshman in high school. You were a junior, and Marty, Bert, Scott, and Tony Campbell were sophomores. Reggie Campbell was a freshman, and we started hanging out together that spring."

"Yeah, go on," Wanda Nell said when he paused.

"Marty and Bert were the cool guys in the class. They were the ones the girls was always after, and Scott and Tony, too. Hotshots on the football team, real studs." He laughed bitterly. "And me and Reggie wanted to be just like them. We tried tagging along with them, and they even let us in on a couple of their parties."

"They were pretty wild, I guess," Wanda Nell said.

"Yeah, especially Marty," Rusty continued. "I guess because his daddy was the sheriff, he thought he could do anything and get away with it."

"Sounds like he did," Wanda Nell commented wryly.

"Pretty much. There was a lot of drinking and even

some drugs, though I don't know where Marty was getting the stuff. I think it was him, or maybe Bert, but they always seemed to have plenty of pot and some other stuff."

"Were you smoking pot and taking drugs?" Wanda Nell tried not to sound shocked, but she couldn't help remembering the lectures their daddy had given them against drugs and drinking.

"Yeah, I tried them a few times," Rusty said. "Mostly they just made me sick, but I did drink some. We all got a little wild. There were plenty of girls around, too." He stopped suddenly.

"And you had sex with some of them," Wanda Nell said.

"No, I couldn't," Rusty said. He sounded almost embarrassed. "I mean, not with everyone else around. They always had these parties at a hunting camp Scott's daddy owned, and if you were gonna do it, you pretty much had to do it in front of everybody else." He laughed, still embarrassed. "I just couldn't, even when I was drinking."

"Well, I'm glad about that," Wanda Nell said. The thought of those orgies made her sick to her stomach. She could never look Bert Vines or Marty Shaw in the face again, though she wouldn't have much choice until this mess was settled.

"Okay," she continued, "so Marty and Bert threw some wild parties and had sex orgies. Is that what you're using to blackmail them with? It's pretty bad, but I can't see that it's worth killing over, or even committing suicide over."

"It's not only that," Rusty said. "I mean, all that's bad enough, especially with the two of them being successful and respectable now. But if I told about all that, I'd also have to bring in all the girls who took part, and I can't do that to those girls. Most of them were too drunk to know what was going on."

"Then what kind of hold do you have over them?"

Wanda Nell couldn't imagine anything worse than what Rusty had already told her.

"There was this girl in my class," Rusty said, his voice soft and low. "She was real pretty, and kinda smart, too. I sat next to her in a couple classes, and we started talking a lot. I really liked her, and she liked me. I wanted to ask her out, but I was afraid to."

"Why?" Wanda Nell asked. She had a sneaking suspicion who the girl had been.

"Because if anybody had seen us together, there would've been hell to pay," Rusty said. "Her name was Lavinia Golliday, and she was black."

Wanda Nell stretched out a hand and touched her brother's shoulder. He sighed and sat back, crossing his arms over his chest.

"I called her Veenie," he said. "She was so cute and so much fun. She had a great sense of humor, laughed at everything. I couldn't look at another girl."

"So what happened?" Rusty and Veenie had been together somehow, Lily was evidence of that.

"I asked Scott if it was okay for me to take a date to his daddy's hunting camp, and he said it was," Rusty said, his voice devoid of inflection. "Reggie already had his driver's license, and he was going to take me and Veenie out there so we could be together. What I didn't know was that Marty and Bert found out about it.

"Reggie drove me and Veenie out there, and I took some food and some Cokes. We were going to have a picnic, and Reggie was going to come back for us after a couple of hours." Rusty paused for a moment. "We had barely been there for ten minutes before Marty, Bert, and Scott showed up. Reggie was right behind them."

Wanda Nell felt like she was going to throw up. Rusty didn't have to tell her what had happened after that. She had realized the truth.

But Rusty talked relentlessly. "I tried to stop them, and so did Reggie. But I think Reggie was getting a kick out of it. They were already drunk and ready to party."

Wanda Nell tried to put her arm around Rusty's shoulders, but he shrugged her off.

"You remember what I was like then. I was still thin and scrawny. They all outweighed me by at least fifty pounds, and they were all taller. I tried to stop them, but Scott knocked me down and sat on me. They made me watch while they raped her."

Rusty started to cry, and this time, when Wanda Nell slipped her arms around him, he didn't resist her. They cried together.

Twenty-eight

How long they sat like that, Wanda Nell had no idea. She had never seen her brother cry like this, not even at the funerals of their parents. During those he had been stoic, remote. If he had cried over their deaths, he had not let her see him do it.

Finally the tears stopped flowing. Rusty wiped his eyes with a semiclean corner of his shirt and reached for his water bottle. Wanda Nell delved into her purse for a pack of Kleenex. She brought it out and pulled several from the pack, offering them to Rusty. He took them and blew his nose while she mopped her own face.

"I just don't know what to say." Wanda Nell's throat ached from all the crying. She took several sips from her bottle of water. "I never imagined anything so awful."

"I still have nightmares about it," Rusty said. He rocked back and forth on the blanket beside Wanda Nell. "I wish I could have done something to stop them. But I couldn't. They held me down until they were finished." His voice trailed off.

"The bastards," Wanda Nell said, a feeling of cold fury enveloping her. "I'd like to castrate all of them with a dull knife." Those sorry excuses for men would pay for this somehow, she vowed.

"Too late," Rusty said bitterly.

"What happened . . . afterward?" Wanda Nell hated to push him into talking more about it, but she had to know the rest of the story.

"When they were done, they let me go," Rusty said, his voice once again flat. "I told them I'd kill them, and they just laughed at me. Said why was I getting so worked up over a nigra gal. Said that's all she was good for anyway. I was so mad I would have killed all of 'em if I'd had a gun." He shook his head. "They weren't afraid of me. They laughed, and then they went off and left us there.

"Reggie at least waited to give us a ride back to town," Rusty went on. "I wanted to knock him down and run over him, the bastard. He could have gotten away and gone for help, but he just stood there. He didn't rape her, but he might just as well have."

"Did you kill him?" Wanda Nell asked. "I can't blame you if you did. I couldn't blame you if you killed all of them."

"No," Rusty said. "I didn't kill nobody. I might have wanted to, but I didn't." He sounded ashamed of himself.

"I got Veenie in the car, and I begged her to let me take her to the hospital, but she cried and cried. All she wanted was her mama. She didn't even want me to touch her, to help her into the car." Rusty paused a minute. "Marty told her I had brought her there for them, and by the time I could talk to her to tell her it was a lie, she wasn't listening to me. She thought I had betrayed her."

"Surely she knows better now," Wanda Nell said, appalled.

"I guess, but it don't make a whole lot of difference," Rusty said. "If it hadn't been for me, she wouldn't have been there in the first place. She was really messed up after that. I tried to see her, but her mama wouldn't let me. Told me to stay away, and finally I just gave up."

"Did you tell Daddy and Mama?"

Rusty sighed deeply. "I told Daddy. I didn't know what else to do. I wanted Marty and the others to be punished for what they'd done. I thought about taking one of Daddy's guns and just killing them, but I chickened out. I couldn't go through with it."

"What did Daddy do?"

"He was real upset," Rusty said. "At first he didn't want to believe me. He thought maybe I had gotten involved in something and was trying put the blame on the others, but when he calmed down, he knew I wasn't lying. I never lied to Daddy or Mama." He stopped for a moment. "Then he went to the sheriff and told him what happened."

"All this happened after Mama and Daddy sent me to stay with her cousins, didn't it?" Wanda Nell asked. "Surely I would have known something was wrong if I had been here."

"Yeah, it was a week or so after you went to Arkansas," Rusty said. "By the time you came back, when Daddy died, I just couldn't talk about it to nobody."

"What did the sheriff do when Daddy talked to him?"

"Not a damn thing," Rusty said. "He told Daddy it wasn't none of his business. He said Marty had told him all about it, how they'd paid this girl to come with them and that she knew exactly what was going to happen. Marty said I was just mad because she wouldn't let me do it with her, said I was too ugly."

"And the sheriff believed that?" If Wanda Nell had had a gun in her hands right that moment, she would have shot Marty herself and been happy to do it.

"Who knows if he did or not? The main thing was, he wasn't going to do a damn thing about it. He and Daddy had a big fight about it, and Daddy swore up and down he'd spit in the sheriff's face every time he saw him after that. I don't think they ever spoke to each other again."

"I can't believe that man had the absolute gall to come to Daddy's funeral after that," Wanda Nell said. She had lost all the respect she had ever had for Sheriff Shaw. She would like to get him in a room and tell him exactly what she thought of him. Time enough for that later, though. "Did Mama know about any of this?"

"Not at first," Rusty said. "I think Daddy told her not long before he died. It was awful, Wanda Nell. Daddy looked like he'd aged twenty years overnight. You were lucky you weren't there to see him like that. Then he had that massive heart attack. He was too young to die." Rusty stifled a sob. "And I killed him. I should have kept my mouth shut, and Daddy might still be alive."

"Now, don't you say that," Wanda Nell said. "You had to talk to Daddy. You did the right thing. It's not your fault what happened after that. Mama told me Daddy had a weak heart, some kind of problem with his arteries. They found that out when he went into the hospital. They said it was a wonder he hadn't died before that."

"That don't make me feel no better," Rusty said.

"I know," Wanda Nell said gently. "I understand how you feel, but you're not to blame here. If you want to blame somebody, blame those bastards Marty and Bert and the others. They're the ones who did wrong."

"They did, and I'm trying to make up for it, although it may be too late."

"How?"

Rusty moved restlessly on the blanket. "I'm sure Lily told you what her problem is. She needs a kidney transplant, and she needs money. Her mama's in too bad a shape to donate a kidney, and she don't have any other family. Except her father."

"And one of those men is her father," Wanda Nell said. She thought a moment. "That's why you had that information about DNA testing places, isn't it?"

"Yeah," Rusty said. "One of them is her daddy, and I want to be able to prove it."

"So you were trying to force them into taking paternity tests and owning up to being her father?"

Rusty nodded.

"How did you find out Lily needed help?"

"I used to call Veenie sometimes to check on her and Lily. Sometimes she'd talk to me, and sometimes she wouldn't. Sometimes they didn't have a phone, and so I'd send her a money order and tell her to call me." He fell silent a moment. "Then Veenie called me out of the blue about three weeks ago and told me how ill Lily is and asked could I help."

"And that's when you decided to blackmail Marty and them into helping?"

"Yeah," Rusty said.

"How were you going to do that? It was just your word against theirs, and after all this time, who would listen to you? The sheriff sure ain't going to."

"I've got some evidence," Rusty said with great satisfaction. "A few years ago, Reggie turned up in Nashville, and he looked me up. At first I wasn't going to have anything to do with him, but I got an idea. I invited him over to my place, and I got him good and drunk." He laughed. "When Reggie got drunk, all he wanted to do was talk. He'd tell anybody anything if you got him drunk enough."

"And you recorded him?"

"I sure did," Rusty said. "On video, no less. I had borrowed some equipment from the studio where I was working at the time. The dumb bastard never even knew I was doing it."

"Where's this video now? Is it somewhere safe?"

"Yeah," Rusty said. "It's somewhere they won't ever think to look, and I've got plenty of copies. They'd never be able to find and destroy them all."

"Did you confront Reggie when you got to town?" Wanda Nell could almost see the way events had unfolded.

"Yeah, I did," Rusty said. "I went by the gas station late that night. I knew if I told him what I had and what I wanted, he'd tell the others for me. So that's what I did. I told him I wanted Marty, Bert, Scott, and Tony to take DNA tests, and whichever one was her daddy was going to do whatever he had to do to get Lily her transplant and the medical care she needed. The others would have to contribute, too."

"How did Reggie react?"

"He was stunned, and then mad," Rusty said. "He was going to come at me, but I told him to back off. If anything happened to me, a copy of that tape would go to somebody who would make sure it got seen by the right people." He laughed. "Reggie backed off then, and I could tell he was scared."

"After you left him, he must have called the others," Wanda Nell said.

"Yeah, and one of them killed him. He was such a stupid jerk, and he was the one who'd given me the evidence to fry their asses. Poor sucker didn't stand a chance after that." Rusty didn't sound too regretful over Reggie's death, and Wanda Nell couldn't blame him. By all accounts, Reggie Campbell had been nasty, violent scum.

"Lily told me you'd been kidnapped, but that you managed to get away from them."

"Yeah, they ambushed me when I was leaving the sheriff's department the other night. They were waiting in the parking lot. Can you believe that?"

"Marty must be pretty sure of himself."

"Because his daddy's going to protect him, no matter what," Rusty said.

Wanda Nell was beginning to have an idea about that, but she wasn't ready to discuss it just yet.

"How did you get away from them?"

"They took me to Tony Campbell's fancy new house and locked me in an upstairs bedroom. The assholes even tied my hands to the bedpost, but I saw this show once about how to hold your hands so you can get out of the rope. If they hadn't all been drinking they might have figured it out. After that, all I had to do was wait until the middle of the night. I got loose and climbed out the window."

"I wish I could have seen the looks on their faces," Wanda Nell said, laughing.

"Yeah, me, too. They hit me a few times. That's how I got this shiner," Rusty said, touching his cheek.

"Then you went to see Veenie and Lily," Wanda Nell said, prompting him.

"Yeah, I stayed with them until about dawn. It took that long to talk Veenie into letting me have a blanket and her car. I was just going to hide out here a day or so and let Marty and them sweat a bit. But then the damn ceiling came down on me, and I was stuck till you come along."

"Thank the Lord I was able to find you," Wanda Nell said. "And now that I found you, I want to make sure you stay in one piece. We can't let those bastards find you."

"I could go back and stay with Veenie and Lily for a day or two, till we figure out what to do," Rusty said.

"But they might come looking for you there," Wanda Nell said. Surely Rusty didn't want to put Veenie and Lily at risk of further harm.

"It would probably take them too long to find her, even if they knew where to look."

"What do you mean," Wanda Nell asked, completely floored, " 'if they knew where to look?' They can probably find her faster than I found Lily."

"Naw, when I talked to Reggie the other night, I told him they were in Memphis hiding out till I got everything arranged. I told him there was no way they could get to Veenie, even if they tried. I was bluffing, but they had no reason to know that."

"Maybe not," Wanda Nell said, "but to be on the safe side, I don't think you'd better go back there."

"Then I'll just stay here."

"No," Wanda Nell said. "The condition this house is in, it's just too dangerous."

"I can't come home with you," Rusty said, getting exasperated. "Or go back to Mayrene's. They'd find me in a heartbeat. You ain't suggesting, I hope, that I go to the sheriff's department and ask them to look after me."

"No," Wanda Nell said, "though that might not be such a bad idea." She shook her head. "No, I've got a better idea. We're going to need to be able to push them into a corner they can't get out of. We can't trust the sheriff, but we may be able to trust one of his men."

"You mean Elmer Lee?"

"Yeah, much as I hate to admit it. He's a royal pain in the rear most of the time, but I'm pretty sure he's honest."

"So is Elmer Lee going to be the one to push them into a corner?"

"He can help," Wanda Nell said, "but I've got somebody even better. Somebody they can't—and won't—ignore." She got up from the blanket. "Come on, let's go outside. I want some fresh air, and I need to make a couple phone calls. We're going to get this mess settled today."

Twenty-nine

Wanda Nell and Rusty had to walk all the way back to the clearing where Wanda Nell had left T.J.'s truck before she could get a decent signal on her cell phone. She speed-dialed T.J. at the office to let him know she was okay and that she had found Rusty. She couldn't take time to answer his questions, but instead she asked him to look up a phone number for her.

He was obviously annoyed with her as well as worried, but he complied with her request. She jotted the number down on a scrap of paper.

"Look, honey, I know you're worried," Wanda Nell said, "but Rusty and I are just fine. I'll call you back in a little while to let you know what's going on, but I've got to take care of some other things first. Just be patient, and don't worry."

She didn't give him time to argue with her. She ended the call, waited a moment, then punched in the number T.J. had found for her.

The phone on the other end rang several times, and Wanda Nell was beginning to think she was out of luck when someone answered it.

"Thank the Lord, Ernie," Wanda Nell said, enormously relieved. "I don't know what I would have done if you hadn't been there."

"Wanda Nell, what's the matter? Are you in trouble?" Ernie didn't waste any time on preliminaries. "What do you need?"

"I've found my brother, and I need your help. He needs a safe place to hide for today, and I have a plan for taking care of everything, if you can help."

"Bring him here," Ernie said without hesitation. "Or do you need me to come and get him?"

"I'll bring him there," Wanda Nell said. "We'll be on our way in a minute. Till we get there, you be thinking of somebody who can help us. Somebody who ain't afraid of the sheriff and who'll be willing to make sure he can't cover this up."

"Will do," Ernie said. "Drive carefully."

Wanda Nell ended the call. "Come on, Rusty, hop in the truck and let's get going."

"I can't just leave Veenie's car out here," Rusty said, not moving. "Can't we take it by her house and drop it off?"

"We don't have time," Wanda Nell said, her patience wearing thin. "If everything goes okay, we'll be able to get her car back to her by sometime tonight. Now get your rear in this truck and let's get going." She didn't wait for a response, she simply got in the truck and cranked it.

Rusty hesitated a moment, but evidently he saw no point in arguing further with his sister. He went around to the passenger side, opened the door, and climbed in. "All right. Let's go."

Down the old road toward the highway they went, with Wanda Nell driving as fast as she dared without shaking either the truck or their bones into a thousand pieces.

As they neared the highway, Wanda Nell said, "Can you get down on the floorboard, Rusty? I think it might be better if nobody could see you until we get through town."

Rusty grumbled, but he did as she asked. He scrunched himself down in the floorboard and rested his arms and head on the seat. Luckily for him, the cab of T.J.'s truck was pretty spacious, so he wasn't too cramped from what Wanda Nell could see.

Before she turned onto the highway, Wanda Nell fished in her purse for her sunglasses, grateful that she hadn't left them in her car. She also asked Rusty for the dirty gimme cap he had brought with him. With the sunglasses on and the cap jammed down on her head, she hoped she would have enough of a disguise, just in case anybody was watching for her.

Wanda Nell drove pretty fast on the highway, but she was careful not to go too fast. The last thing she needed right now was to get pulled over for speeding. Traffic was fairly heavy in Tullahoma because it was nearly noon. She kept a wary eye on the rearview mirror, watching for anyone who might appear to be tailing her.

"Where are we going?" Rusty said. "You ain't told me yet, and I'd kinda like to know."

"Sorry," Wanda Nell said. "I forgot about that. You remember our English teacher from high school, Miss Carpenter?"

"Yeah," Rusty said. "So that's who you were talking to. I thought her name sounded familiar when you called her. What's she got to do with all this?"

"She was a big help when I was looking for information," Wanda Nell said. "And she said if there was anything else she could do to help, I should call her. Her family is pretty prominent here, and she knows a lot of people. I figure if anybody can help us spike the sheriff's guns, so to speak, it'll be Ernie."

"Ernie?" Rusty said, surprised. "You call her Ernie?"

Wanda Nell laughed. "Yeah, pretty funny, ain't it? Her name's Ernestine, but she told me to call her Ernie."

"Well, I'll be damned," Rusty said, laughing.

Wanda Nell was breathing a little more easily by then because they were now out of Tullahoma. In ten or fifteen minutes they would be at Ernie's.

The rest of the short drive transpired without incident, but Wanda Nell insisted that Rusty stay down in the floor of the truck until they reached Ernie's house, just in case.

When Wanda Nell pulled up in front of the Carpenter home, she had to go around to the passenger side and help Rusty out. One of his legs was cramping, and he was having a hard time getting out by himself.

Ernie had the door open and was halfway down the walk by the time Rusty could straighten his legs. She stuck out her hand. "Rusty, how are you? Wanda Nell's told me about the trouble you're in."

"Yes, ma'am," Rusty said, shaking his former teacher's hand awkwardly. "It's a mess, and I sure do appreciate you helping us out like this."

"I'm glad to do it," Ernie said. "Now y'all just come on in here. I imagine by now you must be pretty hungry, and I've got more than enough lunch ready for the three of us."

"Good Lord," Wanda Nell said, turning to her brother. "I never even thought to ask you if you needed something to eat. You must be starving."

"I am," Rusty said as he followed his sister and Ernie into the house. "I had some candy bars and stuff with me at the old house, but I could just about eat a horse right now."

"You're going to have to make do with vegetables and cornbread," Ernie said as she showed them into her dining room. "Have a seat, and let me pour you some tea. Dive right in."

Rusty didn't wait for a second invitation. He pulled out a chair, sat down, and immediately began piling his plate with steaming creamed corn, field peas, and string beans. Wanda Nell passed him the cornbread, still warm from the oven, and then handed him the butter.

Ernie returned with glasses of iced tea, and Wanda Nell filled her own plate. She was just about as hungry as Rusty was, though she ate with less haste.

They all ate for a few minutes in silence, then Ernie turned to Wanda Nell. "Tell me what's going on, and how you think I can help."

Without going into too many of the horrifying details, Wanda Nell explained the situation to Ernie. Ernie didn't say anything while Wanda Nell talked, but she did push her plate away, half of it untouched, before Wanda Nell finished.

"How horrible," Ernie said. "Rusty, I am so sorry. I'll do everything I can to help you and Lavinia and Lily." She shook her head. "I always wondered why Lavinia never came back to school that fall. I had heard she moved away, but we all lost track of her after that."

"I think her and her mama did leave town for a couple of years," Rusty said. He pushed his plate away too, but his was empty. Wanda Nell was glad to see him looking better. The hot food had obviously done him good.

"I have a very dear friend," Ernie said, her face turning slightly pink, "an old beau, actually, who is a retired justice of the state supreme court. He still has quite a lot of influence, and I know he will be very interested in this story. With him on our side, I can assure you that justice will be done."

"See, it's like I told you," Wanda Nell said, looking at her brother.

Ernie pretended not to hear that comment. Instead, she said, "Now, as I see it, we need to confront these vermin about what they've done and the steps they're going to take to rectify the situation. Obviously they can never make it up to Lavinia for what they've done to her, but they *can* save young Lily's life. It's the very least they can do."

"And whoever it was that killed Reggie has to pay for that, too," Wanda Nell said.

"Most assuredly," Ernie said.

"But how are we going to do all that?" Rusty asked. "The sheriff ain't going to do a damn thing about it. Pardon me, ma'am," he added hastily, ducking his head in embarrassed fashion.

Ernie chuckled. "I've heard stronger words than that, Rusty, and even used a few myself. You don't teach in a public high school for forty years without learning some vulgar language."

"No, ma'am," Rusty said, his face still a bit red.

"But you're absolutely right about one thing," Ernie continued. "The sheriff can't be allowed to cover this up. The truth is going to have to come out, and in such a fashion that it can't go back in again."

"Exactly," Wanda Nell said. "We need to corner those rats and not let them loose. We need to get them all together and hit them with everything we've got."

"Yes," Ernie said, "and I'd be delighted to help with that. What were you thinking, Wanda Nell?"

Wanda Nell shrugged. "I was just thinking maybe I could lure Bert and Marty somewhere where they thought Rusty was hiding, confront them with everything, and then turn them over to Elmer Lee Johnson. I believe he's honest, and I don't think he'd let the sheriff intimidate him, not over something like this."

"I think your basic idea is a good one," Ernie said, "but I do believe it calls for certain refinements." She paused, thinking. "Yes, I think I know what we can do. My old beau, the retired supreme court justice, lives in Senatobia, and I'm sure he'd be delighted to join us. I think I might also invite a couple of other people, but more about that later. What do you say we invite the vermin, otherwise known as Bert, Marty, and Tony Campbell, to my house this evening for a little party?"

"Are you sure?" Wanda Nell said.

"Yes, ma'am, it could be dangerous," Rusty said. "No telling what they might try to do."

"Oh, I think we can take care of that," Ernie said.

Wanda Nell nodded slowly. She was thinking of Mayrene, who would be mighty disappointed with her if she wasn't included in this. "Yeah, I think we ought to have quite a little party."

"Good," Ernie said. "Now here's what I think you should do."

Thirty

Wanda Nell and Rusty listened carefully to the plan Ernie proposed, but there were several things about it that made Wanda Nell uneasy. For one thing, Ernie wanted to invite the three men to her house for the confrontation. Wanda Nell worried over that because Ernie's house was so isolated. Her nearest neighbor was a half mile away. Besides which, Ernie was just plain taking over, although she meant well. Wanda Nell was grateful, but she didn't feel comfortable with Ernie putting herself in that position.

After Ernie finished talking, Wanda Nell exchanged glances with Rusty. She saw her uneasiness mirrored in his face. For a moment she felt like she was in high school again, about to talk back to a teacher. "I think the basic idea is a good one," she said, watching Ernie carefully for signs of annoyance. "But I don't like the idea of anything happening here in your house. It's so far away from everything."

Ernie nodded but didn't reply.

"I think it would be better to do it in a public place," Wanda Nell said. Then she laughed. "My first idea was to lure them out to that old house where Rusty was holed up, tie them up, and leave them there for a few days."

Ernie grinned. "An eye for an eye?"

"Yeah," Wanda Nell said. "And I thought about telling them we were going to send some friends out to visit them, some friends who didn't take kindly to the way they had treated a friend of theirs."

"Would you really have done that?" Ernie asked.

"No, but it sure wouldn't hurt them to sweat it out for a few days," Wanda Nell said.

"Amen to that," Rusty said.

"But I like the notion of putting them in a corner where they can't get out, in full view of people who aren't going to be intimidated just because the daddy of one of them is the sheriff," Wanda Nell said.

"That's why I think you should get them here," Ernie said. "I think they're more likely to come here than they would be to some public place in town. Here they would feel less threatened."

Wanda Nell thought about that for a moment. Rusty shrugged, as if leaving the decision to her.

"I think you're probably right," Wanda Nell said finally. "I guess I hadn't thought about that part of it. But are you sure it won't be too dangerous for you? I couldn't live with myself if something happened to you because of this." She really didn't want to put Ernie in danger, but she also knew that, having enlisted the woman's help thus far, she couldn't rely deny her if she wanted to be there.

"Don't worry about me," Ernie said. "I don't think anything is going to happen to me. But I'm doing this of my own free will. I want to see justice done, and I think I can help. There is strength in numbers, after all."

"What about Lily?" Rusty asked. "Do you think she should be there?"

"No," Wanda Nell said. "The poor girl still thinks that maybe you're her father. She obviously doesn't know what happened to her mother, and I'd sure hate for her to have to find out like that."

"I hadn't thought of that," Rusty said. "I guess at some point she'll have to know, though."

"Yeah, but I think her mama will have to be the one to tell her," Wanda Nell said. "If she can."

Rusty shrugged. "What about Veenie? Should I try to get her here?"

"I don't think that's a good idea either," Wanda Nell said. "Things could get out of hand if she shows up. Besides, would Veenie really want to see them all again?"

"No, I guess not," Rusty said.

"I should get on the phone to Porter," Ernie said. "Porter Tillman, that's my old beau the retired judge. What time shall I tell him to be here?"

"I guess I'd better call Melvin first and tell him I'm going to have be off tonight," Wanda Nell said. "May I use your phone?"

Ernie waved a hand toward the instrument sitting on a nearby desk. "Help yourself."

Wanda Nell punched in the number and waited. She glanced at her watch. The worst of the lunch rush would be over by now.

"Hey, Ruby, it's me," Wanda Nell said. "Can I speak to Melvin, please? Tell him it's important."

"Sure thing, Wanda Nell," Ruby Garner replied. "Hang on a sec, he's at the cash register."

When Melvin came to the phone, Wanda Nell launched right into a terse explanation. Melvin heard her out completely before he made any comment.

His first few words almost blistered Wanda Nell's ear. Melvin had always had a very poor opinion of men who abused women. "Those sons of bitches. We oughta just line them up against the wall and shoot 'em," he said in a slightly less irate tone.

"Then I guess you don't mind if I take off tonight," Wanda Nell said.

"You're welcome to," Melvin said. "I just wish I could be there to see those sons of bitches get what's coming to them. You be careful, you hear?"

Wanda Nell promised she would be, then hung up.

"Now I'll call Porter," Ernie said. "You two just relax for a few minutes." She disappeared into another room.

"Are you okay with all this?" Wanda Nell said as she sat down.

"Yeah," Rusty said. "I appreciate all this, Wanda Nell. I hate involving you in this mess, though."

"I'm just sorry I couldn't do something before," Wanda Nell said. "I wish I had known about all this sooner."

"Wouldn't have made much difference," Rusty said. "I don't think it would have changed things much."

"It might not have changed some things," Wanda Nell said. "But maybe you and me wouldn't have spent so much time not talking to each other. You're my brother, and it's not right for you and me not to know each other anymore."

Rusty shrugged, not saying anything.

"Look," Wanda Nell said, starting to get annoyed with him, "I know you were mad at me for a long time because you thought I didn't care, or maybe that I was too involved in my own problems to worry about yours. And I guess I was. Right after Daddy died, I went a little crazy. I got pregnant, and then I got married, and I guess I just didn't make time for anybody else. The last thing I ever wanted to do was push you out of my life, Rusty."

"I know that," Rusty said, his face reddening slightly.

"But I was real screwed up. I was so angry at everybody, but mostly I guess I was mad at myself because I didn't do anything to stop them. After Daddy died, I couldn't talk about it to anybody. I sure couldn't talk to you and Mama."

"We would have understood," Wanda Nell said.

"You were going to have a baby," Rusty said, "and Mama was grieving so over Daddy. How could I burden y'all with something like that?"

From the hallway came the sound of a throat being cleared, and loudly. Moments later Ernie walked into the room, a bright smile on her face.

"Porter will be happy to assist," she said. "He was outraged, as I expected he would be, when I outlined the circumstances for him. He'll be on his way here shortly, and we'll be able to fill him in on the full picture."

"I've got some things I need to take care of," Wanda Nell said. "I'd better be getting back to town."

"Okay," Ernie said. "Rusty will stay here with me, and he can meet Porter and tell his story to him. You should be back here by six-thirty."

"That's fine," Wanda Nell said.

"Good," Ernie said. "And in the meantime, I expect Rusty wouldn't mind having a good bath and a little rest. I can wash your clothes for you while you're doing that."

Rusty looked slightly embarrassed, but all he said was, "Yes, ma'am. Thank you."

"I'll see you later then," Wanda Nell said.

Ernie escorted her to the door. They paused on the threshold, and Wanda Nell turned to the older woman. "I don't know how we can ever thank you for all your help," she said.

"Don't you even think about it," Ernie said, smiling. "It's my pleasure. I want to see justice done as much as you do."

Impulsively Wanda Nell hugged Ernie, and Ernie patted her firmly on the back. "I'll see you later," Wanda Nell said as she pulled away.

"Be careful," Ernie called as she hurried to the pickup. Then the door closed behind her.

Wanda Nell drove back to Tullahoma as fast as she dared. The early afternoon traffic was surprisingly heavy, and several times she fumed over getting stuck behind something slow moving. As she drove into town, she got out her cell phone and called T.J. to let him know she would soon be there.

"Mama, what's been going on?" T.J. said. "Tuck and I have been getting nervous, but I didn't call because I knew you'd get mad."

Wanda Nell laughed. "Now, honey, I wouldn't get mad at you. I might be slightly annoyed if you interrupted me, but don't you two start worrying over me. I'm just fine, and so is Rusty. I'll be there in a few minutes and I'll explain everything." She ended the call before he could say anything else.

As she approached the square she debated whether to drive to the back of the building and go in the rear door or simply to park out front. At this point, did it really matter if the guy following her realized he had been tricked?

Just to be safe, Wanda Nell decided on the former course of action. There was no harm in letting the guy think she had been inside the building all this time. Wanda Nell hoped he been bored out of his mind and desperate for a pee all the time she was gone. It would serve him right!

She made a slight detour in order to approach the square indirectly. Her revised route brought her to the back of the office building without her having to drive around the square. She got out of the truck and locked it, glancing around to make sure no one could see her. The alleyway was deserted except for T.J.'s truck.

Upstairs in Tuck's office, Wanda Nell offered a breezy greeting to his new secretary, then proceeded back to Tuck's office, where she found him and T.J. waiting impatiently.

"Thank the Lord you're okay, Mama," T.J. said, jumping to his feet and enveloping her in a fierce hug.

"Amen to that," Tuck said, also hugging her when T.J. released her.

"I'm just so relieved I was able to find Rusty," Wanda Nell said, "alive and in one piece. But I tell you, what he's been through is pretty awful."

Tuck buzzed his secretary and asked her to hold his calls. "Now, Wanda Nell, we want to hear everything."

As quickly as she could, Wanda Nell told them the events of her day. When she reached the point of divulging everything Rusty had told her, she felt her stomach contract. The horror on the faces of the two men mirrored her own countenance, she had no doubt. When she had finished, both Tuck and T.J. had a few choice words for the rapists.

"What are you planning to do?" Tuck asked. "I'll help in any way I can. If Ms. Golliday wants to pursue a case against them, I'll take her on for free. There's no statute of limitation on rape in Mississippi."

"I don't know about that," Wanda Nell said. "I haven't met her yet. I'm sure Rusty will talk to her about it. Frankly, I hadn't even thought about that."

"It's an option," Tuck said. "Not to mention a paternity suit."

"That might be necessary," Wanda Nell said. "Once we figure out which one of them is really Lily's daddy, she and her mama might have to go to court to get any assistance from him."

"In the meantime," T.J. said, "what's the plan?"

"Rusty and I are going to throw a little party out at

Ernie Carpenter's house tonight at seven, and the guests of honor will be Bert, Marty, and Tony Campbell. Y'all want to be there, too?"

"I wouldn't miss it," T.J. said, grinning. "I have a feeling they're going to be real sorry for themselves by the time you get through with them, Mama."

"What about the sheriff?" Tuck asked. "Is he going to be invited? Or anyone from his department?"

"I'm going to ask Elmer Lee to join us, along with a couple men he feels he can trust. But I'm going to ask him to come at seven-thirty."

"Do you think he'll go along with this? You asking him to do something is like waving a red flag in front of a bull," Tuck said.

"Will Elmer Lee and a couple of deputies be enough?" T.J. asked, frowning.

"The rest of us will be there, and I don't think those three jerks will try anything. Besides, we also have an ace in the hole, in case the sheriff does show up."

"Who's the ace?" Tuck asked.

"A retired state supreme court judge, Porter Tillman," Wanda Nell said. "He's a good friend of Ernie Carpenter's, and she's going to make sure he's there. She says he's very well connected and that he'll be able to make sure the sheriff can't get Marty out of this or cover any of it up."

Tuck whistled. "I'll say he can. He has connections all over the place, not just in Mississippi, but in Washington, too. I'd hate to be on his bad side. We may have us a new sheriff pretty soon, if Shaw gets in Tillman's gun sights."

"I think it's about time he retired," Wanda Nell said. "After all this, I don't have much respect left for him. I can't ever forgive him for the way he treated my daddy and my brother, not to mention poor Veenie Golliday. She deserved a helluva lot better than what she got."

"Sounds like a pretty good plan," T.J. said. "So you're just going to invite them to show up, and then hit them with everything you know about what they did?"

"Yeah," Wanda Nell said, "and doing it in front of a lot of witnesses will make sure the story gets out, one way or another. They won't be able to cover it up after this."

"What about reprisals?" Tuck asked. "Aren't you afraid that they might try to get back at you or one of your family?"

"They might," Wanda Nell said. "I've thought about that. But I can't just stand by and let them get away with all this. One of them, or maybe all three of them, murdered Reggie Campbell and made Scott Simpson kill himself. They need to pay for that, and they need to pay for what they did to Veenie Golliday. And they damn sure better be willing to help Lily." She paused for a moment. "I don't like the idea of putting my family at risk, but once all this gets out, I don't think they'll dare do anything."

"I'm with you, Mama," T.J. said. "We can't let this go. We'll take care of ourselves."

"And speaking of that," Wanda Nell said, "I'm going to have to arrange for Miranda, Lavon, and Juliet to stay with Miz Culpepper tonight. Do you think you could pick Juliet up from school, T.J.? Take her home to get some clothes and stuff for Miranda and Lavon, too?"

"Sure, Mama, no problem." He glanced at Tuck, and Tuck nodded approval. "You want me to call Grandmother and ask her?"

"If you don't mind," Wanda Nell said with relief. "She'll probably take it better coming from you. And please explain to Miranda. Maybe by tomorrow things will be kinda back to normal, and they can all come home." *I hope*, she thought, and added a quick prayer.

"There's one thing I'm still a little puzzled by," Tuck said. "Wanda Nell, you said your brother told you he had proof, that he had recorded Reggie Campbell confessing to what happened. Where is that proof? Will he be able to produce it quickly?"

"You know, I had forgotten about that. I meant to ask him where it was, but so much was going on," Wanda Nell said, frowning. "Let me call him right now." She got up from her chair and went to the phone on Tuck's desk.

She punched in Ernie Carpenter's number and waited. Ernie picked up on the fifth ring, and Wanda Nell asked to speak to Rusty.

"I think he may still be in the shower," Ernie said. "Let me check."

After a few moments Ernie was back. "He's just getting out of the shower now, Wanda Nell. He'll pick up the phone in a second."

"Thanks," Wanda Nell said. She tapped her foot on the carpet while she waited.

"What is it?" Rusty asked a couple of minutes later.

"I'm here talking to Tuck and T.J.," Wanda Nell said, "and Tuck reminded me about this proof you said you have. That recording you made of Reggie Campbell. Where is it? What if we need to show it to somebody?"

"Do you know how to use a computer?" Rusty asked.

"No," Wanda Nell said. "What does that have to do with it?"

"Everything," Rusty said. "What about T.J. or that lawyer? Do they know anything about computers?"

"Sure they do," Wanda Nell said, irritated.

"Then let me talk to T.J."

Sighing, Wanda Nell motioned for T.J. to take the phone. "It's something to do with computers," she said, "and he won't tell me."

T.J. shrugged as he took the phone. "Hey, Uncle Rusty, what can I do for you?" He listened for a moment, then he started laughing. "No problem. I'll get it, and we'll make a couple more copies, just to be safe."

He hung up the phone and turned to his mother and Tuck with a smile.

"So what is it?" Wanda Nell demanded. "What is it? Why is he being so mysterious about it?"

"I'm going to start teaching you how to use the computer soon," T.J. said. "It's really not that mysterious, Mama. Uncle Rusty has this recording in a computer file. It's like watching a movie on the computer."

"Where's the computer file?" Wanda Nell asked. "What does it look like?"

"The file is actually stored on something. It's what they call a thumb drive." T.J. stuck out his pinkie. "It's about the size of my little finger. You just plug it into your computer, and you can store lots of stuff on it."

Wanda Nell shook her head. She felt completely stupid because she didn't know any of this. T.J. and Juliet both spent a lot of time on computers, and she guessed she was going to have to learn about them.

"Where the heck then is this thumb drive?" Wanda Nell asked.

T.J. started laughing. "You're never going to believe this, Mama. Uncle Rusty stuck it into the bottom of the makeup drawer in your bathroom."

Tuck laughed along with T.J. and, after a moment, Wanda Nell joined in. Rusty was right. Her makeup drawer was the last place anybody would have looked. She couldn't wait to tell Mayrene.

Thirty-one

From her vantage point at Ernie's front door, Wanda Nell glanced nervously at the clock on a table nearby. It was already five to seven. Surely Bert, Marty, and Tony were coming. After the conversations she had had with each of them, she didn't think they'd dare not show up. "I have something you want, and the only way you're going to get it is to come talk to me," she had said. "You give me what I want, and you'll get yours." When pressed, she had refused to say what she wanted, simply insisting on their coming to her. She had given them directions, but she was sure they knew exactly where the house was because Bert had followed her here.

Everyone was in place waiting for the "guests of honor." Ernie Carpenter and her friend, Porter Tillman, occupied two chairs in the front sitting room, just a few feet away from where Wanda Nell stood watch. As Wanda Nell caught Ernie's eye, the older woman nodded her head as if to say, "Don't worry. They'll come."

In another room down the hall—Ernie called it the den—sat her brother Rusty, T.J., Tuck, and Mayrene, accompanied by her shotgun, Old Reliable.

Wanda Nell had called Elmer Lee Johnson at six-thirty to tell him to be sure to come out to Ernie's house with a couple men he was sure he could trust. She had her fingers crossed he wouldn't ruin everything by showing up too early.

"What the heck is going on?" he asked. "I don't have time for any of your shenanigans, Wanda Nell."

"Just listen to me, you big doofus," Wanda Nell said, trying to keep her tone light despite her rapidly rising temper. "Something important is going to happen here tonight, and you need to be here. I'll tell you this much. If you get here at seven-thirty, you'll find my brother here. Plus you'll be able to wrap this case up real quick."

"If you know where your brother is, you better tell me right now," Elmer Lee said, practically growling into the phone. "Don't waste my time."

"I'm not," Wanda Nell said sweetly. "I just told you, if you get here at seven-thirty, he'll be here. And not a minute before, you hear me?"

Elmer Lee muttered a few words under his breath, but Wanda Nell decided not to call him on it. The important thing was for him to show up on time. She had allowed for half an hour for the confrontation between Rusty and his three tormentors. If they didn't show up soon, though, Elmer Lee might arrive right in the middle of everything.

Wanda Nell tensed suddenly. Headlights from a car swept across the front windows. They had finally arrived.

The house was completely still around her. Once more she glanced back at Ernie, who grinned encouragement. Beside her, the judge glowered. Wanda Nell was glad he was on her side.

A knock sounded at the door, and Wanda Nell forced herself to breathe in and out a couple of times to steady her nerves. Then she opened the door.

Marty Shaw pushed past her, with Bert Vines practically stepping on his heels. A man Wanda Nell recognized as Tony Campbell was a few steps behind the other two. She shut the door and turned to face the men.

Spying Ernie Carpenter and the judge, Marty Shaw came to an abrupt halt, and Bert Vines stumbled into him. Marty didn't say anything to Bert. He turned and stared at Wanda Nell for a moment, and she had to fight hard not to look away from him. The depth of hatred she saw in his eyes chilled her right to the bone.

She took a deep breath, then walked past them, closer to Ernie and the judge. "Good evening, gentlemen," she said with a bright smile. "I'm glad you could make it. If you'll come with me, we'll get this over with." She didn't give them a chance to say anything. She whirled and headed down the hall to the den.

As they walked past the sitting room, Wanda Nell glanced over at Ernie and the judge. Ernie winked at her. Then she said, "I haven't seen you in ages, boys, but I am going to need to talk you, Bert, about my insurance. I think some changes are in order." She laughed.

Marty spoke quickly. "How do, Miss Carpenter. It has been a long time." Behind him, the other two muttered greetings before lapsing into silence.

"But where are my manners, boys?" Ernie said. "Let me introduce to my dear friend, Porter Tillman. Porter, I'd like you to meet three of my former pupils, Marty Shaw, Bert Vines, and Tony Campbell. I'm sure you'll remember what all I've told you about them."

Remaining seated, the judge, a stately, almost cadaverous man of seventy-two, inclined his head in greeting. His face was impassive, though Wanda Nell would have sworn she saw his nostrils flare for a moment.

"Boys, Porter is retired from the State Supreme Court. Isn't that fascinating? He knows so many people, all over

the state. Why, he even has a nephew in the Justice Department in Washington." Ernie laughed again. "But don't
let me keep you from your meetin'." She waved a hand in
dismissal.

The judge eyed them all for a moment longer before
looking away.

That was about as subtle as an eighteen wheeler, Wanda
Nell thought. She had to hand it to Ernie, though. Only a
steel magnolia like Ernie could make an introduction
sound both utterly charming and sinister at the same time.

Marty, Bert, and Tony didn't say anything further to
Ernie or the judge. As Wanda Nell lead them to the den
and opened the door, motioning them through, Bert muttered just loud enough for her to hear, "I can't believe this
freaking circus. What the hell do you think you're doing?"

"Y'all just come on in, boys," Wanda Nell said. "Take
a seat." She pointed to three chairs arranged side by side.
They faced an arrangement of a sofa and three chairs a
few feet away. Rusty and Tuck occupied the sofa, and T.J.
and Mayrene sat in chairs to one side. Wanda Nell had
purposely wanted this to look like the setup for a trial.
"Make yourselves comfortable, and I'll introduce to
some people." Without waiting, she launched into her in-
troductions. Bert and Tony sat down, but Marty remained
on his feet, arms crossed over his chest, glaring at her.

"Y'all know my brother, Rusty," Wanda Nell said.
"And I know y'all are glad he finally turned up. Y'all sure
have been anxious to see him. Even going to the trouble
of following me around, thinking I knew where he was
all this time." She shook her head as if she were scolding
a misbehaving child.

Rusty didn't say a word to them. He simply sat in his
chair and stared at them.

"What the hell is this?" Bert Vines stood up. "What
kind of sick game are you playing, Wanda Nell?"

"Kinda interesting that you should mention *sick games*," Mayrene said. "Howdy, boys, I'm Mayrene Lancaster. I'm an interested bystander, you might say. I'm a good friend of Wanda Nell's and Rusty's, and I wouldn't have missed this for the world." She laughed. "Oh, and before I forget it, let me introduce my good friend here." She reached behind her and pulled out her shotgun and placed it across her lap. The barrel was pointed straight at Bert. "I call him Old Reliable, because when I aim him at some filthy piece of vermin, he just never misses."

Wanda Nell was watching the three men when Mayrene brought out the gun. Privately she thought her friend might be overdoing it a bit, but she was more than satisfied with the reaction. Bert sat down, swallowing visibly, and even Marty took a step back. Tony paled, and Wanda Nell could see sweat beading on his forehead.

"Next let me introduce my son, T. J. Culpepper. You might remember his late grandfather, the judge? Yes, I thought you might." *Those blasted Culpeppers do come in useful sometimes*, Wanda Nell admitted to herself. "And this is Hamilton Tucker, the lawyer. He's taking a special interest in all this."

T.J. and Tuck nodded at the men.

"What do you want?" Marty Shaw said, directing his question at Wanda Nell. "What the hell is going on here?"

"I'll let my brother tell you that," Wanda Nell said. "Rusty is the host of this little get-together." She walked over to where Mayrene sat and took a chair next to her. She made sure to leave plenty of elbow room between her and Mayrene, just in case her friend needed to grab hold of Old Reliable for any reason.

Rusty got up from the sofa and faced the three men.

"You three and Scott Simpson gang-raped a girl," Rusty said. "Marty lied about it and said she consented, but you all know she didn't. You all should've been hauled off to jail back then, but you got away with it because Marty's daddy wouldn't do a damn thing about it."

"I'm not going to sit here and listen to this crap," Bert said. "Come on, y'all." He got up from his chair and started moving toward the door.

"You'd best come back and sit down," Mayrene called out. "Because if my buddy Old Reliable and me have to follow you outside, we will. You just sit yourself down and behave."

Bert turned slowly and came back to his chair. Wanda Nell could see the fear in his eyes. She felt no pity for him.

"What's the point of all this?" Marty said. He was doing his best to pretend he was bored by what was going on, but he was twisting his wedding ring around and around. Wanda Nell didn't buy his cool act for a minute. He was worried.

"The point is, you bastard," Rusty said, keeping his voice flat and unemotional, "you three are going to pay for what you did. You got away with it then, but you're not going to get away with it any longer. One of you murdered Reggie, the poor dumb jerk, and you have to pay for that, too."

Tony Campbell was sweating profusely now. He pulled a handkerchief from his pocket and wiped his forehead. Marty continued playing with his ring while Bert twitched restlessly in his chair.

"One other thing happened that night," Rusty said. "One of you got her pregnant. You didn't know that, did you?" He paused for a moment, and it was clear from the reactions of the three men that they hadn't known. "Her daughter is real sick now. Her kidneys are failing, and she needs a kidney transplant. Her mama's in no shape to donate one, and so it's up to y'all. We're going to find out which one of you is her daddy, and he's going to take care of it. Plus, I think the other two ought to chip in for her medical care."

"This is ludicrous," Bert said. "Ain't no way I'm putting up with this. I didn't kill anybody, and I didn't rape that girl."

"Bullshit," Rusty said.

"What kind of proof you got?" Bert said, sneering openly. "You think anybody's gonna listen to some black tramp? Or you? Who the hell are you to tell us what we're going to do?"

Despite the bravado, Bert was clearly uneasy. Otherwise, Wanda Nell thought, he wouldn't be squirming so much.

"I've got a confession," Rusty said, appearing unruffled by the taunts. Wanda Nell was proud of him for standing up to these three jerks. "From Reggie. He was a witness to it all, and he confessed everything. I recorded him on video, and there are several copies of it. There's no way you can find them all and destroy them."

None of them appeared completely surprised by the news, though Tony Campbell was starting to look like he wanted to throw up.

"You kidnapped me to try to find the video," Rusty said in the same cool voice, "but that didn't work. And one of you killed Reggie when you found out about it. I don't know for sure which one of you did it, but I don't really care. The only thing that concerns me is the girl."

"I don't give a shit about some bastard nigger girl," Marty said. "How do we know that one of us is even her daddy? You're lying about that."

"In that case," Wanda Nell said, deciding it was about time she chipped in, "if you're so sure, then having a paternity test won't matter that much. Will it?"

Marty didn't respond. He simply stared at her with loathing.

Wanda Nell stood up. She was determined she was going to make him react because he was really pissing her off. "What kind of monster are you?" she asked. "You practically destroyed one life by what you did, and now there's a beautiful girl who's dying. A girl one of you could save, if you're man enough." She laughed derisively. "But if you were decent men, you never would have raped this poor girl's mama in the first place."

Tony Campbell broke into sobs at those words, and even Bert appeared shaken. Marty remained stone-faced.

The door opened, and Elmer Lee Johnson walked in, trailed by two other deputies.

"Evening, everybody," Elmer Lee said. His eyes swept the room, lighting on Rusty. "What the hell is going on here?"

"One of these men killed Reggie Campbell," Rusty said, pointing at Bert, Marty, and Tony. "And I can tell you why."

"I'm not listening to any more of this," Marty said. He turned and headed for the door. He didn't get very far because one of Elmer Lee's men blocked the door.

"I'd hold on there a minute if I was you," Elmer Lee said.

Marty stopped and turned. "Who the hell are you to tell me what to do? Are you forgetting who my father is? He's not going to like you treating me this way." He made as if to push by Elmer Lee.

For a moment, Wanda Nell was afraid he was going to get away with it. Beside her, Mayrene tensed, and Wanda Nell put out a restraining hand, just in case.

Elmer Lee stood his ground though. "I know damn well who your daddy is, Marty. But you're not going anywhere until I find out what's going on. You just sit yourself down over there, and I'll tell you when you can leave."

Marty didn't move, and for a moment Wanda Nell thought he would try to make a break for it. Then suddenly he gave in and went to the chair Elmer Lee indicated. Wanda Nell breathed a shaky sigh of relief.

"What's this all about?" Elmer Lee asked, looking pointedly at Wanda Nell.

She glanced at Rusty. He nodded.

"About twenty-four years ago," Wanda Nell said, "Marty, Bert, and Tony Campbell, along with Scott Simpson, raped a young black girl. Rusty and Reggie Campbell were witnesses. At the time, Rusty went to our daddy and told him what happened. Daddy went to the sheriff, who was a good friend of his, and told him about it." She paused for a moment. "The sheriff refused to do anything, because Marty told him the girl consented. That was a damn lie. My daddy was so upset by the way the sheriff behaved, and by the whole godawful mess, he ended up having a heart attack, and it killed him. All these years they've gotten away with it."

She half expected Marty to utter another denial, but he didn't say anything. He just kept his cold dead eyes fixed on her.

"One of them got the girl pregnant," Wanda Nell said, "and the child, a girl, is now very ill with some kind of kidney disease."

"And that's why I came back to Tullahoma," Rusty said. "Her mama got in touch with me and told me what the situation was. So I decided to do something about it. A few years ago, Reggie was in Nashville. He confessed the whole thing, and I recorded him doing it. I was using that confession to persuade them"—he waved a hand toward Marty, Bert, and Tony—"to take paternity tests, so one of them could donate a kidney maybe. Plus help pay her medical bills. It's the least they could do after what they did to her mama."

"Rusty went to Reggie and told him about the tape he'd made," Wanda Nell said, "and that's when they had that argument. But when Rusty left him, Reggie was still alive. Reggie must have called one of them and told them about Rusty. That's when one of them killed Reggie."

Elmer Lee stared back and forth between Wanda Nell and Rusty. He was about to say something when Tony Campbell forestalled him.

"Reggie called me, real upset," he said, his voice hoarse with emotion. "I didn't know what to do, so I called Marty right away." He paused. "Next thing I knew, I got a call to say that Reggie was dead."

"You asshole," Bert said. "Why don't you keep your mouth shut?" He started to get up from his chair.

Elmer Lee's two deputies moved closer to the three men. Bert sat back down.

"Reggie was my brother. He was an asshole, but he was still my brother," Tony said. "You shouldn't have killed him." He was facing Marty as he spoke those last few words.

Marty's calm finally broke. He lunged at Tony, grabbing him around the throat. They went down on the floor. Marty was throttling Tony and trying to pound his head against the floor.

The two deputies went into action and separated Tony and Marty after a brief struggle.

"I think we'd better move this little show down to the sheriff's department," Elmer Lee said. "Cuff 'em and move 'em out, boys."

Thirty-two

Three weeks later, on a beautiful, sunny Sunday afternoon in October, Wanda Nell was in her kitchen singing along with Emmylou Harris on the radio as she worked. She stepped back from the counter to examine her handiwork. She had baked a chocolate cake for Miranda's birthday, and she was pleased with the way the icing had turned out.

She set the cake to one side and rinsed the knife she had used in the sink. Drying her hands, she considered what else she needed to do. Her guests would be arriving in an hour, and just about everything was ready.

Except her, that was. She glanced down at herself and realized she had better go get changed right now in case anyone showed up early.

Twenty minutes later she was ready. Miranda had woken Lavon up from his nap and was dressing him. Juliet had finished setting out some party decorations, and Wanda Nell retrieved the presents she had bought Miranda from the closet in her bedroom. They made a nice small pile on the coffee table in the living room. There would soon be others to join them, and Wanda Nell hoped that Jack, T.J., and Tuck hadn't gone overboard and bought Miranda expensive things.

On the other hand, she hoped that Mrs. Culpepper would bring something nice. The old woman never stinted where T.J. was concerned, but sometimes she could be a bit cheap when it came to Miranda, Juliet, or Lavon. But there was not much she could do about that, Wanda Nell knew. The old witch would always do exactly as she darn well wanted to.

Miranda appeared with Lavon toddling behind her, dragging his favorite bunny with him.

"Happy birthday, honey," Wanda Nell said. "How does it feel to be eighteen?"

Miranda ducked her head shyly. "Okay, I guess. Not much different, really." Lavon poked her leg and shoved his bunny up toward her. She accepted the bunny. "Thank you, sweetie." A moment later Lavon wanted the bunny back, and Miranda and Wanda Nell laughed. He took the bunny and put him on the couch, then climbed up after him.

"You stay there for a minute, okay?" Wanda Nell hoped he might stay there for a little while, but he was at the stage where he hardly sat still unless he was eating or sleeping.

"Thanks for having a party for me, Mama," Miranda said, eyeing the presents on the table. "I can't wait to see what's in those."

"You will soon enough, honey," Wanda Nell said.

"You sure you don't mind that I invited Teddy?"

Wanda Nell did have a few qualms about meeting Miranda's new boyfriend for the first time, but she was determined to be cheerful and welcoming, no matter how dreadful he might be. Given Miranda's track record with boys, Wanda Nell wasn't expecting much.

A knock sounded at the door, and Wanda Nell went to

open it. "Come on in," she said to Jack. She stood aside to let him enter.

He kissed her first, and she laughingly pushed him inside and shut the door. He grinned at her, then went to give Miranda a hug. "Happy Birthday, Miranda."

"Thank you," Miranda said, her cheeks rosy.

He pulled an envelope from his jacket pocket and handed it to her. "This is for you."

Miranda accepted it with a smile. "Thank you," she said again. She placed it on the coffee table with the other gifts. "Would you like something to drink? Mama made some punch, or maybe you'd like a beer?"

"How about some punch?" Jack said. Miranda nodded and went to the kitchen for it.

Jack turned to Wanda Nell. "Come here, you," he said, holding out his arms. Behind him on the couch, Lavon had started chanting "Jack" over and over. "In a minute, buddy," Jack said, "but I've got something to give your grandmother first."

Wanda Nell walked into his arms and raised her face to his. He smiled down at her as he kissed her, and they stood together for a moment, until Miranda coughed discreetly behind them.

"Here's your punch," she said, offering him the glass as Jack and her mother stepped apart.

"Thank you," Jack said. He accepted the glass and took a sip. "Tasty." He smacked his lips and arched his eyebrows at Wanda Nell. "And the punch is pretty good, too." He went over to the couch and patted Lavon on the head. The boy smiled up at him and then resumed chattering to his rabbit.

Wanda Nell laughed, watching the two of them.

"It's good to hear you laugh like that," Jack said, coming back over to her and putting his arm around her. "You sound completely relaxed."

"I am," Wanda Nell said. "For once everything is calm and not crazy."

"There's a lot to celebrate," Jack said. "Miranda's birthday, and other good news."

"Yes, thank the Lord," Wanda Nell said. "Come on into the kitchen with me while I check on things." Her eye fell on her grandson. "Miranda, you'd better stop those busy little hands, or he'll unwrap every single one of your presents."

Miranda grabbed Lavon and started tickling him. Lavon shrieked with laughter, and Miranda sat down on the couch with him. Smiling at their antics, Jack followed Wanda Nell into the kitchen.

"Things between you and Miranda seem pretty good at the moment," he said.

Wanda Nell added some ice to the punch bowl as she talked. "Yes, thank goodness. She's been acting more mature lately, and I don't know whether it's her new job or this boy she's been seeing." She laughed. "If this Teddy has that kind of influence on her, then I guess I'm going to have to like him."

"Maybe so," Jack said. He set his empty glass on the kitchen table and pulled out a chair. "Come on and sit down a minute. Looks like everything is ready."

Wanda Nell sat down across the table from him. "I guess so. You know me, I have a hard time sitting still if I think there's anything to do."

"Yeah," Jack said. "But I'm going to make it my personal mission to teach you how to relax more."

"I see," Wanda Nell said. "I think I'd like to hear more about this mission of yours."

Jack grinned. "All in good time. Who all's coming today?"

Wanda Nell ticked the list off on her fingers. "T.J. and Tuck, of course. And Miz Culpepper and her cousin Belle are supposed to come, too. Wait till you meet Belle. Just don't let her get you in a corner, or she'll talk your ears off."

"Frankly, after everything you've told me, I'm actually looking forward to meeting her. She sounds like a hoot."

"She is," Wanda Nell said. "She's very sweet, and it's amazing to me how she gets along with that old battle-ax. I just wish she wouldn't go on and on sometimes about next to nothing."

"Who else?" Jack prompted her.

"Miranda's boyfriend, Teddy," Wanda Nell said, resuming her count. "And Mayrene, naturally. They should all be here soon."

"What about Rusty?"

Wanda Nell shook her head. "He had to go back to Nashville yesterday. I wish he could have stayed, but he had to get back to work. He's already taken off a lot of time."

"How are you two getting along? You haven't said much about him lately."

Wanda Nell sighed. "Better, for the most part. At least he's talking to me now and not treating me like his worst enemy. I wish he was living here, though, instead of Nashville. It would be nice to have him close by."

"Maybe he'll at least come to visit more often," Jack said.

"He said he would come down for Thanksgiving and for Christmas," Wanda Nell said. "I'll be looking forward to that. I know Mama and Daddy would be happy that we're acting more like family now."

"You've done everything you can," Jack said. "But Rusty has to meet you at least halfway."

"He's trying," Wanda Nell said. "But he's so worried about everything. Once the trial is done, and once Lily is finished with her treatments and her transplant surgery, I think he'll feel a lot better."

"I was pretty surprised when the sheriff resigned like that," Jack said.

"Me, too," Wanda Nell said. "You know, I saw him the other day, and he looked like he'd aged forty years. I feel sorry for him and his wife. All this mess with Marty has just about killed them."

"I don't feel sorry for Marty Shaw, though," Jack said.

"No, he's getting what he deserves. What he should have got a long time ago."

Marty was in jail waiting for the grand jury to meet to indict him for murder. His young wife, Tiffany, had publicly disavowed him, saying she never wanted to see him again. His partner at the car dealership was said to be trying to buy him out, too. No one wanted to have anything to do with him now.

"I still can't believe Marty was stupid enough to keep the baseball bat he used on Reggie Campbell in the trunk of his car," Jack said, shaking his head.

"It wasn't stupidity," Wanda Nell said. "Just plain arrogance. He never thought anything could happen to him because his daddy would take care of it."

"Do you think they'll ever be prosecuted for rape?" Jack asked.

"I doubt it," Wanda Nell said. "Veenie Golliday is in no condition to go through all that." She sighed. "I talked to Lily last night, and it sounds like Veenie is in real bad shape. There's something bad wrong with her liver, and Lily says the doctor thinks it's cancer."

"What a horrible life that woman's had," Jack said. "I can't even imagine what it's like, all that she's been through."

"I know," Wanda Nell said. "And every time I think

about it, I get mad all over again. I'd still like to string up those jerks and beat the tar out of them."

"I don't blame you," Jack said, "but I think they're getting pretty badly beat up as it is."

"Yeah, and they're just lucky they're not sitting in a cell with Marty," Wanda Nell said. "I think Bert's about lost all his business. He had to let Karen Marter, his secretary, go. Karen's daughter Marijane and Juliet are friends, and I talked to Karen a few days ago. She said people were calling up right and left canceling their insurance. I know I sure did."

"Was he the one who was following you around?"

"Yeah, he finally admitted to that. He borrowed a truck from one of his buddies," Wanda Nell said. "And he was the one that spray-painted the trailer and slashed my tires, too. Marty put him up to that."

Jack had a few choice words for Bert and Marty, and Wanda Nell just grinned.

"Tony Campbell at least had one shred of decency left, I guess," Jack said, cooling down a little. "I figured none of them would ever admit to being Lily's father, but he acknowledged her when the test results were in. And didn't you tell me he even paid a lot of money to get them to rush the tests?"

"Yeah, he did. He's not as big a jerk as the other two, though he's still a pretty sorry excuse for a man," Wanda Nell said. "I hear his young wife isn't too happy with him, but she's at least sticking by him, unlike Miss Tiffany with Marty."

"The whole thing's a big mess," Jack said.

"The only good thing to come out of it," Wanda Nell said, "is Lily finally getting some medical help. She was telling me last night that Tony is willing to donate a kidney if everything goes well."

"I sure hope it does," Jack said. "She deserves some good luck in her life."

"Amen to that," Wanda Nell said. "You know, looking at Lily and all that has sure made me stop and think. I get tired of having to work so much, and sometimes my kids drive me crazy, but I feel incredibly lucky. I can't complain about anything."

"I think the rest of us are the lucky ones," Jack said. "I can't imagine what it would be like not knowing you and having you in my life."

"Probably a lot quieter, and no dead bodies popping up all over the place," Wanda Nell said wryly.

Jack threw back his head and laughed. "It's never boring with you, love, that's for sure."

Wanda Nell grinned. "I don't know. Sometimes boring sounds pretty dang good."

A knock sounded at the front door, and Wanda Nell got up from the chair.

"Come on," she said. "I think it's time to have a birthday party."

Recipes from the Kountry Kitchen

Country-fried Steak with Gravy

1 tenderized round steak (per person, or cut into smaller portions if desired)

2 beaten eggs

⅛ cup milk (2 tablespoons)

flour

salt

pepper

garlic powder

Gravy:

3 tablespoons flour

milk

Season meat and cut into serving sizes. Place a cup or so of flour into one shallow bowl and mix in salt, garlic, and pepper to taste. (Note: for a spicier taste, use a touch of cayenne.) In a second bowl, beat the 2 eggs and add milk. Mix together. Dip meat in flour, then in egg mixture, then in flour a second time. Shake off any excess flour. Fry in cast iron pan with about ¼ to ½ inch heated oil. (Note: make sure the pan is hot enough to fry but not too hot to burn the oil.) Cook until meat is done and coating is a deep golden brown.

Next, make the milk gravy by using 3 tablespoons of the grease used to fry the steak and add 3 tablespoons flour, mix well, and add milk to the consistency of gravy you like.

Add some homemade biscuits, green beans, and iced tea.

Belle Meriwether's
Lemon Icebox Pie

1 can Eagle brand condensed milk

½ cup lemon juice

2 eggs, beaten

Mix the beaten eggs with the condensed milk, then add the lemon juice and mix well. (If you want to be completely certain the eggs are cooked, pop the mixture into the oven for a few minutes at 350 degrees.) Then pour the mixture into the graham cracker crust. Set into the icebox until firm.

If you'd like to make the mixture fluffier, add either cream cheese (2 to 4 ounces) or whipped cream (up to 10 ounces).

Graham Cracker Crust Recipe

1 package graham crackers (makes about 1⅔ cups crumbs)

¼ cup granulated sugar

⅓ cup melted butter

Crumble graham crackers. Combine crumbs and sugar first, then add melted butter. Press crumb mixture inside 9-inch pie plate and spread evenly over bottom and sides. (Note: Belle Meriwether always makes her own pie crust, but if you don't want to go to the trouble, well, Belle says you can find some decent, ready-made pie crust at the grocery store, though she really doesn't know why someone would go to all the trouble of making a pie and then use a pie crust made by somebody you don't even know.)